The Industry of Souls

Also by Martin Booth

FICTION

Hiroshima Joe

The Jade Pavilion

Black Chameleon

Dreaming of Samarkand

A Very Private Gentleman

The Humble Disciple

The Iron Tree

Toys of Glass

Adrift in the Oceans of Mercy

CHILDREN'S FICTION

War Dog

Music on the Bamboo Radio

POETRY

The Crying Embers

Coronis

Snath

The Brevities

Extending upon the Kingdom

The Knotting Sequence

Devil's Wine

The Cnot Dialogues

Meeting the Snowy North Again

Killing the Moscs

NONFICTION

Carpet Sahib: A Life of Jim Corbett

The Triads

Rhino Road

The Dragon and the Pearl: A Hong Kong Notebook

Opium: A History

The Doctor, the Detective and Arthur Conan Doyle

EDITED BOOKS

The Book of Cats (with George Macbeth)

Contemporary British and North American Verse

The Selected Poems of Aleister Crowley

The Industry of Souls

Martin Booth

St. Martin's Press / New York

THOMAS DUNNE BOOKS.
An imprint of St. Martin's Press.

THE INDUSTRY OF SOULS. Copyright © 1998 by Martin
Booth. All rights reserved. Printed in the United States of
America. No part of this book may be used or reproduced
in any manner whatsoever without written permission
except in the case of brief quotations embodied in critical
articles or reviews. For information, address St. Martin's
Press,
175 Fifth Avenue, New York, N.Y. 10010.

ISBN 0-312-24203-4

First published in the United Kingdom by Dewi Lewis
Publishing

First U.S. Edition: October 1999

1 0 9 8 7 6 5 4 3 2 1

for Vera and Volodya
who know of such things,
with love

*It is the industry of the soul, to love and to hate;
to seek after the beautiful and to recognise the ugly,
to honour friends and wreak vengeance upon enemies;
yet, above all, it is the work of the soul to prove
it can be steadfast in these matters...*

1

It was only this morning and yet it seems much longer ago. I might have lived a week since dawn.

Perhaps it is that, in my dotage, the god who controls time has seen fit to play the fool with me either by inexorably slowing down the clock or awarding me more hours than he does my fellow man, more than are my fair due. Perhaps the truth is that he is a sympathetic god who knew that, today of all days, I needed more time.

I woke as I always do, just after six, regardless of whether the summer sun is up and the birds contesting the day, or it is still night with the land clutched in winter's Arctic fist, and lay quite still. Usually, this is a quiet time when I empty the jug of my mind in readiness for whatever the coming day may pour into it. Yet, this morning, I came to consciousness with an inch or two of life's murky liquid already sloshing about in the bottom, and remained in my bed cogitating upon it: it had already occupied some sleepless hours of the night.

Eventually, there came the inevitable knock upon the door, quiet but assertive. From its insistence, I could tell the sound was Frosya's knuckles playing upon the bare vertical planks. Through the crack that appears a few centimetres to the left of the middle hinge every summer, when the air is dry, the sky is a washed lazy blue the colour of ducks' eggs and the little house breathes, I could see her shadow. I cannot be sure but, on occasion, I think she tries to peer through the crack.

'Shurik!' she called, her voice not much above a half-whisper. 'Shurik! Eight o'clock. It's time to wake up.'

Shurik. That is her pet name for me and has been since the very start, since the tide of time cast me onto the beach of her life and left me stranded there.

She must know I am already awake when she comes for me

every morning. I am sure she is aware of the fact that the habits of half a life-time are far too ingrained in me to change and that I have long since been awake. Yet, as I do every day, I did not let on for this is a part of our daily routine, the teasing little game I play with her.

'Shurik!'

Her voice took on a sudden, slight yet discernible tension. I knew what she was thinking. It was the thought which passes through her head every morning these days, that I will not answer and she, lifting the latch, will come into my room to discover me stiff, cold and no longer giving a damn.

'Shurik!'

She was a little louder, my name tinged with the fear which was momentarily lingering in her heart. If my hearing was better, I'm sure I would have picked up her pulse as it accelerated with her apprehension.

'Yes,' I replied at last, the game having reached its climax. 'Good morning.'

'Shurik!'

Her anxiety vanished: her pulse was slowing and there was a hint of chastisement in her words.

'It's time to open your shutters.'

As I heard her steps retreat across the floorboards, changing pitch as she went out onto the porch, I wondered if, by shutters, she meant my eyelids or the aluminium panels Trofim fashioned and put up last autumn to cover the window, replacing the iron ones which had rusted. After a few moments, the musical tumble of water pouring from the spout of her kettle reached me.

I swung my legs over the edge of my bed, feeling for the floor with my toes and careful not to catch the loose skin on the back of my thighs between the mattress and the raised wooden rim of the frame. There is so much loose skin on me these days: I am forever watching out not to nick it.

Every morning, as I perch on the edge of the bed like an old turkey, with my wattles hanging loose around me, I take stock of all

8

I am, all I have to show for my timeless journey upon this earth.

The bed is not mine: nor is the little table bearing my steel fountain pen and a sheaf of paper, the upright chair and the wooden chest under the window. The cushion embroidered with a tapestry butterfly on the chair is mine as are my steel-framed spectacles and the row of books on the shelf. The shelf, however, is not mine. The oil lamp with the smoke-stained glass chimney which I use when the electricity fails, the small framed photograph hanging from a nail in the wall above my books and, of course, my clothing which I keep in the chest, belong to me. However, the tumbler containing water on the floor beside my bed, the plate from which I ate one of Komarov's apples in the night and the curtain folded away beside the window belong to Frosya and Trofim whilst the Afghan rug is on loan to me by Sergei Petrovich, a neighbour. The cutlery on the plate is mine. As Frosya once pointed out to me, a man who does not possess his own knife and fork is a stranger to dignity.

Footsteps approached again and there was a knock on the door once more. Before I could bid her enter, it opened and Frosya came in carrying a chipped blue enamel basin of steaming water in which a flannel floated just under the surface, looking vaguely like a miniature grey sting-ray.

'Time to greet the new day, Shurik,' she announced and, lowering the basin to the floor by my feet, bent over and kissed me on my brow. She smelt strongly of soap and faintly of roses. 'It's a fine summer's morning.'

'And what day is it?' I enquired.

She snapped the catches on the shutters and swung them open but slowly so the brilliant sunlight did not catch my old eyes unawares and temporarily blind me.

'Thursday,' she answered. 'August 14.' She turned and held out a small packet which she had had secreted in her pocket. 'Happy birthday, dear Shurik.'

I looked from the little package to her face. Her eyes were wet with tears which had not yet started to spill down her cheek.

'So,' I said, in English, 'how old am I today?''

'Today, Alexander Alanovich Bayliss,' she replied, also in English, 'you are eighty years old.' She Russianified my name, giving me the middle patronymic for she knows my father was called Alan: then she rubbed the rim of her right eye with her finger and, reverting to Russian, ordered, 'Open your present.'

My fingers pulled at the wrapping of silver foil. It might have contained a bar of dark, bitter chocolate. She knows I have a penchant for it. Yet it was not. It was a small icon, hand-painted upon wood with a thin halo of gold round its head.

'And who is this?'

'Saint Basil,' Frosya replied.

With my glasses out of reach on the bookshelf, I held the icon closer to my face to get a better look at it. The colours of the painting, which lacked any sense of perspective whatsoever, were deep and rich and ancient. The saint had a bland unimpassioned look, neither a smile nor a frown. It was the stereo-typical look of the disparaging innocent, characteristic of all men who would be holy or profess power, gazing out upon a corrupt world from the safe cave of their belief, high up the mountain of their dogma, regarding human fallibility as a petty, passing flaw on their god's creation, nothing more than a raindrop bending light on creation's window. His hand was raised in front of his chest in a begrudging benediction.

'His halo is gold,' Frosya said. 'Real gold. Thin, but solid gold. Not plated silver. The icon comes from Romania. The criminals there are selling them. Trofim purchased it when he was in Volgograd last month.'

I made to stand up but she put her hand on my shoulder. Now, the tears were seeping down her cheek. Just the weight of her hand was enough to keep me seated.

'You should not have bought this,' I remonstrated with her. 'It will have cost far too much. And in dollars, not roubles.'

'How many dollars buy love?' she answered softly.

She knelt on the floor at my feet and dipped her hands in the basin, wringing out the flannel and holding it open upon her palms.

'It depends where you are,' I told her. 'In St Petersburg, where I understand from the television there are a copious number of foreign visitors these days, love probably costs twenty-five American dollars at the eastern end of the Nevsky Prospekt, near the Metro station, whilst outside the Astoria Hotel in ulitsa Gertsena it must be about fifty. Within the Astoria, out of the rain and the snow, inside the cocktail lounge, the price will be higher...'

'You're a naughty old man!' she chided me. 'You know what I mean.'

I put my hand on the crown of her head. I might have been Saint Basil himself, giving her a blessing or, had I a beard the colour of wood ash and as dense as a blackberry bush, Father Kondrati who lives in the house by the bridge, below the church at the other end of the village.

'Yes, I know exactly what you mean.'

Frosya looked up at me, like a child before her uncle or a sinner in front of her confessor.

'We love you, Shurik,' she said simply. 'So much. So very much.'

I did not reply. There was no need to and she expected no answer. Between the two of us, much passes that requires no words of thanks, no explanation, no interpretation or extrapolation.

A movement at the door drew my eye. Just over the lintel lurked Murka, Frosya's handsome tabby cat, with white socks on its front paws and a white flash on its forehead. I raised my hand from its mistress's head in greeting. The cat, in the way of haughty women and supercilious felines, stared an *ennuyant* acknowledgement then strolled off.

Frosya draped the flannel over the side of the basin and rolled up the trouser legs of my pyjamas almost to my groin. The veins in my legs looked like a relief map of a particularly bizarre and byzantine underground railway system.

'Now to get your blood warm,' she said in the matter-of-fact and falsely jovial tone of a nurse. 'Get you moving. Today, you must go round the village. Everyone wants to see you.'

With that, she spread the hot flannel over my shin, pressing it down with her left hand whilst the fingers of her right kneaded my skin just above the knee. The heat of the water seemed to run through me like the first vodka of the day in a confirmed drunk. No drug could have coursed its way so fervidly through such old flesh and brittle bones as those of which I am now constructed.

I sat quite still, my eyes fixed on the cloudless sky outside. The sun was warm upon my face. Somewhere in the village, a dog was barking. Sparrows in the gutter above the window were chattering gaily.

Gradually, the barking subsided and the sparrows' twittering conversation faded until all I could hear was the voice of Kirill Karlovich, Frosya's father, not ten centimetres from my ear. He was speaking as if his mouth were full of grit.

'Shurik,' he was saying. 'Go to Frosya. One day, a million years from now. Even if you are a ghost. Go to her. Tell her it was good.'

'What was good?' I heard myself asking, my voice echoing as if from the end of a long, dark tunnel.

'To die with a friend,' Kirill replied. 'To die by the hand of a man whose name you know.'

∗

To the side and rear of the house, there is a yard surrounded by a flower bed in which Frosya grows marigolds and, closer to the wall under the window of my room, dahlias the tubers of which she pulls up every autumn to nurture safely in a box under her bed until spring. In this yard, as soon as the warm weather breaks, Trofim sets up a table under a silver birch which he has carefully pruned and trained into a weeping tree about three metres high to the crown. It is here I sit on sunny days, the leaves rippling in the breeze, the hanging tresses of the branches giving me a living cave from which to observe Frosya going about her chores and Trofim, when he is not working at the garage, tending his vegetable plot or looking after his hens.

This morning, Frosya laid out my breakfast on the table. It was a meagre repast for, in my advanced years, I do not eat much: a small piece of hard cheese, a slice of bread, a pared and cored apple and a cup of plain tea without milk or sugar.

As I cut into the cheese, Frosya joined me, sitting opposite me across the table. She, too, had a cup of tea.

'You are such a man of habit, Shurik. A man of schedules. Every day, cheese, bread, apple. Do you never want something different? An egg?'

She looked up the gentle slope behind the house, towards the distant tree line where the forests begin that run, without interruption save for occasional roads and railway lines, clear to the Volga. Twenty metres in from the trees was Trofim's chicken run built around an old, solitary oak tree.

'I am not that fond of eggs,' I informed her. 'As for habit, I feel secure in knowing how my life pans out. A day with a timetable feels safe.'

I smiled at her and, placing the sliver of cheese I had cut on the edge of the slice of bread, raised it to my mouth and bit into it. The bread was dark, dense, slightly moist and grainy.

'What will you do today, Shurik?'

'The usual,' I replied. 'Take my walk down through the village, across the river, through the forest and back here. My customary route, to my customary schedule.'

'You will take longer today,' Frosya predicted. 'People want to talk to you.' She cradled her cup in her hands as if the weather was chilly and she was warming her fingers. 'Today is special for you and for them. If you want to be back on time, you will have to leave earlier than usual.'

'I shall leave when I'm ready,' I declared. 'No sooner, no later.'

Frosya sipped her tea. She had something on her mind and

was not sure whether to broach the subject or leave it be. I knew what she was concerned about, too: yet I did not intend to say anything. She would come to it in her own good time.

'Do you like your St. Basil?' she asked.

'He's very fine and I'm very grateful to you for him.' I took a swallow of tea: a crumb of the bread had lodged in my gullet and I washed it down. 'A remarkable man from a veritable clan of saints. As I recall, his grandmother, father, mother, older sister and two younger brothers all feature in the hagiographies. He was a friend of St. Gregory and upon his principles are based the monastic paradigms of the Orthodox church. He showed much sympathy for the poor, always took the side of the under-dog and was critical of wealth even though he came from a very well-to-do family. He was also said to be obstinate, argumentative and querulous. In short, he was an ideal saint for Russia.'

Frosya laughed and declared, 'For an atheist, you know a lot about the church.'

'To defeat your enemy,' I justified my knowledge, 'you must know him in all his guises.'

'You, too, are a remarkable man, Shurik.'

'No,' I complained. 'That is not right, Frosya. I am not. I am merely a man shaped by his destiny.'

For a long moment, she was silent. She was, I could feel it, about to bring up the subject which was haunting her. Casting me a quick glance, she then looked into the distance, steeling her courage.

'When will they arrive?' she enquired at last, still not looking in my direction.

'This afternoon. The letter said they would get here about five o'clock. It is a long drive for them.'

'Are they coming from Moscow?'

'Not directly, no. I suspect they will have stayed last night somewhere. In Voronezh, perhaps.'

She was silent for a moment then opened her mouth to speak.

'Do not ask, Frosya,' I warned her.

Yet she had to. It was in her feminine nature to need to know.

'But have you decided, Shurik?'

I did not reply but reached out and, unfurling her fingers from around her cup, took them in my own. I looked at our hands. Mine are old, gnarled as the roots of a cypress: hers are soft, not as a young girl's might be but as a caring woman's. Frosya was 48 last month.

'How long have I lived here?' I asked her.

'Twenty years.'

'And still you don't know me? You who can tell everything that is happening in your husband's mind? Surely you know what is going on in mine, too. I have lived here with the pair of you for all your married life bar the first four years.'

She smiled. It was a loving smile.

'Yes,' she admitted, 'under normal circumstances, I can read your thoughts as well as I can my Trofim's. But these are not normal circumstances and I am at a loss.'

'Don't worry, Frosya,' I said. 'Trust in fate. In destiny. What more can you or I do?'

'Shape it!' she answered quite firmly yet I knew she did not believe it. We have been through too much to do so.

I let go of her hand.

'I want nothing more to eat. Save the apple for later.'

'It will go brown.'

'Then feed it to the hens and I shall break my habit and eat an egg in a few days made from it.'

She laughed, stood up and started to collect in the crockery. I drained my cup of tea. When she had returned to the house, I felt inside my jacket and removed the letter from the inside pocket. I slipped it from its envelope and, once again, unfolded it. I did not immediately read it but just looked at it. It was crisp and official, neatly typed upon a heavy bond paper, the expensive sort with the paper-maker's watermarked lines evident as a faint grid in the weave of the pulp. The letterhead was printed in black, the letters embossed, shining and raised in relief from the surface of the page. I balanced my steel-framed spectacles upon my nose and, yet again, studied what was printed there.

*

I was five weeks making my way to Myshkino, the village in which I now live, travelling mostly by jumping freight trains, sleeping crouched up in box-cars parked in sidings or hiding in track-side maintenance huts. From time to time, I was moved on by railway officials or the transport authorities but usually I was simply ignored. They did not know who I was but they certainly knew what I was without asking for my papers. Some were sympathetic and gave me a few kopeks: others were antagonistic, punched and kicked me and stole the kopeks. Most were apathetic and paid me no heed whatsoever.

For food, I begged. Knowing instinctively the importance of appearing at least reasonably presentable, for a tramp in any society gets short shrift at all times, I managed to wash myself now and again in the public conveniences in stations, keeping my beard down to a trim stubble with a pair of nail scissors I filched from a street vendor's stall in Kazan. My clothes, however, suffered on the journey and, by the time I had walked the thirty kilometres from Zarechensk to Myshkino, I looked more like a hobgoblin than a human.

With difficulty, for no one would offer the information to a vagabond, I found Frosya's house around midday, opened the gate in the low fence and made my way up the path to the porch. I knocked on the door but there was no answer so, cupping my hands, I peered in a window. The living room was tidy, with comfortable furniture, a carpet and a radio on a table. Exhausted, I lowered myself down in the shade by the door and dozed fitfully, awaiting her return from wherever she was.

'Who the hell are you?' were Trofim's first words when he found me at about five o'clock, hunched on the steps of the porch, my arms hugging my legs to my chest, my chin resting on my knees.

I woke from my semi-slumber and squinted at him in the afternoon sunlight. He was of average height, with dark hair and a handsome face, and dressed in a mechanic's overalls. I could smell the syrupy scent of warm gearbox oil on his clothing.

'You look like a thief who's found nothing to steal,' he added.

Slowly, I got to my feet and cast a quick glance at my reflection in the window. My face was grey and rough with several days' stubble, my hair short but not to the extent of still being a criminal's crop: it had had five weeks to grow. My jacket was soiled and my shirt, an old-fashioned clerk's shirt with the collar missing, was grimy about the neck. My trousers looked as if I had slept in them which, save one or two nights, I had and the leather of my boots was cracked for lack of polish and too frequent soakings in the rain.

'Go on!' he exclaimed, waving his hand at me as he might a mangy cat routing round the garbage pail, dismissive rather than belligerent. '*Otvali!*'

'My name is Alexander,' I said quietly.

'Fine!' Trofim replied. '*Otvali*, Alexander!'

I felt weak and leaned against one of the posts holding up the roof over the porch. I had not eaten for several days except for some handfuls of wheat I had snatched in a field not yet harvested.

'Are you are the husband of Efrosiniya?' I asked, my voice hoarse and consequently not much louder than a whisper.

He looked at me, suddenly very suspicious, and said with no small degree of defensive menace, 'What's it to you?'

'And was your wife's mother Tatyana Antonovna?'

He was immediately on the offensive, glared at me and said, '*Poshol k chortu!*'

'I will go to hell,' I responded, my voice quiet with fatigue, 'but first I must speak to your wife.' I sucked on my own spittle to lubricate my mouth. 'I have come from Kirill Karlovich.'

Trofim stared at me for a long moment then, his demeanour

utterly changed, he stepped quickly forward, taking my arm and guiding me towards an upright chair under the window. It was the very same chair in which I still frequently sit on the porch on a warm evening, which over the years has become somehow shaped to my body, or my body has become formed to its curves and peculiarities.

'Frosya!' he called urgently as he let go of my arm. 'Frosya! Come quickly!'

In a few seconds Frosya appeared, her sleeves rolled up. Her hands and forearms were wet from doing the laundry in a tub behind the house. She must have been in the house all along without my knowing. Her face was blushed from the effort of scrubbing. When she saw me, she stopped in her tracks. A dog, sauntering down the village street, spied me and started to yap.

'Where have you come from?' she asked, her voice barely audible over the dog's noise. Trofim bent to pretend to pick up a stone. The dog fell silent and slunk off.

'Sosnogorsklag 32,' I told her.

'Where are you going?' Trofim asked.

I looked at him and said, 'After I have given you my message, I am going to hell.'

'I'm sorry,' Trofim began to explain. 'When I first saw you...'

I raised my hand to silence him and smiled weakly.

'Sosnogorsklag,' Frosya mused quietly.

'Not a pretty town, I'll bet,' Trofim remarked soberly.

'Labour camp number 32 was not in the town,' I informed him, 'but some way out. South of Pasn'a. Not far from Vojvoz.'

'I think,' Frosya said, 'you must have come from hell.'

She came forward, then bent over me and kissed my cheek. As she did this morning, when she entered my room and gave me my present, she smelled of soap.

It was the first kiss I had experienced in many years, since that terrible, unforgettable winter which I have never been able to excise from my mind.

'Get some water,' Trofim suddenly ordered her, as if coming

to his senses. 'Make some tea. Prepare a bed.' Turning to me, he said, 'You will stay here. With us. For as long as you wish.'

I stayed that night, promising myself I would leave the next morning: but the night turned into a week which evolved into a month that metamorphosed into two decades, the remnant of my life.

*

Folding the letter once more and returning it to my pocket, I sat on for a short while, gazing out from the leafy parasol of the silver birch. From this vantage point, I had as usual a fairly panoramic view of the village.

The house is on a slight rise with most of the buildings below, on the gentle incline that goes down to the river and the road which crosses it by way of a concrete bridge. Now, in high summer, the gardens are a blaze of colour. Sunflowers stand against walls, smaller blooms in front of them. Where there are no flowers, there are vegetables.

In front of Trofim's porch are several rows of raspberry canes and a patch of herbs and small onions. Between the house and the woodland up the slope behind it, Trofim's plot is filled with cucumbers and marrows trailing on the ground, beans hanging like plump green fingers from a trellis of sticks, tomatoes tied against stakes, dark-leaved potatoes with their tiny white blossoms and rows of cabbages. The ranks of carrots, beetroots and radishes are protected from marauding birds by a thin black netting suspended from poles like a miniature, transparent Bedouin tent.

Beyond the gate, across the lane, stands a quaint little house made of age-blackened wood with a fretwork boarding around the eaves over the porch which is as deep as a room. The chimney leans precariously but has done so for at least a decade. I cannot look upon the house without being reminded of the world of Pasternak and Dostoyevsky.

The property is owned by a widow, Vera Dorokhova, whom

the villagers refer to behind her back as The Merry Widow for she has been happiest since her spouse disappeared into the forest one January winters ago, not to be found until the spring when his half-thawed body, gnawed by foxes, was discovered beside a woodsman's hut in which he had taken shelter. A lathe operator in a small engineering works which turned out tractor wheel bearings at Zarechensk, his wife may have been Vera but his mistress was Madam Vodka under whose instruction, as people put it, he frequently beat her and generally made her life miserable. In the first few years of my residency in Myshkino, the sight of him returning from work, his clothing powdered with iron filings and his shoes trailing the odd shiny turning like a weak spring embedded in the rubber soles, sent involuntary shivers down my spine. Had I the hackles of a dog, they would have been instantly erect but not on account of his cruelty to Vera Dorokhova: I had seen far worse cruelty than anything he could have devised, sober or sozzled. It was because, at a distance, he reminded me of a brute I had known called Genrikh.

Since Madam Vodka's lover was planted in the graveyard by the church at the other end of his village, I have been haunted by a newer ghost in the form of his widow. She watches out for me and I watch out for her. Despite my being 20 years her senior – twenty years today, as it happens – she has a yearning for me, a longing she will only satisfy by getting me to the altar down the road. That I am past caring for women, that I have been past caring for them for decades, does not seem to put her off. Perhaps she has developed a macabre taste for burying men. I do not intend to find out.

One of Trofim's cockerels crowing in the distant brought me back to my senses and I glanced at my watch. It was time for me to go, to set off on my constitutional, to go and meet all those who would pass the time of day with me and who, according to Frosya, were keen to talk to me, to see me on my birthday.

My daily walk is important to me: I may be old and becoming frail but I like to keep myself fit and my daily neighbourhood perambulation sees I stay in good condition, body and brain.

As Kirill always said, a fit man fights and therefore survives whilst a weak man wails and goes to the wall.

2

I first met Kirill in the primary shaft chamber on Gallery B of the coal mine six kilometres from Sosnogorsklag 32 labour camp.

After descending for two levels, the wire mesh door of the lift cage was opened by a shifty little man not over one and a half metres tall whose large skull with its bulbous forehead and huge hands were out of all proportion to the remainder of his body.

'Get out! Get out!' he squeaked in a falsetto voice. 'Line up! Line up! You!' He pointed at me then at the rock face behind me. His arms were short and also incongruous. 'Mr. Soft Hands! Form a rank! Form a rank!'

I moved back. The dozen or so other new arrivals joined me, chivvied onto parade by the miniature martinet.

'Silence! No communication!' he shrilled again.

The cage door was slammed across, the safety bar swung down into place and the cage began its descent down the mine shaft, the cables humming, the grease on the guide wheels sucking.

Standing with my spine pressed to the rock, I studied the subterranean world into which I had been plunged, no wiser nor any more blessed than a kitten, surplus to the breeder's requirement, dropped onto the carpet to the sound of water being run into a pail.

The main shaft contained two cages, one for the transportation of miners and the other for trucks of coal. The passenger cage had a sliding door to it but the truck cage door had been welded shut. Gallery B was mined out and was now used, I discovered from a board bolted to the rock, as a storage area. From the roof were suspended bare 60 watt light bulbs protected from breakage by wire baskets and hanging at five metre intervals. I could see them disappearing down the perspective of the gallery which ran off at right angles to the shaft, curving gradually out of sight as the tunnel turned to the left. Water dripped with melancholic monotony from a pipe overhead into a puddle below but, when I pressed my hands against the rock behind my back, I was surprised to find it dry and cool.

From a side chamber a little way down the gallery appeared three men who came towards us. As they passed under a light, their faces were momentarily illuminated from above, casting strange shadows downwards across their features.

'Attention! Attention!' squealed the little man. All his orders seemed to be repeated. The men drew closer. He waited until they were not ten metres away then he shouted, 'You! Mr. Soft Hands! Stop shuffling! Stop shuffling!'

I was standing quite still. He was blustering for effect.

'Shut up, troglodyte!' said the tallest of the men. The martinet stepped aside and gave a semi-salute.

Despite his prison cropped hair, the grimy coating of coal dust blotching his skin as if he were in the early stages of leprosy, his grey and filthy uniform, he cut a handsome figure. His eyes, surrounded by two circles of comparatively clean skin, were filled with humour, his lips just touched by the faintest of wry smiles.

'Number off,' he commanded.

We each announced ourselves by our prison numbers. Mine was B916. Our voices sounded dull in the flat acoustics of the shaft chamber.

'Good!' he exclaimed and he ran his eye over us. We might have been auditioning for some macabre play. 'So you are all new to the gulag,' he divined accurately. 'New to the concept that Labour is Dignity.' There was an unmistakable sarcasm to his voice. 'Has anyone here less than twenty years?'

I glanced along the line. No one put up their hand or stepped forward.

'In that case,' he said with a grandiloquent and ironic sweep of his arm, 'welcome to the rest of your lives. And take a word of advice. Do not dream of the day of your release. Do not think about it for if you do, it will not come. Like the kettle you watch, it will not boil. Men go mad thinking about the past, the future.

Here, there is no then and no next. There is only now. Live for now.' He paused to let his words sink in. 'There is no point in being morbid about it. Do that and you die. Inside.' He put his hand on his chest. 'In your heart. The blood will still pump but the spirit will be dead. The spirit is what they want to kill. Not the body. The body has a use.'

The cage sped by, heading upwards, the steel guide wheels hissing on their well-greased rails. A draft of fetid air preceded it.

'You at the end,' he said: it took me a moment to realise he was addressing me. 'You come with me. The rest...'

The other two men divided the remainder of the group amongst themselves.

'So, B916, what is your name?' he enquired as I followed him along the wide tunnel.

'Alexander Bayliss,' I told him.

He stopped and studied me.

'A good Russian name for the start. But the other? And your spoken Russian? Not so good. A curious accent.'

'I've only picked it up recently,' I admitted.

'So where do you come from, comrade?'

'I'm English.'

'Ah!' he wagged his finger at me. 'So you are the Englishman.' He held out his hand and I accepted it. This was the first time I had shaken a friendly hand for months: most hands I had come across had either pointed accusingly at me or slapped my face. 'I am a Work Unit leader and you are joining my team.' We walked on, passing a side gallery piled to the roof with crates and boxes. 'My name is Kirill Karlovich Balashov. They call me Kirill. And you? Alexander is a bit of a mouthful. Do you know the diminutive for Alexander? It's Shurik. So, from now on, you are Shurik.'

I nodded my head. At the next offshoot, we turned right and, in a short distance, arrived at a table upon which had been placed rows of kit.

'Take one,' Kirill said. 'Don't worry about anything but the metal hat and the gloves. If they fit, you'll be all right. If they don't you'll spend twenty-odd years with your hat falling into your eyes or tipping off the back of your head.' He grinned then added more seriously, 'They must fit. Your life may depend upon it one day.'

I gathered up one of the piles. It consisted of a thick gauge aluminium hat, a pair of heavy duty gloves, a small hand axe and a ball-headed hammer, both attached to a worn leather belt. The hat fitted, the gloves did not. Kirill swapped them for a tighter pair then reached over to one of the other piles and removed a small battery-powered lamp from it.

'Not everyone gets one of these,' he said. 'You are a lucky one.' He flicked the switch. It did not come on. He thumped it on the table then against the palm of his hand. 'No battery,' he declared then, finding another lamp, he snapped open the reflector and unscrewed the bulb. 'Get a spare. Best be on the safe side. You don't say much.'

'What is there to say?' I replied and, nodding at the lamp, added, 'Except thank you.'

Kirill laughed and put his hand on my shoulder. His teeth were white and pure against his besmirched face.

'We'll get along just fine. I can't stand blabbermouthers. Put your kit on.'

When I was dressed, we returned to the main shaft, passing the other new arrivals heading for the store chamber. At the cage door, we halted. Kirill pressed a button to summon the cage. A tinny electric bell rang far above our heads.

'This is Gallery B,' he explained. 'B for Beria who banged us in here.' He smiled. 'Two down from the surface. We are working at present on Gallery L.'

'L for Lenin who invented Dignified Labour,' I suggested.

For a moment, he looked at me and I felt a twinge of fear. He might, it suddenly occurred to me, have been testing me. Trust no one. That was the motto of the gulag: trust no one until you were so intimate with them that you knew the given names of every louse living in their pubic hair. Even then, you should still be wary. Yet I had no need to worry. Kirill exploded into laughter.

'L for Lobanov who...'

The cage arrived, the noise drowning out Kirill's metaphor. We stepped into it and descended at increasing speed, decelerating so quickly at our destination that I felt my legs bend and my head swirl. Kirill put his hand under my armpit to steady me.

'You'll get used to it,' he said. 'We all do. Unless you're the troglodyte.' He leaned conspiratorially towards me. 'You ever wonder how the little bastard got so small?'

He opened the gate and we stepped out into Gallery L. Another prisoner carrying a wooden box got in and the cage rose out of sight.

The shaft chamber was not like that in Gallery B. A railway line ended here in a loop. Men stood around in the glare of three bare lights which did not hang from the roof but were mounted on the rock wall. Stripped to the waist, they were caked in coal dust, striped like zebras where their sweat had coursed in runnels over their skin. They wore their metal hats squarely on their heads. The air was surprisingly warm and there was quite a breeze blowing from the depths of the mine. Along the roof ran cables, pipes and a square, galvanised iron ventilation duct, air whistling out through a poorly sealed joint.

'He was crushed?' I asked incredulously.

'It was his first day. At the time, the mine only went down to Gallery P. For the Politburo which pisses on us all. That was where he was headed. P is over two kilometres down. The last hundred metres... He didn't brace himself like the old hands.' He squeezed his palms together. '*Phapp*! He went from one metre eighty-seven to what you see now in less than two seconds. Thirty-nine centimetres he lost. His balls got caught between his thighs. He went from a bass to a soprano.'

'How could he have survived?' I said.

Kirill slapped me on the back and replied, 'What do you think? Is the moon made of marzipan? No, it's just my joke. A story we tell to get his goat up. His real tale is much funnier. Let's

27

go. I'll tell you as we walk.' He looked at my hands. 'Put your gloves on.'

We set off along the gallery, keeping to one side of the railway track. Every fifty metres or so, chambers had been hollowed out on either side of the gallery. Some were shallow and empty, others filled with boxes. One had a door fastened across the entrance with a picture of a globular cartoon terrorist's bomb nailed to the panelling.

'The troglodyte,' Kirill said, 'was a trapeze clown in the Moscow State Circus. One of a troupe called the Flying Fedeyevs or something like that. All of them were dwarfs or not much bigger. They jumped and chased each other across a mesh of wires about ten metres up, scampering around like monkeys, playing the fool, bursting bladders of water, throwing talc. The children liked them. The troglodyte was the boss clown.

'Anyway, some years ago, the circus went on tour to Czechoslovakia, giving performances at Prague, Decin, Ostrava, Brno. And Breclav. You know where that is?' He did not wait for an answer. 'Ten kilometres from the Austrian border. The little bugger couldn't resist it. There was the usual brigade of KGB stoolies and minders along on the tour, occupied watching who did what to whom, where and why, and noting it all down for the files. But he still thought he could outsmart them. So, you know what he did? I will tell you.'

A rumbling sound reached us. A light rocked from side to side far down the tunnel. Kirill took my arm and pulled me to one side. A train of ten trucks laden with lumps of coal and rock juddered by, towed by a much dented and scratched electric locomotive driven by a man who gave Kirill a cursory wave as he passed. Kirill nodded in reply.

'For the climax of the act, the troglodyte dressed up as a gorilla. Blacked face, hairy suit. He swung about scratching his belly, tickling his armpits and beating his chest. The big top tent had been erected close to the railway station. He had worked out that he could swing from rope to rope across the tent, out of the big door through which they brought in the larger acts, over the guy ropes, along a heavy telephone wire to the railway line and drop onto a train heading south.

'The show began. It was a matinée. That was his first mistake. If he had moved at night, he might have stood an outside chance. He's not one of nature's brightest candles. Anyway, he's up there, monkeying about. He hears a train whistle. It's going the right way. He's off. The minders don't realise he's done a runner until he doesn't return through the big door to take a bow and throw a bag of talc. They unholster their Makarovs and set off in hot pursuit. By the time they get outside the tent, he's well on his way down the telephone line. They run after him, taking a pot shot or two at him to impress their officers but they miss and they can't get near the telephone line because it's over the other side of a tall railing fence.'

The gallery widened, the rails dividing into two to provide a passing place with a short siding running into a side tunnel. From ahead came the faint, insistent but unidentifiable sounds of machinery.

'At last,' Kirill recounted, 'he gets near the train. All he has to do is swing from the telephone line to a trackside cable and then jump. The comrade brothers are going berserk. If he gets away, they're bound for Siberia. The troglodyte gets to the train, swings out from the phone line and grabs the cable. The momentum of the swing will carry him onto the train. He swings. Next he knows, he's in a prison ward of the local hospital with his hands bandaged, his head aching and his eyelashes gone.'

'What happened?' I asked.

'Why don't birds get fried on power lines?' Kirill asked. 'He short circuited the telephone system with the railway high voltage supply. Like any cautious trapeze artist, he didn't let go of one hold until the next was firm.'

The noise in the gallery grew louder until it was almost deafening. The air tasted of coal dust. Ahead was the working face, men bent to hydraulic-powered drills, water spraying onto the bits where they wormed into the coal seam. Behind them, others shovelled coal into a row of parked trucks, jammed pit props into place with lump hammers and laid another section of track.

'Welcome to hell!' Kirill shouted, his mouth close to my ear.

*

Imagine this.

It is a rest break, one and a half kilometres down. There are six of us, and Kirill. We are Work Unit 8, gathered in one of the side chambers six hundred metres back from the coal face, lounging on piles of sacks or sitting on boxes. At the face, the explosives team is setting the charges.

Around me, in the gloom cast by a single light, are my fellow workers, my comrades in coal, Kirill's boys. From my perch on a crate of drill parts, I look from one to the other of them, observe their faces and the bend in their bones, share in their exhaustion, their aching muscles and tired souls.

Leaning against a pit prop under the light is Avel. Avel the Aviator, we call him. He is slightly shorter than I am with pointed features. His chin is sharp, his ears flat against the side of his narrow head and his fingers, despite the manual work we do, slender: they might be a pianist's or a violinist's. Before he fell foul of the system, arousing some jealousy or enmity in a colleague who shopped him to a cadre who passed his name on down the line, he had been a fighter pilot in the Soviet Air Force.

Even when they came for him, beat his shins with canes and imprisoned him for a crime he did not realise he had committed, he remained a dedicated Communist, a Party man through and through. In his early months in the mine, he had accepted his lot with the sangfroid of the unquestioning zealot. A mistake had been made but he was not going to complain: this was his fate, his sacrifice for Mother Russia. After all, he reasoned, someone had to mine coal.

As a pilot, he had actively fought the American Aggressor in

Korea, at first as an advisor to the Chinese and North Korean air forces but, later, as a combat flyer. From late in 1950 to the summer of 1952, he had flicked and jived his MiG-15 in the deadly aerial ballet of dog-fights with American F-80 Shooting Stars and F-86 Sabres, being twice shot down and having to bale out. His had been a simplistic world of speed, sky and the red fire button on his control column spitting bursts of 37- and 23-millimetre calibre cannon shells at an overt enemy.

Now, as I watch him, he has changed. No longer a devoted follower of Marx and Engels, he has seen the error of their ways and his own.

He stands under the light for a purpose: none of us tries to rob him of his place. He might have been an air ace with eight kills to his name but he has the heart of an artist. With his dexterous fingers, he passes his time carving chess pieces out of coal and shale. Admittedly the shale chess-men, being grey, are not as white as they might be and are sometimes hard to distinguish from their opponents, but they are better than nothing. At this moment, as I watch him, he is concentrating on a black rook, turning a fragment of coal in his hand, shaping the battlements of the little tower with an awl he has fashioned from a broken drill bit.

Across from Avel, Kostya fumbles with his lamp. It is some weeks since we were last issued with batteries and his is the only one still charged: however, the bulb is ill-fitting and flickers irritatingly. He is intent on trying to repair it, wrapping single strands of copper wire round the base in the hope he might increase the diameter of the thread.

Although we are an informal band, only two of us are perpetually known by nicknames, myself and Kostya, which is short for Konstantin.

Poor Kostya! He was the one who felt imprisonment the hardest at first. Avel had possessed the freedom of the skies, but only saw it from the cell of a cockpit, surrounded by switches and dials, levers and gauges, buckles and belts. Before the darkness, as he put it, Kostya had been a warrant officer in the Soviet Navy, in charge of his own mess deck. For him, the world was huge, a vastness of empty ocean and sky which he could cross for days without seeing anything other than clouds, flying fish and the tail fin of a diving whale.

During his eight years in the service, he had been based in Vladivostok and sailed the Pacific and Indian Oceans in a frigate, stationed in Archangel and traversed the Atlantic watching out for American submarines from destroyers, and assigned to a battleship whose home port was Odessa and aboard which he had sailed the Mediterranean and the South Atlantic. He had been to Cuba and smoked an Havana cigar in Havana, to Shanghai where he had dined on snake, to Bombay where he had seen dead bodies being eaten by vultures on the top of a funereal tower and to Naples where he had taken a tour round Pompeii and caught a dose of the clap. Kostya has more stories than the rest of us but he keeps them suppressed for the sake of his sanity.

Ylli, who sits hunched up on a box, his eyes closed, is the only other foreigner working in the mine. His name means *Star*. He is an Albanian who came to the USSR as an engineering student. For two years, he lived frugally in a foreign students' hostel and studied hard, rose to the top of his class and thereby engendered the envy of his peers. It was his girlfriend who turned him in when he beat her by one mark in a mechanics test upon which depended placement in the next term's seminar groups.

They came for him at dawn, snapped the handcuffs on him, bundled him into a car and drove him straight to prison without even touching base in the KGB cells. He was beaten up a few times, questioned about subjects of which he was utterly ignorant, beaten again for his insolent non-compliance, accused of nothing, held for a month then transported east without so much as a rigged trial. He is a natural pessimist, and it is not unusual for him to fall into an incommunicative sulk every so often, his pessimism and the gulag getting the better of him: no doubt, he cannot quite rid himself of memories of the bleak, historic shores of his native Albania, basking under a Mediterranean sky, the sea unchanged since Julius Caesar crossed it to fight Pompey, the villages unscarred since Ali Pasha raided them for tribute.

Lying on a pile of tarpaulins farthest from the mouth of the side chamber, which luxury we take in turns, is Titian. Once a mathematics teacher, he is a cultured man of quiet intellect and charm who, in the sorry and typical catalogue of betrayal which put most of us here, was grassed on by a pupil to whom he gave low grades. It was foolish of him and he knew it at the time: the boy's father was a Party official of some standing in the town. Yet he still gave the youth a D because that was all he was worth in the race for academic honours. In the race for personal survival, he was a certain A++.

Titian's eyes are closed but he does not sleep. None of us sleep in rest breaks. If we did, we should be all the more tired when we returned to our labours.

Look closely. His lips are moving silently. He is not praying for release, or escape, or death, nor is he losing his mind. In fact, he is reciting a poem to himself and I think I know which one for, from the timing of the movement of his lips, I can tell it is a poem constructed in four couplets and his favourite is so written.

It is by the Korean poet, Yi Yuk-sa, who was arrested in Peking by the Kempetai, the Japanese secret police, who tortured him to death in 1944. Entitled *The Peak*, it goes

> *Lashed by the bitter season's blast,*
> *At last I am driven to the north.*
>
> *I stand upon the sword sharp frost,*
> *Where senseless horizon and flat land meet.*
>
> *I do not know quite where to kneel*
> *Nor where to place my fretting steps.*

There is nothing to do but close my eyes
And think of the steel rainbow of winter.

Next to me, perched on the end of a crate marked *Track ties and assorted fittings*, is Dmitri who has, in his time, been a Soviet army conscript, a cook, a stevedore, the janitor of a block of sumptuous apartments for the exclusive use of the *nomenklatura* and a shopkeeper. With an irrepressible sense of humour, often scatological, and a treasury of stories, most of them either risqué or risky, depending upon your political standpoint, he comes from what is now known once again as St. Petersburg. He survived the Fascist siege towards the end of which he was reduced to surviving solely on soup, made by boiling algæ gathered from the Moika canal, where it joined the Fontanka canal just north of the Mikhailovskiy Castle, his belt and the leather straps from an old wooden trunk he had long since burnt for fuel.

Unlike the others, who were betrayed into the gulag, Dmitri put himself there. It was a slip of the hand, a momentary aberration, a miscalculation of infinitesimal insignificance but it did for him. A woman entered his shop, which sold household articles, one Thursday afternoon to purchase a colander: of course, when I say it was Dmitri's shop, he was not the proprietor but the manager for the establishment belonged to the state. The colander was made of pressed aluminium and cost one rouble, 15 kopecks. He had wrapped the item up in brown paper, tied it about with cord with a loop that she might carry it more easily and given her change for a five rouble note. As he was counting out the change, his wife dropped a glass preserving jar. It shattered, glass flying in all directions. For five seconds, ten at the most, his attention was diverted and he lost count. The woman checked her change: she had received 3.35. not 3.85. She did not make a fuss, just gave Dmitri a sour look and demanded fifty kopecks. He apologised profusely and stumped up. Twelve hours later, he was in a cell being accused of anti-Socialist sentiments, of undermining the principles of Socialism, of

34

harbouring greed and capitalist tendencies.

Despite his self-betrayal, Dmitri is an optimist. He survived the Nazis and a stretch in the army so the gulag is, for him, just another tribulation life has chucked in his way. He will, he is convinced, get through it.

Penultimately, there is Kirill.

From my first day down the mine, we have been good friends. He is about my age, tall enough to have to duck in many of the side chambers where the coal seam is narrow or the nature of the rock overhead demands the use of extra thick pit props and cross-members. Even now, sitting on a barrel gazing down the main gallery in the direction of the coal face, he gives off a sense of authority, a certain charisma which commands respect and might, in other circumstances, occasion fear.

This is hardly surprising for he was an officer in the local militia before he arrested a young official called Nikolai Georgievich Krivopaltsev for corruption and fell from grace. It was not until after he had signed the charge sheet, slammed the cell door shut, turned the key and filed the arrest papers that he discovered his prisoner was the nephew of Innokenty Ivanovich Andronikov, First Secretary of the Communist Party for the entire region.

Upon making his discovery, Kirill immediately returned home, kissed his wife and two-year-old daughter, patted their Borzoi bitch and sat down on the porch of their house in the twilight of a late summer evening to await the inevitable. It was two hours in coming.

And finally, there is me.

Alexander Bayliss, bachelor, graduate of English Literature from the University of Durham, one-time representative of Scott, Pudney (Steel Stockholders) & Sons, Ltd., of Doncaster, England, arrested in Leipzig whilst on a trip to buy scrap iron, charged with espionage (erroneously, as it happens), accused of being an enemy of the Soviet peoples and reported tragically killed when my car was struck by a lorry on a bridge over the River Elbe. I was presumed drowned.

My trial, such as it was, was held in camera. It was short, efficient in the extreme and utterly irrelevant. I was dressed in prison clothing, taken to a corridor and seated on a bench alongside an assortment of other miscreants, some innocent, some foolish, some guilty. We were ordered to look to the front, not attempt to communicate at all with each other and to edge forwards as the queue shortened.

The court was nothing more than a large room. The judges – there were, I recall, three of them – sat behind a scratched table on a dais a few inches higher than the bare floorboards. On the wall above them hung a portrait of Stalin, his moustache prim and bristling, his piggy eyes glinting. I was marched in and stood on a low pedestal. The presiding judge shuffled some papers, looked up, stared at me for a moment then made his pronouncement speaking, for my convenience, in heavily accented English although I had acquired a reasonable smattering of Russian during my interminable and pointless interrogation.

'B916, Bayliss Alexander,' he said in a bored monotone and without taking a breath. 'You are charged under Section 6 of Article 58 of the Criminal Code. The charge is that you are suspected of espionage against the Union of Soviet Socialist Republics. Your sentence is twenty-five years of hard labour.'

With that, he stamped and signed several sheets of foolscap one of which was handed to me by a clerk. I looked at it. The rubber stamp was smudged. It was triangular and contained the letters SVPSh. I enquired what it meant and was told it was an acronym meaning I was accused of making contacts which might have led to my being suspected of espionage.

From that moment on, as the rubber stamp chopped down, I was – like Avel, Kostya, Ylli, Titian, Dmitri and Kirill – a filed dossier in a locked cabinet in the vaults of the Lubyanka, a lost man, a non-person.

Kirill sits up.

Listen.

Far away down the gallery, someone is blowing a long blast

on a whistle. It stops. There is a silence deeper than that on the inert surface of the moon. A dull thud reaches us as if someone far away has slammed shut a heavy dungeon door. The light over Avel's head flickers a few times. The air seems momentarily dense and stifles breath.

Kirill puts his hands on his knees and pushes himself up. Avel slips the half-shaped rook into his pocket and secrets his home-made, contraband tool into the folds of his clothing. Kostya stops fidgeting with his lamp.

'They've blown the charge,' Kirill announces laconically. 'Time to be dignified again.'

We set off towards the coal face, walking in a line between the steel rails. As we reach the passing place and siding which exists in every gallery at every level of the mine, Kostya starts to hum, loudly. The tune is familiar but it takes me several minutes to place it. He must have picked it up at the movies, on one of his many voyages around the world. It is the *Heigh Ho!* song from Walt Disney's *Snow White and the Seven Dwarfs*.

And there are seven of us.

*

Sosnogorsklag 32 forced labour camp consisted of fifty wooden barracks, assorted administrative buildings, stores, quarters for the guards and a large parade ground or mustering area where we were counted before leaving for the mine or returning from our shifts there. The whole camp was surrounded by several five-metre high barbed wire and electrified fences surmounted by watch towers, wire entanglements and a three-metre deep moat filled with more wire and iron stakes. The land around was covered in grass and scrub, more or less flat and treeless. Had it sand and had it not had the Arctic Circle bisecting it, it would have been a desert.

Work Unit 8 was housed in Hut 14, the last barrack in the first row alongside the wire. In it lived 160 prisoners, all of them men. The bunks, one per prisoner, were erected in tiers of four down either side of the hut with just sufficient space between them to allow access. Down the length of the hut ran an aisle, just two men wide. Every three metres, a light socket fitted with a 40 watt bulb hung from the roof beams, protected from any leaks in the roof or dripping condensation by a tin shade. There were no cupboards, foot lockers or the like except, at one end, there was a small and usually empty storage room not much larger than a lavatory cubicle by the door of which a sack of fuel was kept for the stove.

My bunk was on top of the last tier at the end of the hut close to the storage cubicle, bounded by two outside walls which, despite their insulation, did not keep out the cold. It was not unknown for the nails holding the wooden panels in place to conduct the Arctic winter in and become so cold as to have the heads ice up with condensation and crack.

At the farthest end of the hut from the door was an area devoid of bunks. Here, a large table stood surrounded by several benches. It was here we ate, three work units at a time for there were insufficient benches to seat more than twenty-five prisoners. Beyond the table was an open space in the centre of which stood the stove. It was large, made of cast-iron and the only form of heating in the hut other than our own bodies. It was our responsibility to light the stove every day, stoke it up with fuel before we were called out to roll call and a day in the mine. If we could get it really going before we left, and closed the air vent right down, it would stay alight through the day and have the place warm for our return.

It was as a result of this stove that I learnt what Kirill termed my first instruction in the philosophy of endurance from the Faculty of Incarceration of the University of the Gulag.

I had been in the camp about a month when, one morning, it came round to be Ylli's turn to tend to the stove. He was out of his bunk before the rest of us, riddling the ashes, huffing and puffing on a few remaining embers which he had surrounded with several fistfuls of wood shavings one of the pit head carpenters had filched from the workshop where they cut the pit props. The fuel we were issued with consisted of lumps of compacted coal dust and clay which were bastards to ignite but which smouldered slowly for hours once they were alight.

As I settled my feet into my *valenki*, the Russian felt boots with which we were issued, there was a commotion by the stove. A Muscovite thug called Genrikh, the leader of the *blatnye*, had discovered it to be barely warm. The shavings were only just catching.

The *blatnye* were the criminal class inmates, arrested not for crimes against ideology and dogma but because they had broken heads and bones, slit some sucker's throat in a dark alley and made off with his wallet. They lacked the close-knit camaraderie of our little group, were a more disparate bunch, individuals thrown together in a brotherhood of disdainful violence rather than souls, forced by a common circumstance rather than the powerful wills of sadistic men, into a common predicament.

There were eleven *blatnye* under Genrikh's leadership. He was serving twenty years for murder, arson and the rape of six women which, he was proud to proclaim, he had had over a period of 65 hours. The murder charge was for the third woman, whom he had strangled because of her resistance to his fornication, the arson for the sixth whose apartment he torched. His fellow *blatnye* called him the Tsar, in which sobriquet he revelled for he saw himself as an emperor although he would have preferred himself to be coupled with Ivan the Terrible rather than Nicholas II, whom he referred to as His Milksop Majesty.

'You!' he shouted at Ylli. 'You! The Balkan turd. The Mohammedan shit cake.'

Ylli turned. He was not the sole Muslim in Hut 14 but he was the only Albanian.

'You! Allah's bum-boy! You call this a fire?' Genrikh growled, stepping towards his victim.

Ylli made no reply. Genrikh grabbed him by the scruff of his collar and shook him, thrusting him towards the stove, forcing him down on his knees in front of the fire-door through the stained mica window of which the first flames were beginning to flicker.

'You call this a fucking fire?' Genrikh repeated. 'Feel it!'

He slammed Ylli's head against the cast-iron carcass of the stove. The metal was hot but not enough to scald him. Ylli, with an animal cunning, allowed himself to go limp, to be completely at the mercy of the Tsar. After a moment, the *blatnoi* dropped him to the concrete floor and kicked him, not too viciously, upon the thigh.

'You limp prick!' Genrikh said, his voice thick with contempt.

Ylli, doubled at a crouch, headed back in our direction and did not stand upright until he was out of Genrikh's sight between the rows of bunks.

We said nothing, just gave him a quick smile of encouragement and got on with readying ourselves for the day ahead. Ylli was no less in our eyes for his cravenness. We were there to survive. Any one of us might have done the same. He lost his dignity, perhaps, but he kept his life, his self-respect and our esteem and that was what was valuable.

Lining up at the door to go out for muster and counting, Kirill leaned over to me.

'Are you ashamed, Shurik?' he enquired.

'Ashamed?'

'Yes. Ashamed for Ylli, ashamed you did nothing to help him, ashamed we live like this.'

I nodded my head, embarrassed to admit I was. Outside, the guards were calling for Hut 13. It would soon be our turn to head out into the freezing darkness.

'Don't be,' Kirill advised. 'Just learn the lesson, Shurik. Take it to heart and hold it there, like a long-lost love. After all, what is the difference between Genrikh and the Politburo? Or, come to that, Genrikh and Winston Churchill? President Eisenhower?

General De Gaulle? Nothing! All you have seen is the exercise of authority, the exploitation of power. It is always cruel, to suit its purpose. As for us? We fight and die, or adapt and live.'

*

The drill hit an unexpectedly hard vein of rock, the bit screaming. I flicked the switch to increase the flow of water from the spray nozzle by the chuck but it made no difference. The screeching continued, rising in pitch to the intolerable level of a dog whistle.

'You see him?' Titian yelled, jerking his head over his shoulder.

Glancing in the direction his head indicated I nodded, partly in recognition of his question and partly in response to the vibration of the drill. By the coal trucks stood a man with a scar upon his left biceps which showed white against the coal-caked remainder of his arm. The damaged tissue was devoid of hairs and was so smooth his sweat consistently sluiced it clean.

I eased back on the trigger. The drill slowed to a dull whine. Unclipping it from its tripod, I swung it back on its bracket, retracting the bit from the coal face. The cutting surfaces at the tip were as bright as molten mercury and just as blunt.

'Lousy Ukrainian steel,' Titian remarked. 'Wrong carbon content. They can never get it right. You know his name?' he added in an undertone, no longer competing with the drill to be heard.

I shook my head and, turning the compressed air tap shut, started to release the chuck. Dmitri, seeing what I was doing, went off down the gallery to fetch a new bit.

'Vachnadze, a Georgian from Kutaisi. He's the leader of 39. They usually work at the pit head.'

'What's he doing down here?'

Titian shrugged and said, 'Someone blotted his copy book. But he'll be back up in a week or two. Safe above ground with the birds and the clouds. You know what they call him?'

41

I shook my head again. The chuck was loose and the bit starting to slide out. I tilted the drill forward, the bit clattering onto the rock at my feet, spitting where the hot metal touched a puddle of standing water.

'They call him Odds-On.' Titian saw the puzzlement on my face. 'He was caught embezzling Party funds,' he continued, 'to pay off his debts. He's a gambler.'

'What did he gamble on?'

'Football matches, boxing fights, cards, dice.'

I looked at Vachnadze. He was leaning on a shovel, looking like any other prisoner in the mine but, now I knew his story, he took on a different aura. It was always like this: we were such a uniform-looking bunch in our regulation prison issue clothing and layering of coal dust that all that really distinguished us, apart from our heights, was our backgrounds. When you learnt that so-and-so had been a rocket scientist or a farm-worker, a general or a tram driver, it coloured them in your eyes. You started to perceive those pieces of their past which fitted their present character and you used the information to judge them and know them.

'I would imagine,' I said, 'that a long stretch in the gulag will cure him.'

Dmitri returned with a new bit wrapped in oiled paper which he started to strip off.

'Don't bet on it!' Titian replied with a broad grin. Even his teeth were speckled with coal. 'He's still at it.'

'Wagering on what?' I asked, somewhat incredulously.

'Anything. Anything at all. He has to gamble just as a miser has to count money, a whore screw or a priest pray.' He gave Dmitri a glance. 'Shall we?'

Dmitri slid the bit into the chuck and I started to tighten the teeth on it. He thought for a moment as he held the bit in place.

'Shame to miss the chance,' he mused.

'Could do...' Ylli contemplated.

'We'll have to be good, comrades,' Titian commented. 'He's as cunning as a viper.'

'Could do what?' I wanted to know.

Titian glanced at Vachnadze. He was now back at work, shovelling the last of the previous shift's coal and rubble into one of the trucks.

'Lay a bet with him,' said Titian.

'And where do we get so much as a kopeck, never mind a rouble, to put on the table?'

'Ah, Shurik!' Dmitri exclaimed. 'You have been here now for - how long? Don't say. We don't count such things. But still you don't know Russians.'

'We don't need money,' Titian said. 'Do you have any *makhorka*?'

'I don't smoke,' I reminded him.

'No, but you get the issue all the same and you trade it like the others who don't use it. Now, have you any?'

The bit was tight in the chuck. Some way down the pressure hose, compressed air was escaping from a weak seal. If I did not turn the tap on soon, it might blow, we would be forced to stop drilling, the holes would not be ready for the explosives team, we should be docked rations for not meeting our quota and life would be tougher than it was already.

'No, I don't,' I admitted and I began to open the air valve, the chuck starting to spin once more.

'But tomorrow is issue day,' Dmitri pointed out over the rising whine, 'so when you get some, keep it. Don't trade it. And in four days, when everyone's smoked their *makhorka*, we'll have a bit of fun.'

In the next rest period, whilst the dynamite charges were set, Titian and Dmitri huddled together with Kostya. They whispered and chuckled. When I enquired what they were up to, they just smirked and told to me save my tobacco. By the fourth day, their plan was in place.

We were hard at work shovelling newly-blasted coal into the trucks. Odds-on Vachnadze was attached to the team installing the new props. Dmitri and Titian kept exchanging glances and winks.

At one stage, Titian leaned over to check I had my tobacco ration on me. Finally, the new props were installed and the trucks filled. The locomotive appeared down the track, its wheels grinding and its brake pads sparking, to tow the filled trucks away and bring down an empty train to replace them. This gave us three or four minutes' respite from our labours.

'What I'd like right now,' Titian observed in a marginally louder than normal voice, 'is a smoke. A good long drag on a Virginia, an American cigarette. A Lucky Strike would do.' To add emotion to this statement, he mimicked putting a butt to his mouth and drawing on it, exhaling with a leisured sigh.

Kostya interjected, 'Lucky Strike! I'd like a fat cigar, thicker than a negro's penis. And longer. A real three-hour smoke. Cuban tobacco. One of those cigars that comes in a metal tube like a toy torpedo.'

Dmitri said, a little wistfully, 'I'd just settle for *makhorka*. But I'm clean out. The old trouble. Smoke it all at once. We *zeks*,' it was the slang word for an occupant of the gulag by which we referred to ourselves, 'savour a cup of soup with gristle like an old tart's lips in it, and sip it as slowly as if it was French champagne just to make it last longer. But tobacco...' He turned to me and winked. 'You don't puff, Shurik. You still in possession?'

'Yes,' I said, taking my cue.

Vachnadze, I noted, was standing by a pit prop, watching us and listening to the conversation.

'Will you trade it?' Dmitri enquired, but his eyes told me to refuse.

'I don't think so,' I said.

'How much do you have, English?' asked Vachnadze, stepping forward.

'My full ration.'

'Why haven't you traded yet?'

There was a touch of suspicion in his voice. Just as Titian had said, he was, I thought, a crafty sod.

'It's best to wait a day or two after the issue,' I explained.

'Then I get a better deal.'

I could sense the machinations of his mind shift into motion, the gear wheels of thought beginning to churn.

'You got it on you now?' the Georgian enquired.

'I've got it where I can get it,' I replied, sliding my hand over my waistband.

'What do you want for it?'

I caught Titian's eye. He was willing me to refuse to trade, to up the stakes, to play the game.

'I haven't thought,' I said. 'What do you have?'

'Dried fish,' Vachnadze answered. 'Not the usually salty shit we get in the stew. Not crushed into dust. Whole fish. Head, gills, tails – the lot.'

I pretended to give his offer consideration then rejected the offer.

'Salted fish makes me thirsty,' I complained.

'And dried meat,' Vachnadze continued.

'What meat?' Avel asked, joining in the conversation.

'He doesn't want cat,' Kostya butted in.

'Some beef, some reindeer,' Vachnadze declared. 'Good quality jerky. Tough but you can chew it or boil it.'

'How much do you have?' I asked.

'Enough,' Vachnadze assured me. 'How much tobacco do you have?'

'Why trade?' Titian suggested. 'You're said to be a gambling man, Georgian. Make a bet. What do you say, Shurik?'

Vachnadze looked at me for confirmation of my agreement and I knew then he was hooked.

I nodded my agreement and said, I hoped not too nonchalantly, 'Why not? I shan't be smoking it. It seems a fair risk.'

The wager was made: forty grams of *makhorka* against two hundred and fifty grams of jerky. Then, of course, the question arose as to what the bet would be based upon. A few ideas were mooted – how many trucks full of coal would be carted in the next shift, how many times the lights would dim when the dynamite was detonated, how many drips of water would fall from a certain cracked pipe in a certain length of time. These were all discarded. What constituted a truckful of coal? It could be manipulated. Who would count the dimming of the light, which was not finite? How could we time the drips when none of us possessed a watch?

The quandary was answered by Ylli who had taken no part in the discussion at all so far. Indeed, for the preceding few days he had hardly spoken to any of us when down the mine and I had assumed he was in one of his periodic huffs. Yet it was all part of the grand design. Ylli was our ringer.

'What have we in the mine, which is unpredictable, often seen, easily counted and does not require timing?'

Everyone looked at him.

'Well what?' said Vachnadze testily.

'Mice,' replied Ylli.

It was true. There were mice in the mine, as far down as the very bottom-most gallery. They lived by nibbling crumbs of bread the prisoners accidentally dropped, seeds carried in the mud on the soles of our boots and the packaging of machine parts: it was even rumoured they gnawed sticks of dynamite.

'I suggest,' Ylli said, 'that you bet on the likelihood of a mouse appearing during the next rest period. When the blasting team blow the charges, the little buggers sometimes show their heads.'

'What do you say?' Titian offered. 'If a mouse appears, Shurik gets the jerky, if no mouse turns up, you get the tobacco.'

Vachnadze thought about it for a moment before his face broke into a grin and he held his hand out.

'Done!' he stated.

Titian slapped his hand against Vachnadze's and the bet was sealed.

In the next rest period, he quit his own work unit and joined us in a small side chamber quite empty of stores. We all stood in the semi-darkness alert, watching the entrance to the chamber for a mouse to enter or run by. The leader of the team setting the charges blew the long blast on his whistle, the lights flickered, there was the customary dull thump and thickening of the air.

'That's it,' Vachnadze declared. 'It was odds on no mouse would turn up. You get plenty of them in the summer months, but not so many in the winter.' He pointed to the roughly hewn roof of the chamber. 'It's December up there, comrades.'

I put my hand in my clothing and tugged the packet of *makhorka* free of the lining where I had secreted it. It was forbidden to bring tobacco down the mine.

'What's that?' Kirill remarked in an off-hand manner, pointing to the rear of the chamber. As our leader, he had kept himself aloof from the business of the wager.

Kostya switched on his lamp. Cowering against the rear wall was a grey mouse, its whiskers quivering and its tail straight out behind it.

'A mouse!' exclaimed Dmitri. 'A bloody mouse!'

Vachnadze stared at the rodent with a mixture of annoyance and disbelief. Its beady eye shone in the lamp light: then it was gone, running for cover in a crack in the rock.

'Some you win, comrade, some you lose,' Titian remarked with a smirk he could not control.

Vachnadze handed over a package and stomped out of the side chamber. I replaced the *makhorka* in my clothing and shone my lamp around to see if I could catch sight of the rodent but it had vanished.

Six hours later, as we queued for the cage to lift us to the December night above, shuffling on our padded jackets in readiness for the sub-zero temperatures awaiting us, each of us chewing on a wadge of the jerky, I noticed Dmitri was holding his thumb in the palm of his hand.

'Problem?' I asked.

Unfurling his fingers, I saw the coal grime was darker than usual and shiny. He was bleeding from a gash behind his thumb nail.

'No problem,' Dmitri said.

'Drill bit?' I enquired. 'If it is you'll need to clean it well. The grease they come in...'

'No, no drill bit,' he cut in then, whispering, added, 'Those little buggers have quite a bite.'

3

I have always thought myself to be safe here in Myshkino.

Not from enemies, you understand. I have no concern for them now. Most, if not all, of them have died off, or been demoted, or sacked from whatever service bound them by its codes of hate and fear. The gulag is shut for the likes of me and, until I join a crime gang in St. Petersburg and peddle dope, or attempt a coup in Moscow which fails for lack of commitment or lousy planning, it will remain closed. The only wire that holds me in now is that which also encloses Trofim's chickens which, from time to time, I enter with a bowl of scraps or a handful of corn: the key to their door hangs by a length of string from a hook by the back door.

As I totter towards eternity, a crusty old cove in a tidy jacket in a small village in the middle of Russia, you would think I was beyond care, beyond the reach of elements that might shake my security. What, you would think, could possibly happen to the old boy now. He's been through hell's kitchen – and the adjacent pantry, too – and has still come out with a smile in his heart. What, you could surmise, could possibly test him further.

Until this last week, I would have agreed with the conjecture. I thought I was done with earthquakes of the soul twenty years ago when the gates of the camp swung open and I was cast adrift, a remnant of human flotsam to wash up on Frosya's shore. Time's passage, winter storms, angry words and aching bones held no terror for me now. I was not afraid of them. They could not affect me. But fate, carrying in its basket the disconnected fragments of a long-forgotten past – that was a different matter altogether. Believe me.

As the dawn broke this morning, to turn the eightieth page of the chronicle of my trespass upon earth, I woke to discover the relentless clock taking me closer to being tested yet once more and, as the day drew on, I sidled inexorably nearer to the moment when fate was to knock its gavel on the block and, pointing at me with a finger like a malformed talon, shriek, 'Decide! Decide!' And, just as it was in the gulag or down the mine, I knew I should have no choice but to square up to the inevitable, take what chance served to me and dance to the pipes of fortune.

In truth, I thought, I would rather face death than five o'clock on this sunlit day, the sky dotted with fair weather cumuli, the world at peace with itself and the harvest in the fields half done. Over towards Stargorod, the wheat is already gathered in and the barns are blizzarded by sparrows and finches. Here in Myshkino, they are still gleaning the stubble rows or filching from the uncut ears. The apples in the orchards are early this year, some already suitable for picking, the first of the ripe fruit falling into the grass which, every morning, glitters with dew bedecking the webs of field spiders. Butterflies vie with Stepanov's bees for the bounty of the blossoms.

At least, where death was concerned, I considered, I was prepared, have been so for most of my life.

As I brushed my white and – at last – gradually thinning hair, I studied myself in the mirror. Make no mistake, mine is a face that has seen the action. Gazing into my own eyes, I could spy the past slipping by not in detailed pictures but in moments of love and hatred, terror and joy, elation and depression. The lines on my forehead are furrows you could plant seeds in yet they are not frowns of disgruntlement or cantankerous age but channels of experience, rails to guide me into my thoughts. My cheeks are slightly pink, a sort of healthy glow such as one sees in the faces of children or old men like me who might, if their minds were weak, revert to infancy, spending their days drooling, fingering their privates and waiting for the god to beckon.

Even as the bristles scarified my scalp and tidied my not-too-short locks, for an old man with hair slightly longer than decency dictates has a certain dignity, I could see particles of that past which I have so long denied, to such an extent that now it is little more than a series of disjointed shards of time, like badly edited film, connected by short breaks of darkness.

There was a dog, possibly an Old English setter with a liver and white coat, running under trees the ground beneath which was a carpet of what might have been bluebells. It must have been spring-time although of what year, or of my life, there was no way of telling. A woman in an ankle-length, dark skirt and lace-trimmed, long-sleeved cream blouse called after the dog but it ignored her and scampered on. I could not make out the features of her face nor could I hear so much as a whisper of her voice nor the faintest of yaps from the dog. This was a silent film. A flash of time's void and a house appeared across a wide lawn. The roof was indistinct, the windows nothing more than glass oblongs reflecting a grey sky, the chimneys squat but vague although the upper section of one of them might have consisted of a pattern of double twisted bricks. All that was plain to see was a rampant wisteria hung with lilac bunches of flowers like gossamer grapes. Another flick of black and I was moving down a street, turning a corner and facing a shop the window of which was filled with colourful objects although I was not certain quite what any of them were save three. These were tall, narrow-necked glass bottles with ornate stoppers, each a metre high. One contained liquid red as a blood ruby, the second hyacinthine blue and the third chartreuse green. Above these hung a sign upon the polished black background of which were painted, in gold leaf shadowed with deep vermilion, two indistinct letters and a name I could read as clearly as I saw my own visage in the mirror.

That was enough! Be gone! I had seen sufficient to know what I am and what, as the afternoon drew to an end, I had to decide.

✱

The lane outside Frosya's and Trofim's house is not surfaced but merely a dirt track about three metres wide running down the hill towards the centre of the village. The house is, with the Merry

51

Widow's, the last habitation before the forest begins. In winter, the lane is either a glassine slope of ice upon which Trofim throws the ashes from the fire to give the soles of his *valenki* some purchase, or a morass churned up by feet, Spitsin the pig farmer's horse and cart and the occasional motor vehicle. Now, in summer, it is a dusty track made uneven by the winter's traffic. When it rains, the wheel ruts act as gutters and the hoof-prints as little pools from which, when the sun reappears, swallows and swifts come to dip their beaks and sip. The verges, where the lane runs unevenly along the edge of people's vegetable plots or flower beds, are rank with grasses and wild flowers visited by bees from Stepanov's hives and wild bees'-nests in the forest or butterflies drifting across the world on the currents of their trade winds.

I stepped gingerly along the lane. At my age, a twisted ankle is no laughing matter. It could be the death of me.

A few years ago, Trofim made me a walking stick out of a length of hazel, with a carved boss shaped like an eagle's head and occasionally, so as not to hurt his feelings, I carry it about with me, but I refuse to rely upon it. I needed no stick in the gulag, when I was often bowed by the burden of my labours, and I will not depend upon one now. Today, being my birthday, I left the thing behind. It was not a matter of pride: it was a matter of surrender. I will not – I have never – surrendered, not to circumstance, not to man and certainly not to the tyranny of time.

Halfway down to the village, on the left of the lane, is Komarov's property behind which extends his orchard of about a hundred apple trees, many of them far more gnarled and decrepit-looking than I, but all considerably more fruitful.

As I advanced, making my way cautiously over the rock-hard ruts, I heard a rhythmic squeaking. It emanated from a large shed twenty metres to the right side of the house, approached by a path neatly lined with smooth stones collected from the bed of the river. Against the side of the building were piled hessian sacks tied with twine, dark stains upon them.

Drawing still nearer, the sound suddenly stopped to be followed by a noise akin to a man dropping a load of rubber balls into a wooden bucket. It had a curious music to it, somehow primeval like the throbbing of drums in the jungle or distant thunder in imaginary mountains and meant Komarov was hard at his seasonal work.

It had been my intention to make Komarov my first call on this auspicious day but, as he was clearly busy at his toil, I decided to move on. It was not yet mid-morning: there was plenty of time. Yet it was not to be for, just as I reached the gate and passed through it, Komarov appeared at the door of the shed and, seeing me, shouted out.

'Shurik! Where are you going?'

'On my rounds,' I said. 'As usual.'

'Your rounds?' he echoed, then he remembered. 'Your rounds! As usual! Today is your day, my friend. Nothing usual about it! Come!' He waved his hand, frenetically beckoning to me.

'I don't want to interrupt you.'

'Interrupt me? You won't. I can work and talk. Would welcome it.' He looked towards his house and called out, 'Katya!' There was no reply so he shouted louder. Komarov has a deep booming voice which can carry half a kilometre. 'Katya! Shurik is here.'

I turned back through his gate and started up the path. Had I my walking stick with me, I should have trailed it against the round, grey stones like a boy running his ruler along a fence. Old men have puerile ways and I am no exception.

'Happy birthday, Alexander,' Komarov said somewhat formally, stepping out from the shade of the shed.

'Thank you, Komar,' I replied.

His nickname is an ironic play upon his surname: komar means mosquito. It is most inappropriate for Komarov is a big bear of a man, with a full black beard just starting to grey, hands the size of dried herrings and a laugh so jovial one would think it could draw nails from wood.

'Shurik, step into my lair,' he invited me, shaking my hand, his fingers softer than at any other time of the year. 'Enter the den of the happiest man in the world.'

'It is that month,' I remarked.

The interior of the shed was cool and dark, but not without light. There were cracks in the roof through which sunlight was filtering, spaces between the boards of the walls. Indeed, the building is less of a shed and more of a temporary shelter. Against the far wall was piled firewood for the winter and split lengths of kindling next to three bales of straw the size of steamer trunks, the topmost cut open and trailing stalks on the earthen floor. Yet the function of the shed is not as a store or a winter byre. Komarov keeps no sheep or cows.

In the centre of the structure stood a tall contraption made of wood. At the top was a square funnel below which, projecting from a sturdy oak casing, were two large wooden wheels, one connected to a crank with the other acting as a governor. Both engaged several toothed wooden gear wheels and a pair of stone rollers set only a few millimetres apart. Below this was an oblong tray. All the wood was either grey with age or blackened with usage. This is Komarov's pride and joy, the one thing for which he is envied not just in the village but in the entire district. It is his apple mill.

'There she is,' Komarov declared. 'My once-a-year lady friend. The only whore who can steal me from my wife's bed.'

'How old is this machine?' I enquired.

He laughed and said, 'If she was a woman, she'd be past bedding and if I was her age I'd be past trouncing her. She is...' he thought for a moment '...just over 150 years old. My great-great-grandfather made her. Every square centimetre of the timber used in her came from trees growing within a five kilometre radius of the village. Of this very house. The same with the press.'

He moved around the mill to the other side of the shed. The apple press stood against the wall, a massive wooden screw thread holding the pressing plate in mid-air.

'You know what I call this?' Komarov asked, resting his hand on the suspended plate.

I shook my head and said, 'Komar, you have told me. Every year when it is time to harvest your orchard, you tell me. And every year I forget.'

'The right of an old man, Shurik. This top part, which presses the fruit, is called the bull and this...' He touched the bed beneath, made of elm planking stained to ebony by year upon year of juice. '...is the cow. Sex,' he added, 'is everywhere in the agricultural life.'

Upon the cow was piled a half-made cheese of pomace, alternate layers of straw and mashed fruit. Yellow and black striped wasps hovered lazily in the air around it, drunk on a surfeit of apple flesh. I followed one as it flew unsteadily up to the rafters to become entangled in a spider's web.

Komarov, seeing my eyes tracing the wasp, said, 'Watch now what happens.'

The wasp started to struggle to free itself. The more it endeavoured to free itself, the more enmeshed it became. Suddenly, the owner of the web appeared on the scene. It was a big, dark grey spider with a leg span of at least eight centimetres. Pausing at the edge of its web, it placed its two forelegs upon crucial strands.

'He's testing the tension,' Komarov observed, 'judging the size of his captive.'

With a sudden rush, the spider crossed the web to within a centimetre or two of the wasp. It paused again.

'Now he knows,' Komarov declared. 'Watch what he does, Shurik.'

The spider, far from leaping on the wasp and sinking its poisoned fangs into it, stepped back one arachnidian pace and began to snip the threads of its own web. The wasp was loosened but was still ensnared. The spider moved round, still cutting the net of the web. Finally, the wasp dangled at the end of a single strand. The spider reached it and severed it. The wasp fell to the ground, still threshing about to get free of its bindings.

'So much for the grey wolf of my rafters,' Komarov stated, 'and the stripped tiger of the forests.' He stamped his foot down. 'Even when they are soporific, the spider knows better than to take on a wasp'.

From a lip in the rim of the cow, juice dribbled into a wooden pail large enough to bathe a baby. It was a dull, cloudy amber.

'Try it,' Komarov suggested. 'Go on! Have a sip of the whole of the summer concentrated in a thimble.'

I held my finger under the trickle and sucked my skin. The juice was sweet but had an edge to it.

There was a movement at the entrance to the shed. Katya, Komarov's wife, was there with a tray bearing three glasses of *kvas*, made from the apple juice. The liquid was the faint golden colour of raw plasma.

'Happy birthday, Shurik,' she said and, placing the tray in the sunlight on the edge of the cow, kissed me lightly. 'Eighty years. Such an age. Just to think, you were born in the year of the October Revolution.'

She handed the glasses round and raised hers to me.

'To you, Shurik,' she declared. 'With thanks to God for you being amongst us.'

I nodded politely, accepted the toast and sipped the drink. It was sweet and I imagined it tasted of warm days and meadows. A small shadow edged across the square of bright morning sunlight upon the earth by the door.

'Stas is here,' Katya announced. 'Come, Stas. Uncle Shurik is here and you know what this day is.'

Into the shed stepped a small, tow-headed boy of about five. He was a handsome child, already showing his father's strength but still in possession of his mother's softness. I sensed he wanted to hide behind the bulk of the apple mill but had been instructed not to.

'What have you say?' his father prompted him.

The child swallowed, stared up at me and brought his hands round from behind his back. He held out a small package wrapped in red paper.

'Well, Stas?' his mother urged.

'Alexander Alanovich Bayliss,' he uttered, his voice not much louder than the drone of the inebriated wasps, 'merry birthday.'

'Not merry birthday!' Komarov exclaimed. 'It is happy birthday.'

The little boy grinned sheepishly. I stooped to accept his present.

'Thank you very much, Stanislav Yurievich,' I told him. 'And you may be sure I shall have a merry day.'

It was, in part, a lie. I knew I should not actually be unhappy. That much was the truth. But later on, I considered, when the sun started to dip, then my day might take on a different mien.

The package was easily opened. Within was a small cardboard box. I opened this to discover, protected by flakes of cotton wool, a carved model of a wealthy land-owner's *kibitka* about ten centimetres long. It was perfect down to the smallest detail. The runners under the sleigh curved perfectly, the sides were finely cut and decorated and, beside the sleigh-driver's seat, a whip stood up in the air, a thin twine of leather curling away from it as if caught in mid-motion. I turned the model over appreciatively in my hand.

'When Shurik was a little boy like you,' Katya said to Stas, 'if he had lived in Russia, he would have travelled to school every day in a sledge like that.'

'How did you go to school?' the child queried, drawing courage from his mother's presence.

In truth, I do not remember for I have chosen to forget, and time has aided me in my deliberate neglect, but it is the role of an old man to entertain the young so I lied again.

'When I was six,' I said, 'I went to school in an omnibus.

Later, when I was older, I went in a train.'

Stas thought about this: I might just as well have told him I was taken to school in a gondola set with amethysts, mounted on wheels and drawn by a pair of white unicorns. He walks to the school in the village and, although he has travelled on a bus to Zarechensk, he has never seen a train except in pictures or on the television.

'It was a toy, a hundred years ago,' Komarov explained, pointing to the model.

'How did you get it?' I enquired.

Komarov smiled and replied, 'Like the mill, like the press, my great-great-grandfather made it.'

I was deeply touched. These people were not giving me a gift so much as parting with a treasured and, I was sure, a valuable heirloom.

'What can I say? It is exquisite. I am deeply honoured. Yet, surely, you should keep this, for Stas, for his son, for the future...'

Komarov put his hand on my shoulder.

'My dear friend,' he said, 'we are the honoured. That you have chosen to live here, with us, for - how long is it now?'

'Too long,' I teased him.

'Many years. It must be twenty for I was eleven, or twelve, when you arrived.' He paused to gather himself as if to make a speech. 'You chose to live amongst us, after all we had done to you, after all the years of hate, after the pain.'

'Enough!' I complained. 'You did nothing to me, Komar. Nothing.'

'But the Russians,' Katya begins, 'the Soviet...'

'Are you those people?' I replied. 'Are you the chosen eunuchs of the Supreme Soviet? No. You are not. Like me, you are just common people going about your lives caught in the common mesh of history.' I glanced upwards at the wasps receiving their liberty. 'Like them, but without the sting. And as for this hate of which you speak?' I shrugged dramatically and cast an obvious theatrical glance about the shed. 'I do not see it.

58

As for the pain, well, that was in my muscles, not in my heart.'

'The common mesh of history,' Komarov reiterated. 'I like that. You were always good with words, Shurik. When I was a boy...'

'The less said about your boyhood,' I announced, 'the better. I remember you as a rumbustious little sod. Quick to answer back, full of irrepressible impertinence. I am sure you would not wish your son to hear of his father's waywardness. Or your wife, come to that.'

'I learnt from you,' Komarov said.

'Rubbish!' I retorted. 'You merely came to your senses, realised there was more to life than standing in the fields killing jays. Remember that?'

'I remember,' he admitted. 'You shamed me.'

'You shamed yourself,' I said. 'You knew you were doing wrong.'

'And can you recall what you said to me?'

I thought for a moment before speaking and saw, once again, a well-built twelve-year-old with a small bore shotgun standing at the edge of the forest with a dozen jays dead at his feet, their azure plumage catching the sun and speckled with black clots of congealing blood.

'I think I said that for every beautiful thing a man destroys, two ugly ones are born. You were good at arithmetic, looked at the ground and the message sank in.'

'It scared the hell out of me,' Komarov confessed.

'It was meant to. Teach the father and you teach the son.'

I looked down at Komarov's little boy and put my hand out. 'Stas, shake my hand.'

He was cautious again. Katya nudged him. He slowly brought his small hand out and I took it in mine. It was lost between my fingers.

'There,' I said, 'the old world passes on the future to the new.'

Not looking at their faces, for I knew they were sad, I returned the *kibitka* to its box.

Komarov could not let it go. He had to ask me, as he has done before in what he has decreed to be moments of gravity.

'Do you forgive us, Shurik?'

'Forgive you? For what?'

Komarov avoided my eye and said, 'You know, Shurik.'

I sipped the *kvas*. The sun, cutting through the door and striking the jug, had warmed the contents. It was smooth, like honey brought to blood heat.

As for what it is Komarov knows I know, it is this: his father, Vladimir Nikolaevich, was for six years the *nachalnik* – which is to say, the commandant – of a forced labour camp near Ust' Olenëk. I was never held in that camp but that is of no concern to Komarov. It is enough that I was in the gulag and that his father was a part of the apparatus that held me there.

'Komar,' I said, 'are you a religious man?' It was a rhetorical question and I answered it immediately. 'No. Like me, you give no truck for gods and angels and yet you know the text as well as I do. The soul that sinneth,' I quoted, 'it shall die. The son shall not bear the iniquity of the father, neither shall the father bear the iniquity of the son: the righteousness of the righteous shall be upon him. The Book of the Prophet Ezekiel, chapter 18, verse 20.'

For a Russian from peasant stock who possesses nothing more than a small house his grandfather built, a hundred apple trees and a derelict car which cannot move for lack of a new rear axle, Komarov is exceptionally well-read. When most of his peers sit around the long winter fires playing cards, roasting chestnuts or their toes, watching television or lying cosseted under the blankets with their wives, Komarov reads. This, he claims, is why his friends have four children but he has only one to show for ten years' of marriage: and he has spent long nights forsaking his wife's love, seeking to come to terms with the burden his soul has carried, of which I am a constant reminder.

'Horace,' he parried, 'wrote in his Odes, *Delicta maiorum immertius lues.*'

'I know my Horace,' I rejoined and translated the quotation.

'Though without guilt, you must atone for your father's sins. Do you believe that? If this were the case,' I argued, 'the sins of men would be passed on, multiplying with every generation until the whole world was full of nothing but sin.'

'You have been in the gulag, Shurik,' Katya almost whispered.

'That, my dear Katya, was not the whole world. It was a small blot on the landscape west of the Urals and up towards the Arctic Circle, a few kilometres from a coal mine. If you had been with me in the gulag, you would agree with me that the world is not full of evil. Even there, there was friendship, love, compassion. True, human goodness.'

For a long moment, she looked at me with such puzzlement. She cannot understand my stoicism, cannot come to terms with the fact that I bear no grudges and have simply, as she sees it, shrugged off a quarter of a century hacking coal out of the frozen north to feed the power stations of the temperate south.

'Stas,' I said, to break the tension of this awkward moment for us all, 'will you take this box home for me and ask Frosya to put it in my room? If I carry it with me around the village, I may drop it.'

The child nodded gravely and, accepting the box containing the miniature sleigh, went off with Katya in the direction of Frosya's house.

'I have not told this to you before, Shurik,' Komarov said, watching his wife and child turn through the gate and start off up the lane.

'Said what?'

'I have never told you this,' he ignored my question, 'because I have not wanted you to think I was using it as an excuse.'

'An excuse? For what? What are you going on about, my friend?'

'For...' He had to choose his words. 'For the Soviet Union, as it was. For my father.'

'No man, Komar,' I insisted, 'has to excuse his father. I've said this many times to you. Believe it, believe me!' I raised my finger to drive home the point. 'Himself? Yes! His father? Never!'

'Let me tell you, Shurik, this story,' he went on undaunted by my brief didactic outburst. 'It is true. I swear it on Stas' head. On March 5, 1953, the radio announced the death of Stalin. Maybe he died a few days before. Who can tell? That was the official date of his death. All over the Soviet Union, people gathered in the streets, in the town squares, around the local Party offices. In Moscow, people died, hundreds of them crushed to death in the mass of people on the streets, mourning, wondering about their futures. My father was on leave from his posting. Of course, I was not there. I was not yet born. But my mother – he had married her only the year before – told me he was distraught.'

Komarov turned and emptied another sack of apples into the mill. The rubber ball sound resounded in the shed. An apple bounced free and I picked it up, tossing into the gaping maw at the top of the machine.

'The next day,' Komarov continued, 'my father went to Zarechensk. They had opened a book of mourning in the Party office there. He inscribed his name.'

He set the mill in motion. The apples rolled down, slid into the teeth of the mill and were split apart. The sound of each apple breaking open was a sharp click, like a bone being snapped. The air filled with the tart tang of the raw juice. From between the rollers oozed a mush of apple flesh which dropped heavily into the tray beneath.

For several minutes, Komarov evenly revolved the handle. Not until the last of the apples in the funnel had passed through the mechanism did he stop, sweat beading on his brow.

'Just before my father died, three years ago, I visited him,' he went on. 'He lived in Volgograd, in a small apartment they wanted him to leave after my mother died. It was winter, the street full of slush.'

He dug the wooden spade into the apple mush and swung a load onto the press where it bounced on the layer of straw.

'In the apartment, my father was sitting before the fire. It was an old building, once a mansion but now divided into little flats. Not one of your concrete Khruschev cubes. The roof was sloping, the windows big, the eaves deep. A real house, from the old days of Russia. So he had a fireplace in his room. I touched his shoulder but he did not look up. In his hands, he held a small doll, one of those little mannequins in peasant clothing children like to play with. It was of a man dressed in a cap, like Lenin but without the beard.'

He threw another shovel of pomace onto the cheese of straw.

'A doll?' I queried.

'I thought maybe it was my sister's, from when she was a child. My mother kept such things after the measles killed her. But it was not. It was older. "What is this?" I asked my father in a friendly way and reached down to take the doll. But he gripped it fiercely and tore it from my fingers. Something sharp jabbed painfully into my thumb.'

'What was it?'

'The doll,' Komar said, 'was stuck with pins. Like a voodoo charm. Dress-maker's pins, old-fashioned hat pins, safety pins. Even a hypodermic needle.'

He looked at the rollers in the mill. Apple juice was dripping from it. Tears appeared on his cheek.

'"What is this doll?" I asked him again, a little angry. My finger was beaded with dark red blood for the pin had gone in deep. "Tell me." My father said nothing. I was afraid, for a reason I could not explain even now. I thought he was going senile. Suddenly, he jumped up from his chair and threw the doll onto the fire. It was only a few coals, hardly any flames, but the material of the doll's costume quickly ignited. I said nothing. My father turned and faced me. It was then I knew he would soon die. He stared into my eyes and he said, "That's the last of him."'

'Of whom?' I asked.

'He told me later,' Komarov explained, 'when I put him to his bed. As he grew older, my father saw what Stalin had done to

Russia and he was ashamed. He had, in his feeble way, been sticking pins in what he thought was Stalin.'

'You mean,' I said, 'he had forgotten in his dotage that Stalin was dead.'

Komarov looked at me, a terrible weary sadness in his eyes. He wiped a tear from under his eye with his finger, leaving an apple pip adhering to his cheek.

'Stalin is not dead,' he replied quietly. 'He is still here, with us. Just as all evil men are. We cannot be rid of them, no matter how many dolls we torture and throw on the coals.'

'If evil men remain,' I said, 'then so do the good.'

Komarov could not hold back his tears now. He stood next to his weeping apples, the goodness of the orchard seeping into the bucket, and sobbed. This big bear of a man, who could carry the whole of the Russian winter on his back and hurl it into the sea, stood with his shoulders hunched, his head bowed and his tears soaking into his black beard. I stepped to his side, careful not to slip on gobbets of mashed apple strewn on the ground, took my handkerchief out of my pocket and wiped his face for him as if he were my son.

'Remember this, Komar,' I told him, 'The stupid neither forgive nor forget; the naïve forgive and forget; the wise forgive but do not forget. And, if the years have taught me anything, it is a wisdom of sorts.'

'You are a truly good man,' Komarov said, straightening and blinking his eyes to be rid of the last of his tears.

'No, my dear friend Komar,' I replied, 'I am not. I am just a realist.'

I folded my handkerchief, finished my glass of *kvas* and, biding him farewell with a wave of my hand, set off down the path. Looking back from the gate, I saw him bending his back to another sack of apples and heard the rumble of fruit falling into the mill.

It occurred to me, as I reached the lane, that I did not own the model *kibitka* but merely held it on loan. In a few years, when I am

64

dead, Frosya will return it to Komar and it will re-enter the cavalcade of his family's history, where it should be, but with the added tale attached to it of how, once upon a time, it was given for a year or two to the Englishman who lived down the lane, who forgave those whom he never met.

∗

From Komarov's house, the lane drops slowly down a gentle slope past other houses. Some have little fences between them and the thoroughfare, others nothing but a strip of unguarded land.

The first belongs to Yelyutin, the village carpenter: the whine of his electric jigsaw was just audible from the rear of his property as I passed by, not unlike the sound of the wasps in the cider shed. He has for over a week now been cutting out new facing boards for Andryukha, the baker. A sallow man with a complexion not unlike that of his dough, he has made good money in recent years because he has taken to heart the doctrines of elementary capitalism.

In the old days, no Russian village ever had its own bakery. Everybody made their own bread. Russian stoves were constructed to accommodate the weekly bake. Housewives dedicated their Saturdays to the task, kneading and moulding the loaves with a piece of *zakvaska*, a block of the previous week's dough which served in lieu of precious and expensive yeast. With the coming of Communism, domestic bread-making died out and loaves were mass-produced in state-run bakeries. Andryukha's father, a forester, had been plucked by the Party from his shady glens and sent to work in a co-operative bakery in 1941: his son had followed in his footsteps but, when the red flag ceased to fly, and the bakery was privatised, half the work-force were dismissed as surplus to requirements.

Taking a leaf out of the new management's book, Andryukha privatised himself, erected an extension to his house, purchased three old stoves, built two wood-fired ovens out of

65

fireproof lining bricks purloined from his former employers and set up his own small bakery.

Within a month, he was in business. His bread was good, tasting and smelling like the loaves everyone imagined the grandmothers of Myshkino had baked in the good years before memory. Now he not only sells bread to the villagers but he also bakes pastries and buns which he hands over every morning to a callow youth called Durov who takes them on a superannuated motorcycle to Zarechensk. There, in the bus depot or railway station, he hawks them to waiting passengers or patrols the platform, offering up his flat wicker tray of goodies to open carriage windows. For his pains, he is allowed to keep fifteen percent of all he earns. As a result of his business acumen, and Durov's reluctance to ask for a bigger percentage, Andryukha has bought a three-year-old Volkswagen and is having his house repaired and extended.

Beyond that lies Izakov's home, set back from the lane and closed up: the shutters have been drawn across the windows since last summer, as if it was mid-winter all the year round. The chimney is cold. No smoke has risen up the flue for over two years for Izakov and his wife have departed Myshkino.

At first, no one knew where they had made off to for they left suddenly, early one morning, a suitcase in each hand. A taxi from Zarechensk collected them. They bade no one good-bye. For several months, the old women gossiped about them and a number of rumours did the rounds: Izakov was involved with gangsters, had reneged on a debt, had run off with a younger woman. That his wife had departed with him seemed to have slipped from the common consciousness. Then, just as the first snows of winter began to fall, Father Kondrati received a letter which explained all. It bore three stamps with portraits of Elvis Presley upon them and a Denver, Colorado postmark. Izakov's wife, it transpired, had a distant relative who lived in America and had invited them over to visit. They had gone and decided to stay the winter. The letter requested Father Kondrati arrange for the

66

house to be looked after until the spring. One hundred dollars was enclosed to cover the costs. The priest steamed the stamps off the envelope, separated them and gave them as awards to the three children who had best learnt the catechism: such trophies from the West are much prized by the young these days. The money he passed to the Merry Widow. She tended the place for nine months, even keeping the garden trim through the next summer, but nothing more has been heard of the Izakovs. Now, the house is showing the first signs of abandonment. In another five winters, it will be unfit for habitation.

Opposite the Izakov house is the village school. It, too, is set back from the lane, an expanse of mown grass dividing them. In the centre is a bare patch of earth upon which the village name has been spelt out in pebbles collected by the children and set in cement. When I first came to Myshkino, there was a hammer and sickle above the name but it has been removed, the tell-tale cavities filled in with mortar. Next to the name is a flagpole from which used to hang the red flag of the USSR but which, for the last two years, has been supplanted by the white, blue and red flag of the new Russia. To the left of the building is a playground surfaced with concrete whilst to the right is a football pitch with two white goal posts devoid of nets.

The school is a trim, single-storey building constructed of brick under a sloping shingle roof. The walls are painted white with deep-set, metal-framed and triple-glazed windows which are protected by steel shutters. If it were not a school, one might suppose it to be the home of a well-to-do villager. The verandah on the front, running the entire length of the building and lined with plant pots, suggests it might still be a private house.

I made my way up the broad, stepped path to the school. It was easy going: the steps are low, designed for young children and old limbs. The shadow of the building was cool, as if the walls had retained a vestige of the winter snows.

Going up to the verandah, I found the main door was open. It being summer, the pupils are away on their holidays and the school is not in use: but, from the smell of turpentine, it was plain that someone was redecorating the classrooms.

The interior plan of the building is simple. A central corridor runs from front to back, off which there are two classrooms of equal size, two store-rooms, two lavatories (one for each sex), a teachers' office and a room, formerly used by the local Party apparatchiks but now containing three rows of chairs, a slide projector and a television set.

The classroom on the right was mine.

For the first ten years of my life in Myshkino, I taught in this school. I felt it was my duty to repay the community which had taken me in, believed I owed them an obligation. Besides, I was without money, could not pay my way with Frosya and Trofim and was reluctant to sponge off them. They were adamant that I was not a burden upon them but I knew otherwise. Life was hard for them and my presence made it no easier. I informed them that I could not – indeed I would not – remain with them if I was not able to contribute either to my upkeep or to the village as a whole. A meeting of villagers and the local cadre was convened, from which I was expressly excluded, the outcome of which was the suggestion that if I insisted on doing something then I could help out in the school.

I shall not forget my first day. I was excited by the thought and responsibility of teaching and yet I was also unaccountably alarmed at the prospect. That I had faced and survived KGB interrogation was by the way. I was far more terrified of the children than I ever was of an interrogator in a crisp uniform with a glowing cigarette held between his fingers and a revolver in a holster on his polished belt.

At half past eight, I walked into the classroom and made my way to the teacher's desk on a low dais in front of a wall-mounted blackboard. I can clearly picture the room. The walls were painted off-white and the windows were open with early morning sunlight streaming in. Above the door hung a battery operated clock whilst over the blackboard were suspended a portrait of Stalin spotted with fly shit and a fading photograph of Red Square. At the far end of the room, opposite the blackboard, was a huge map of the USSR, at least three metres by two, printed upon cloth and varnished so that it shone like a piece of highly polished furniture in a palace. A notice-board beside the door carried a laminated card of rules to be obeyed by a good Communist child and a chart showing each pupil's progress in the basic subjects.

The pupils, who ranged from six- to eleven-year-olds, stood up in silence. Every eye was upon me.

'Good morning,' I said. 'Please sit down.'

There was a scraping of chairs as the thirty or so children sat at their tables. Unnecessarily, for everyone in the village who had even the most infantile command of language knew it, I gave them my name and wrote it on the blackboard in both Cyrillic and English alphabets. They watched in silence as my hand moved the stick of chalk over the surface.

'I am going to teach you English,' I announced and, facing the blackboard once more, began to write *Good morning* upon it.

A chair screeched on the floor.

'Alexander Alanovich,' a voice said.

I was not taken aback: Frosya had prepared me well, warned me that the correct way for a pupil to address a teacher was by his first patronymic names.

I turned to find a boy had got to his feet, his hand raised in the air.

'What is your name?' I enquired.

'Demyan Simonovich.'

'And what can I do for you, Demyan Simonovich?' I asked with all the refinement I could muster: yet, within, my very soul quaked with fear of this twelve-year-old.

He glanced about the room at his fellow pupils then said, 'Were you an enemy of the people?'

I looked at him for what must have been five seconds before I smiled.

'No,' I told him quietly, looking him straight in the eye, 'I was never an enemy of the people. I have only ever been an enemy of myself.'

He looked puzzled. A few of his classmates cast him bewildered glances and I realised he had been put up to questioning me. I moved round to the front of the teacher's desk and leaned upon it.

'You will not understand this, Demyan Simonovich. Perhaps not even when you are grown up. Sometimes, I do not understand it myself. All I can say, with all truthfulness, is that I have never been your enemy and I never will be.' I ran my eyes over every up-turned face. 'This is so for all of you. I shall always be your friend. Sometimes, I may be strict and make you do your studies, make you work hard. Yet I will never hate you, never disrespect you, never ever be your enemy.'

Demyan Simonovich sat down. Once more, there was silence then a girl at the back of the class rose from her table and walked down the room with her hands behind her back. Everyone watched her. She kept her head bowed with acute bashfulness. I felt for her, understood the courage she must have had to summon to leave her place. She reached the teacher's desk and placed upon it a single red rose. I picked it up. The bud was only just opening and yet already it was giving off its perfume.

Standing by the door, the stink of the turpentine beginning to give me a mild headache, I wondered what became of her. Demyan Simonovich I know about: he left the school, joined the army, entered a staff college and reached the rank of captain before he was killed in Afghanistan, drawn and quartered by a gang of Mujaheddin who ambushed his tank. But the girl? Try as I might, I could not bring back her name.

There was a movement in my former classroom. I pushed open the door. The hinge needed lubricating.

All the tables and chairs had been piled against the far wall and covered in a canvas tarpaulin. Poised on a ladder in the centre of the room was a man in paint-smeared overalls, running a roller over the ceiling, dipping it in a tray balanced on the top rung. At the sound of the hinge squeaking, he peered over his shoulder, saw me and nodded a greeting. I did not know him: he was not from Myshkino but had been sent by the regional public buildings authority.

I passed on through the room and entered the store leading off it. The shelves were laden with books, rolled up posters, packs of exercise books and chalk, boxes of pencils and all the usual assortment of educational equipment. On the top shelf, sticking out into the room and covered with dust, was the vast map which used to hang on the back wall of the room, now redundant and superseded by history and the political whims of a world turning faster and faster by the week. I ran my fingers along the rows of books: Dickens and Swift leaned against Turgenev, Mark Twain and Jack London rubbed bindings with Zola and Pushkin. Pulling one of the posters out of its cardboard canister, I found it was a map of the night sky which I had drawn for an astronomy club I instigated amongst the pupils. In the corner, I had signed and dated it – 1980.

Returning it to the tube, I heard disembodied voices. There was not one to which I could put a name or a face, nor was I even sure of what they were saying: yet they were all young and eager, filled with the zealous vibrancy of children discovering wonders. They spoke in Russian, and in strongly accented English and, mingled with them, I heard a man's voice, confident and filled with love and I knew it was my own.

4

In front of us, the pit head buildings loomed squat and foreboding in the crisp night air, only the lower third illuminated by the lights surrounding the marshalling and assembly yard. Close to the main door to the mine offices, the duty overseer and his sidekick had positioned themselves on a low platform under a brighter than average light. The guards, posted around the periphery of the mustering area, held their Simonov automatics across their chests or stomachs, stamped their feet and watched us from the shadows cast by the peaks of their *ushankas*. To our left, the mine stores and coal sorting sheds ran in a row behind which the slag heap rose like a mountain, darker than the overcast night sky itself. On the other side of the yard were the railway sidings, rows of coal trucks parked under intermittent lamps mounted on posts made of rusting steel girders painted grey. It was along this edge of the mustering area that most guards were stationed, to foil anyone who thought he might like to go for a runner.

No prisoner had attempted an escape for over three years and then, as Dmitri had put it, he had been slowly falling off his bicycle for weeks. He had had to have been: he made his break for it in the summer, during the white nights when the sun never set and the guards could see him three hundred metres off, sprinting over the uneven ground like a hare keeping one hop ahead of the hounds. They had made sport with him, firing deliberately wide, or short, turning him this way and that before the officer on duty took careful aim and brought him down with a single shot through his spine. He was still alive when they reached him to put a bullet through his skull with a revolver.

Yet that made little difference: someone had once tried it on, the precedent had been set and the intractable mind and policies of the mine authorities had been shaped.

Like the guards, we stamped our feet and shuffled about.

73

Partly, this was to keep our circulation going but it also disguised our muted conversations. Talking on muster was forbidden but, like many of the rules, if you could break them and get away with it, you did. The attitude was dismissive for the mine managers could do little. If they trimmed your rations, you lost energy and the production quota was not met. If they put you in solitary, the quota was missed. If they shot you, they were another pair of hands short at the coal face. Everyone tacitly knew the status quo. Of course, it cut two ways: if you were sick, you worked until you dropped. As for the guards, they couldn't care less. So long as no one took it in mind to make a dash for the coal trucks or headed for the gate on a suicide sprint, they didn't give a toss.

A loudspeaker crackled and a metallic voice sputtered, 'Work Units 25 to 49! Forward!'

Five lines of prisoners stumbled forward at a half run, heading for the building which housed the winding gear. Their feet thumped rhythmically upon the leaden, frozen slush coloured with coal dust. In the sidings, a locomotive loudly vented a rush of steam which lazily rose about three metres in the frigid air before, being robbed of its heat, it collapsed, the water droplets freezing and drifting down in strands. It looked like ectoplasm in faked photographs of Edwardian seances. Into the night sky, the locomotive funnel pumped billows of dense black smoke as the pistons took the strain and the wheels began to turn. The locomotive chuffed thrice then died: the crew were testing the axles had not become seized with ice overnight. Over the pit head, we could hear the cables whining as the cages dropped.

Dmitri beat his arms against his sides in time with the locomotive and let out a hiss of breath. Like the steam, it too rose a few centimetres then tumbled to vanish towards his feet.

'There was this little polar bear,' he began. 'A baby, a cub, sitting on an ice flow five hundred kays north of Archangel. With its mummy and daddy bear.'

'Was it an Armenian polar bear?' Kostya interrupted.

For reasons we never divined, Dmitri had it in for Armenians.

74

If it occurred to him, he would twist a joke to denigrate them, ridicule them or lambast them. His hatred was complete. If he met an Armenian, he ignored him completely. Ylli conjectured it was because he had caught a dose of the clap off an Armenian tart when he was serving his time in the army but it was only a guess. Kirill, more wisely, once confided in me that it was something to do with someone he had known in the army, who had scotched his being made up to corporal, but he did not elaborate.

'They don't have polar bears in Armenia,' Dmitri replied, a hint of tired vexation in his voice. 'As an ignorant sailor you wouldn't have come across Armenia. Naval training won't have mentioned it. They've got no coastline for you to go whoring along.'

'So why don't they have polar bears?' Kostya wound him up.

'You want to hear this,' Dmitri addressed the rest of us, 'or shall we continue with sailor boy's geography lesson?' He did not wait for our answer. 'There's a baby polar bear on the ice cap with his parents. He goes up to his mother and asks, "Am I a true-blooded polar bear?" "Why, certainly," his mother tells him. "Absolutely pure polar bear?" "Yes." "Not part grizzly bear?" His mother's getting a bit short on patience by now. "You're pure, 24 carat polar bear. If you don't believe me, ask you father." Baby bear trots across the ice to his father who's sitting by an ice hole eating a seal. "Daddy," says the bear cub, "am I a pure polar bear?" "No doubt about it," Father Polar Bear replied through a mouthful of seal blubber. "You're a dyed-in-the-wool polar bear from arse to ears." "I'm not part panda bear? Or brown bear?" questions baby bear. "Out of the question," his father tells him. "You are absolutely, one hundred and ten per cent, to the very core, a polar bear. So why do you ask?" "I wondered because," says the baby bear, "I'm fucking freezing!"'

We chuckled amongst ourselves. The guards and overseers aside, it was too cold to laugh out loud: below -30°, the air could crack the enamel on your teeth.

In the two and a half decades – and a bit added on for good measure, to make me sure I was not going to trust in miracles or certainties – I was in Sosnogorsklag 32, I cannot recall ever hearing one of Dmitri's jokes repeated. Where he got his fund of tales from remains a mystery to me. I cannot believe he remembered them all from the days before the gulag: most of us lost, either through deterioration of our minds or deliberate erasure, or had few if any pre-incarceration memories. I can only assume that he made them up, that he lay in his bunk and, whilst the rest of us were escaping into the universe of our dreams, he set himself a task to invent a new joke for his captive audience. In more ways than one.

'I know how the cub felt,' Ylli remarked to no one on particular.

'You think this is cold?' Dmitri responded. 'This isn't cold. This is cool. You've too much Albanian Mediterranean sun in your veins. Still,' he added, 'don't worry. They'll drain it out of you yet. As for cold...'

His eyes, squinting against the freezing air, narrowed further. I knew what was coming. Dmitri was going back to Leningrad, in 1942.

'This is not cold,' he continued quietly. 'Cold is when you think you should be warm, when you are in your apartment but the stove is out, the windows are broken, you are wearing the curtains on top of your coat, and there's no food on the table except what is left of your daily 125 grams of bread made out of rye flour and wood shavings. And a haunch of your neighbours' tabby.' He put his gloved hand on Ylli's arm. 'I hope, sincerely, in the name of whatever you hold dear, that you, my friend,' he moved his head in a circle to indicate the whole of the pit head facilities and the lines of waiting *zeks*, 'in this comparatively tropical adversity, will never know real cold.'

The loudspeaker fizzled again.

'Work Units 1 to 24! Forward!'

We set off at the regulation jog, passed the overseer and his sidekick who counted off the units, and in through the wide door over which hung the sign that mocked us every day of our lives.

Labour is Dignity.

At the cage door, we gathered in groups by unit, keeping close together to ensure we all stepped into the same cage together.

'Prepare to descend!' ordered another loudspeaker, screwed crookedly to a girder overhead and caked in grime.

We removed our *ushankas*, replacing them with our aluminium helmets. Those of us with lamps tested the batteries, little lights going on and off like candles during Mass in a monastery.

'Where're we going?' Avel enquired, shouting above the noise of the winding gear.

Kirill held up an aluminium disc the size of a saucer into which had been stamped the letter R.

'R for Rasputin,' he called back, 'who Rogered the Royals.'

The cables started to vibrate. A strong breeze of warm, feisty air swept over us as the cage came into view and the wire doors clanged open. An overseer by the cage held up a disk similar to Kirill's and we pressed forward, competing with the other work units heading for the same gallery.

I managed to get in ahead of my team, to find myself squeezed against the rear of the cage. The doors were swung shut, an electric bell rang discordantly and the cage set off, plunging down the main shaft. By the light of the two bulbs hanging from bare sockets in the cage ceiling, I could see the walls of the shaft rush by, wires and pipes snaking faster and faster as we fell more and more quickly. A strong wind blew upwards past my face and, as we neared our destination in the penultimate gallery of the mine (S for Stalin who sold us into slavery), I closed my eyes and mouth, pinching my nostrils. We all did. The cage nearing the bottom the shaft kicked up a lot of dust in which, mine legend had it, diseases unknown to medical science also lurked, living on the decayed corpses of those of us who had not lived to see the end of a shift.

The cage slowed and stopped, bouncing for thirty seconds

on its steel cables. At over two kilometres depth, the cables were as elastic as a rubber thong. Finally, the cage was opened and we stepped out. Ahead stretched Gallery R, disappearing in the perspective of lights which looked, I thought, like a necklace of ever-diminishing translucent pearls. Under other circumstances, it might have been almost beautiful.

*

Like most of the levels in the mine, Gallery R was not a single entity but consisted of a central tunnel from which a maze of side galleries diverged following the route of a number of coal seams. Some of these side galleries were substantial but others were what the miners called mole holes: and it was to one of these we were assigned.

About one hundred and fifty metres long, it followed a narrow coal seam running at right angles to the main tunnel. Not only was the seam it traced constricted but it was also thin, the gallery not much more than one and a half metres high in places and never above two metres from rock floor to ceiling. These restrictions meant that only one work unit could operate it at any one time.

On first being allocated the Gallery R mole hole, we had groaned with dismay but Kirill had dispelled our concerns, as he always did as leader, by pointing out the advantages as well as the setbacks.

'So,' he had said, 'we're going to be furry little bastards for a bit. And we all know what a mole hole means. It means crouching and crawling, hauling and heaving. No drilling, because the seam's too small, therefore no explosives. This is pick and shovel time.'

'And getting the black crap back?' Kostya muttered. 'Wooden sledges!'

Kirill gave him a look that silenced him and went on, 'I've been talking to Kochetov. His unit had it last. It's true it's a bugger, with no lighting. We'll have to do something about that to

78

avoid depending upon our lamps. But there are advantages. First, because the seam's small, we don't get a fixed quota. We just hack out what we can and deliver it to the main gallery, tipping into any truck that happens to be going by. No one checks our tally. We can do one sledge a shift or we can do one hundred. Who's to know? Second, the overseer never visits. He can't be bothered playing hunchback for three hundred metres to inspect a coal face no bigger than a baker's basket. Kochetov said they never saw him. Not once in a month. Third, we're on our own. No other work unit is involved. We're our own masters. There's no breaks for dynamiting, but so what? We can rest when we like, work when we like. So long as we don't slack right off, and we keep our eyes peeled, we're safe.'

Within the first two days, we had the gallery sorted out. Kirill managed to filch a socket and a four hundred metre roll of electric cable from a store which, when no one was looking, Ylli tapped into the main power supply line in the main tunnel. We ran the line all the way to the coal face and rigged ourselves a light. It was against the rules for mole holes to have electric light but no one could see it for the tunnel dipped and turned after leaving the main thoroughfare and if, by some chance, the overseer did decide to inspect us, we would claim it was there when we arrived. Admittedly, the bulb was dim for the cable was sub-standard and a good fifty per cent of the power was lost on the way from the connection but it was better than relying upon battery-powered lamps. The wooden sledges were cumbersome but Kostya managed to purloin some strips of steel which he screwed to the runners. By the time he was done, we must have had the only smooth sliding sledges in the mine.

The work was hard. The short-handled picks we were issued with had to be swung horizontally for there was insufficient height to bring them down over our heads. When the steel hit the face it often shattered the coal, sharp fragments flying out to pepper our skin: having no goggles, we had to close our eyes with each impact. Two of us hacked at the coal face, two shovelled the cut

79

coal and rock into the sledges and two hauled it away. The seventh member – we rotated the responsibility – kept a fictitious tally and watched out for the overseer. Setting ourselves a target of twenty sledges a shift, which was a fraction of what we normally produced from a primary gallery, we worked steadily, pacing ourselves and generally taking it easy. By the eighth day, we were settled into our routine and plainly getting away with it. Kostya was even wondering aloud how easily Kirill might be able to swing a longer stint in the mole hole without arousing suspicion from the overseers and the other leaders of the work units.

I can still recall, as if they were a dream from which I had just woken, the events of the second half of our fourteen-hour shift on that memorable day.

We had been working for three or four hours when Kirill, who was shovelling coal into the sledges, suddenly stopped. We downed tools and watched him.

'Avel,' he whispered, after a few minutes, 'Shurik! Check the pit props. Dmitri, go down the tunnel, have a listen. Titian, go with him. Kostya, go down to the main tunnel and work your way back. Ylli, watch the coal face.'

Avel and I quickly inspected the pit props we had installed at the start of that shift then began working backwards from the digging. Everything seemed in order. There was no splintering, no buckling, no movement at all that we could detect. We returned to Kirill and gave him the thumbs up. Kostya came back, shook his head and shrugged. No one spoke. Kirill needed silence.

'Do you hear that?' he asked in not much more than a whisper, after several minutes during which the only sound I could hear was Ylli's breathing and my own heart pounding like a kettle drum.

We looked from one to the other. I could see the wells of fear opening their maws in Ylli's eyes.

Of the seven of us, Ylli was the one most afraid of our shared subterranean existence. For most of the while, he suppressed his terror, deceiving himself that there was no need for concern, pretending there was nothing more above our heads than a few metres of loose earth, tree roots and the burrows of Arctic foxes. Yet on occasion, when a prop sighed, a fine shower of gravel spattered down, a stone dislodged itself or Kirill stood motionless, listening – then he had to take a grip on his nerves, lie all the harder to himself, win the argument between logical reason and the basic instinct to see the sky and feel the wind, even if it blew through tangled strands of rusty barbed wire.

'You know what that is?' Kirill continued, his eyes now closed. 'That's the music of sempiternity. It is the cantata of creation, the symphony of all the souls trapped in the earth, all the dead creatures that have ever lived.'

Kostya gave me a quizzical look and put his finger to his forehead, tapping the skin lightly. I could see him mouth, *Is he losing it?*

Kirill said quietly, 'Shurik, put your ear to the rock.'

I did as he bade but, for a moment, I could discern nothing save my own pulse: then, I heard it. It was a minute squeaking, no louder than a mouse on the surface of the moon.

'You can hear it now, can't you, Shurik?' Kirill asked in a faraway voice.

I nodded. The others put their ears to the rock walls of the mole hole.

The squeaking changed in pitch to a brief, low, barely perceptible vibrant hum which ended in an abrupt click. There followed several seconds of silence then a minute whine, not unlike that of a mosquito or a violin being tuned in a heavily padded box a hundred kilometres away.

'The language of dinosaurs played by the orchestras of time,' Kirill whispered.

'What does it mean?' Ylli enquired in a small voice verging on the jittery.

Kirill opened his eyes and said, 'There's nothing we can do about it. Forget it.'

'Forget it?' Ylli retorted. 'All this poetic shit about earth music and dinosaur orchestras! What you mean is the rocks're shifting and there's going to be a cave in.'

'Not necessarily,' Kirill replied, his voice calm and even. 'But even if there is, what are you going to do about it? Run for the surface and get shot as an escaper? Complain to the General Administration of Camps? *Dear Commissar for Camps*,' he mocked, '*I am serving twenty years in Sosnogorsklag 32 where the coal mine is collapsing on me. Please transfer me to an open cast pit. Your obedient servant, Ylli the Albanian*. We can do nothing. This is our fate. If destiny has decreed that we get buried alive under two kilometres of Soviet rock, so be it.'

'Stuff fate!' Ylli responded, his anger rising as his awareness of his impotence increased in exponential relation to his mounting anguish.

We were all silent for a moment then Dmitri picked up his shovel, running it into the pile of cut coal.

'You can't stuff fate,' he remarked. 'What's to be will be.' He dropped the shovel-load in one of the sledges. 'This is a good one. A true story. There was once a man cycling through the countryside on his way to market, his bicycle loaded with onions, when he reached a railway crossing. The bar was coming down. A train was on the way. After a minute, a farmer with a goat arrived and tethered the goat to the bar while he lit a cigarette. Then another farmer arrived with a mule and cart laden with maize on the cob. They are all going to market.'

He thrust his shovel into the coal and deposited another five kilos in the sledge.

'Where?' Kostya enquired obtusely.

'Where?' Dmitri echoed.

'What kind of market?' Kostya went on.

'What kind of market?' Dmitri exploded: he was not used to having his stories disrupted so resolutely. 'What're you talking about?'

The rest of us joined in, temporarily dispelling Ylli's fear, drawing his mind away from the capricious fainéance of the earth.

'What kind of market?' Titian repeated.

'What does it matter?' Dmitri replied.

'Livestock?' I ventured. 'Vegetable? Fruit?'

'Slave-girl?' Kostya added facetiously.

'It was a market!' retorted Dmitri. 'It's a story, for fuck's sake! Who cares?'

'Where?' Kostya reiterated with stolid determination.

'What do you want to know for?' Dmitri snapped. 'Armenia has no interest for sailors.'

'Ah! So it's Armenia!' Avel exclaimed.

'Where else?' I said. 'Dmitri doesn't know any other countries.'

Dmitri gave me a sharp look and spat on the coal to clear the dust from his throat.

'Just before the train came,' he went on, 'a Party official drew up in his car. When the train rattled over the crossing, at 100kph, it startled the mule which kicked the cycling onion-seller on the shin. He, being angry with the pain, slapped the mule's rump. The mule-driver jumped down from the cart to scuffle with the cyclist and the mule, no longer reined in, reversed the cart into the car, denting the front, smashing the head lamp. The Party official climbed out of the car – someone was going to pay for damage to an official vehicle. The farmer, seeing a fight develop, came to try and stop the trouble. The crossing bar rose and the goat had his neck stretched. Now that,' he ended, slapping his hand on the shaft of the shovel with finality, 'is what I call fate.'

Even Ylli laughed, albeit nervously, at the monstrosity of the tale.

'And that's a true story?' Avel asked incredulously.

Dmitri smirked and said, 'In Armenia, anything can happen.'

'What became of the people?' I asked.

'They all wound up in the gulag,' Titian said. 'The onion-seller got five years for inciting a riot, the mule-driver got ten for being negligent in charge of a cart, the official got fifteen for allowing damage to Party property and the farmer got twenty years for associating with three others who were enemies of the people.'

We returned to cutting and carting coal and had almost filled our self-imposed quota for the shift, with three hours to spare when, suddenly, there was a rumble like distant thunder and the rock all around us briefly vibrated. As one, we froze. Ylli's face went white under its layer of coal dust and sweat. Fragments of rock spattered down from the ceiling, bouncing on the floor. In less than ten seconds, it was over.

'We're okay, comrades,' Kirill said softly. 'Don't worry.' He glanced at Ylli. 'Are you all right?'

Ylli was rooted to the spot, turned to stone with the fear he was doing his utmost to suppress. I realised then that he must have lived with the terror of this moment every day since arriving in the camp. Avel put his arm round his shoulder.

'Everything's fine,' he reassured him. 'If it was serious, the power would have failed. Look, the light's still on.'

Ylli moved his eyes and stared at the bare bulb. Very slowly, a smile crept across his face. Kirill patted his cheek.

'Good boy!' he said gently. 'We're all just as shit scared as you are.'

Titian, who had been on sledge duty, appeared running down the tunnel, ducking where the roof dipped down.

'There's been a rock fall in Gallery N,' he reported breathlessly. 'A big one! We're instructed to stay put, do nothing. Down tools. The cages're being used for emergency crews. Nobody's going to the surface until they get things straight up there.'

Kirill, who had experienced a mine collapse before and knew the ropes, gave out his orders. I was sent to the main shaft to refill our canteens with drinking water before the supply was switched off. Dmitri came with me but vanished down another shaft to return with three loaves of bread stashed under his coat. Ylli and Avel inspected the pit props along the entire length of our mole hole: Kirill knew they were sound but he wanted Ylli to share his confidence and the only way to do that was to give him the task of checking.

'That's it for now, comrade moles,' Kirill said as we all reassembled at the end of our tunnel. 'All we do is wait.'

For some time, we sat about and talked but, as time passed, we grew weary of conversation and retreated one by one into our thoughts. Avel set about carving another chess piece whilst Dmitri and Kostya flicked pebbles of coal against the far wall of the tunnel in a game of pitch-and-toss. Titian recited poetry to himself under his breath. Kirill dozed and Ylli lay on the ground, on his side, stifling his fear. As for me, I leaned against the rock and, allowing my mind to go blank, turned my head to one side so as not to miss the opening bars of the next rhapsody of the rocks.

I must have drifted off for the next thing I remember was being gently shaken. I came to immediately, adrenalin sluicing through me. Yet it was not the rocks but Titian touching me on the shoulder. The others were silent, alert and looking down the tunnel.

'What is it?' I whispered.

Titian leaned towards me and murmured, 'Someone's coming.'

Very slowly, we all stood up. I could just hear footsteps approaching. They were slow, soft, careful footsteps, redolent with stealth. Dmitri picked up a shovel. Ylli grasped the broken shaft of a pick that had cracked the day before.

'*Blatnye?*' I muttered.

There was not a single one of them who was not above murdering a political prisoner for fifty grams of bread, a pair of *valenki* with holes in the soles and a spare lamp battery. Our only defence against them was to stand united in the face of their onslaught: the team spirit of a work unit counted for more than just productivity and the meeting of quotas to avoid ration cuts.

'Could be,' Kirill answered softly. 'Not the overseer, that's for sure.'

Glancing around for a weapon, my eye settled on a two kilo

lump hammer we used to smash the larger nuggets of coal which would not fit in the sledge. It would be of little use against a determined *blatnoi* and his razored shiv but at least it would show intent. I would go down fighting.

We waited.

The footsteps halted. There was a shuffling sound.

'It's all right,' Dmitri whispered. 'It's just someone coming down for a shit in what he thinks is a disused tunnel.'

No sooner had he spoken than the shuffling ceased and the footsteps began again.

'Damn quick crap!' Kostya observed, raising one of the shovels to waist height as if it was a pikestaff.

It was now apparent that there was more than one set of footsteps. Whoever was approaching, they were coming in numbers.

A little way from the coal face, the tunnel turned a 30° bend. Just beyond it, the footsteps halted again. We could pick out the incomprehensible undertones of a brief, muted conversation. By now, I thought, they would have seen the faint gleam of our forbidden bulb and it occurred to me that, when they came round the corner, we would be at a disadvantage. They would see us as clearly as actors on a stage but they, beyond the reach of the light, would at best be as disembodied faces in the twenty rouble seats.

The conversation stopped. The footsteps recommenced. They were advancing.

With every nerve primed and ready, we stood our ground. Suddenly, the footsteps were louder. They had turned the bend and could behold us now but we could not yet see them.

Gradually, as ghosts manifesting themselves upon the black void of the grave, or as figures looming out of a jet black mist, the figures slowly materialised. They were dressed in the same prison issue clothes as ourselves and they carried the same aluminium hats.

'Are they *blatnye*?' Avel murmured.

I did not respond. There was something indefinable about

them which counteracted any sense of intimidation or menace.

Yet still no one spoke, challenged them or told them to sod off.

Kirill put down the pick axe he had chosen to defend himself. The steel head briefly rang on the stone by his foot. It was then I noticed the approaching figures were unarmed.

'Who are you, comrades?' Kirill called out with a certain courtesy. It was not a challenge for identification but a request for an introduction.

'Work Unit 91,' came the reply, the voice barely audible in the confines of the mole hole.

'91!' exclaimed Titian under his breath.

'How many are you?' the voice asked.

'The usual seven,' Kirill answered back.

'So are we,' came the response.

'You know what 91 is, don't you?' Titian said, keeping his voice low. 'Any number prefixed by 9 or 11?'

Dmitri nodded and said, 'Women.'

We put down our weapons as the leader of the work unit approached Kirill. She was a thin, sinewy woman possibly in her late thirties, her hair cut close as was our own: indeed, they all had cropped hair, their bodies made shapeless by their clothing. For some curious reason, their faces were cleaner than ours.

'My name,' she said, holding out her hand, 'is Dusya.'

Kirill took it but, instead of shaking it, raised it to his lips and, bowing his head, lightly kissed her fingers.

'I am Kirill,' he introduced himself. 'This is Work Unit 8.'

The remainder of us just stood around like embarrassed schoolboys at their first dance. It had been so long since any of us had addressed a woman that we were temporarily at a loss. Above ground, the women were held in a separate camp two kilometres from our own and although we occasionally saw them at the muster by the pit head, we never spoke to them or gave them any thought. It was beyond all expectation that we would ever meet them.

Dusya smiled and said, 'Such gallantry!'

Kirill smiled back and asked, 'What's happening?'

'There's been a roof collapse on N,' Dusya confirmed Titian's report. 'Two work units trapped.'

'Do they have much of a chance?'

She grimaced and said, 'Not a lot. The emergency teams're there burrowing like rats. They've gone ten metres in but...'

There followed an awkward silence. Somewhere, a few hundred metres above us, men were slowing dying, the air about them growing foul with the stink of their own sweat and dread. I glanced at Ylli. His face was drawn and I knew he was fighting the panic which was trying to engulf him.

One of the women stepped towards me, easing her way past Dusya. She was, I reckoned, in her mid-twenties. Her hair, or what remained of it after the scissors had wreaked their havoc, was blonde under its coating of black dust and her eyes dark blue.

'I am Valya,' she said, stopping within my reach. 'Who are you?'

For a moment, I could say nothing. No words came. Just looking at her eyes was like leaving the mine and travelling to a far and peaceful country.

'I am Shurik,' I replied at last.

She took my hand, pulled me very gently towards her.

'Come and talk to me,' she invited.

We walked a little way down the mole hole and around the bend. Where the roof lowered, she swept the rock floor clear of pebbles with her boot and sat down. I joined her, leaning my back against the side of the tunnel. In the meagre glow coming from around the corner, her features faded. Her spiky, short hair disappeared and her face seemed to glow almost ethereally.

'Where are you from, Shurik?' she enquired.

'I am English,' I said.

She looked at me for a moment, assimilating the information, then she took a square of damp cloth from her pocket and started to wipe the coal dust from my forehead. When she had washed my entire face, and without so much as another word, she kissed me. Her lips touched mine, her tongue just licking at the edge of my mouth. Two figures came towards us round the corner, momentarily blocking out the faint light. Titian and one of the other women stepped over our legs and disappeared into the gloom. I could hear their footsteps receding until they reached the next dip in the tunnel.

Valya took my hand and pressed it inside the waistband of her regulation issue trousers, undoing the top button to ease my access. Her belly was warm and exquisitely soft, the muscles tight with the labour of working in the mine, her pelvis angular with the bone not far under the skin.

'When did you last touch a woman?' she asked in a whisper.

'I do not remember,' I replied and it was the truth.

'No man has touched me since...' Her voice trailed off. 'Well, no man has touched me who loved me since before the world ended.'

She pulled my vest out from my trousers and stroked her fingers along my sternum. Her nails were broken short and a rough patch of skin on the ball of her thumb teased my skin, snagging the hairs on my chest.

'Push your hand down,' she murmured. 'Don't be afraid, Shurik.'

I moved my fingers slowly over her skin, down the flat surface of her belly, slipping them between her legs. Even the muscles on the inside of her thighs were tensioned by her years of cutting and carting coal. She moved her fingers, searching for me in the folds of my clothing. There was an urgency about her movements and yet she did not hurry.

'Have you been to Zagorsk, Shurik?' she asked.

'No,' I answered.

'Do you know where it is?'

'No,' I admitted again.

She laughed lightly and said, 'North of Moscow. Not far. An hour's drive, no more.'

'Is that your home?'

'Does it matter any more?' she answered, her fingers stroking the base of my belly.

At the end of the tunnel, the light went out. It might have been Kirill unscrewing the bulb for the sake of modesty or it might have been the power supply failing. I gave it no thought.

'You and me, Shurik,' she whispered in the Stygian subterranean night. 'Let us go to Zagorsk.'

For a while, we explored each other's invisible bodies, testing each other, touching and kissing. Valya pulled her vest over her head and pressed my face into her breasts. They were small, smooth and firm, the nipples hard against my tongue. Finally, removing her trousers as well as my own, she moved over and sat across me, her thighs solid against my own.

'Can you do this?' she enquired quietly as she lowered herself onto me.

'I think so,' I said, feeling her moist and warm against my groin.

She guided me into her then and put her arms around my neck for I was still sitting against the tunnel wall. Very gradually, she started to rise and fall. I put my hands about her waist to steady her but she did not need my assistance.

'Can you see them, Shurik?' she suddenly asked, her voice disembodied in the darkness.

'See what, Valya?' I replied.

'The houses,' she answered, her voice whispering as if she was praying. 'The houses with their green walls. And the windows of the *izba* with their carved frames. And the sky reflecting in the black glass. The snow on the roof. The drift of smoke.'

She started to move more urgently, pushing herself down lower on me.

'Can you smell it, Shurik? They're burning apple wood. And pine. Someone is roasting chestnuts.'

I could feel her sliding onto me, withdrawing herself almost from me then dropping once more, her belly brushing against my own. Her hands slipped down to my shoulders, her long fingers gripping me.

'Listen, Shurik! Listen! In the church of St. Sergius. They're chanting.' She rose and fell, her breath coming in sharp gasps. 'Chanting. Chanting. Chanting. Can you hear them, Shurik! Shurik!'

'Yes,' I told her. 'I can hear them.'

For just the most fleeting of moments, that lasted no longer than the lifespan of a meteor burning across the heavens between Merak and Muscida, I was far away with Valya: and I could scent the smoke of burning apple wood drifting over a landscape of deep snow, and smell the perfume of chestnuts roasting on a stove plate, and hear a patriarch intoning in a church in which the icons glistened on the gloomy walls like predatory angels, the glow of the incense in the censer like the gleam in the eye of a cruel and vindictive god.

*

That night, as I was sitting on my bunk trying to sew a tear in my coat, Kirill hoisted himself up beside me.

'So, Shurik,' he enquired, 'are you a happy man?'

'How do you mean?' I replied. 'Am I happy because I have survived another day, happy because I have twine to mend my coat, or happy because I was screwed by a scrub-headed girl thousands of metres under the ground?'

'Any of those,' Kirill retorted.

'Then, yes, I am a happy man,' I conceded. 'I could be happier...'

'It's better to count your eggs and plan your omelette than dream of getting a few more and making a plateful of *blinis*.'

'What is a *blini*?' I asked.

'Of course, you never had one!' Kirill replied. 'They don't serve them in the cells.' He lowered his voice. 'A *blini* is - how do I describe such a simply thing? – flat, round. Made of batter...?'

'Thin,' I cut in, 'usually circular with a ragged edge, like a piece of pale yellow fabric. Like an edible table mat.'

'That's it! Exactly! If you had paper other than to wipe your arse on, you should be a poet, Shurik. Such command of language!'

'So what's in it?'

'You want to know?' He wagged his finger at me, playing the KGB inquisitor. 'These are dangerous thoughts, comrade. They can drive a man crazy.'

'Are they a state secret?'

'No, but you can die from them.' For a moment, he was serious. 'Do not forget, just as you must never look forward to your release, so must you never let your thoughts dwell on food. If you want to run for the cover of your soul, dream of other things.'

I tightened the twine and the rip in my coat closed up.

'So, are you going to tell me the secret?'

Kirill glanced around as if he was in possession of a piece of real information any secret agent would be pleased to pass onto his spymaster in the hope of promotion and a comfortable desk job back at HQ.

'Flour, yeast, water, butter, salt, sugar, milk, frying oil. And eggs!'

'In what quantities?'

'I didn't get a look at the formulæ,' Kirill answered conspiratorially. 'Only the basic plan. But,' he closed his eyes, 'you serve them very hot, with a ladleful of melted butter, sour cream, dried fish and caviar.' He licked his lips as if tasting a final smear of butter and opened his eyes.

'Look on the bright side of the street, Kirill,' I told him. 'We get dried fish in our rations. That's a start.'

He laughed. I bit off the remaining length of twine from my coat and spat out the hairs of the cord adhering to my tongue.

'You'll make it, Shurik,' he declared, slapping my shoulder. 'If you can laugh when the world is black, you'll make it. The man who sees the funny side survives.'

Down at the far end of the hut, there were raised voices. Kirill peered down the aisle between the bunks. Several of the men whose bunks were at that end of the hut – which was to say, the warm end near the stove – were arguing. Others climbed down from their bunks, joining in the altercation.

'It's the *blatnye*,' Kirill remarked with obvious loathing.

The shouting grew louder. The argument was getting heated. Kirill nodded to me and we quit our bunks to see what was going on. In the middle of a circle of men, two of the *blatnye* were yelling at each other, waving their hands and fists but holding back from physical confrontation. The other *blatnye* egged them on or took the side of the larger of the two. The rest of us, the *ideinye*, political prisoners who had had their hands caught in the wheel of fortune rather than trying to filch it, merely observed: one did not join in the affairs of the *blatnye*.

'Who are they?' I asked Kirill.

'The little one's called Styopa,' he replied, keeping his voice down to avoid being dragged into the melée, 'a pickpocket from Leningrad, specialised in sailors coming out the navy yards. The big one's Kabanov. They call him Kaban. An appropriate name.'

'Why?'

'Kaban means boar. You ever seen anyone who looks more like a pig?'

'What is he sitting in here for?' I enquired, using the gulag vernacular.

'He was a pimp in Moscow. When his girls grew tired or their cunts grew loose, he killed them.'

'How long did he get?'

'Ten years,' Kirill said. 'For killing girls you've duped onto their backs then rubbed out, you get ten. For standing on the wrong street corner with your hands in your pockets, you get twenty-five. That's Soviet justice for you, Shurik!'

There was no animosity or angst in his voice but neither was there resigned acceptance. This was the way it was for all of us.

We could do nothing about it: we just did the best we could in the circumstances. Better to smile than sulk was one of Kirill's mottoes.

'So where is it?' Kaban the Boar bellowed. 'You've got my fucking...'

'It's not me!' Styopa screamed back. 'Ask Shifrin! Ask Novikov!' He spun round looking for another target for his accusation and pointed at one of the *ideinye*, a man called Zverev with a bright scar on his face. 'Ask old Two Mouth here!'

Zverev went white, the scar all the more livid against his paling skin.

'Zverev!' Kaban roared. 'He was down at the other end, playing with himself.'

The *blatnye* parted and Genrikh came forward. Immediately, the two protagonists shut up.

'What's going on?' Genrikh asked with quiet menace.

Neither Kaban nor Styopa replied. The former looked at a point midway between Genrikh's eyes and belt, the latter contemplated the top of the table.

'Who's up to what?' Genrikh spoke slowly, enunciating each word carefully, as if speaking to an idiot child.

'Styopa's stolen,' Kaban answered.

'Stolen what?'

'A piece of dried herring. It was under my blanket.'

Genrikh faced Styopa.

'Where's the herring?'

'I didn't take it. It must have fallen down the cracks in the boards. Or he's eaten it and forgotten. Or some fucking enemy of the people,' he cast a quick sideways glance at the assembled *ideinye*, looking for Zverev, 'lifted it.'

'Lifted it?' Genrikh said in an almost insouciant tone. 'You mean the best dipper in Leningrad has a rival in the ranks of the run-and-hides?'

Styopa made no response.

'So, let me get this straight,' Genrikh began his soliloquy.

'Kaban's hungry and angry, Styopa's met his match amongst the spies and stoolies, and a bit of fish has vanished down a hole. The question is,' he turned his head to survey the other *blatnye*, 'which hole?'

Like a snake striking, his arm flicked out to grasp Styopa by the throat, hauling him across the floor. He rammed his face into Styopa's.

'What did we have for rations tonight, Pasha?' he asked.

'Stew,' informed one of the *blatnye* behind him.

'Fish or flesh?' he went on, still nose to nose with Styopa.

'Flesh.'

'What did we have tonight, Styopa?'

'Flesh,' hissed Styopa through a restricted windpipe.

'Say, "We had flesh stew for supper, comrade Genrikh."'

As Styopa spoke, Genrikh inhaled hard, like a man pulling on an expensive cigar. His hand shifted round to the back of his captive's neck, preventing him from moving away.

'Now we need an independent opinion,' Genrikh declared and he looked at me. 'You, English!' he ordered. 'Come here.'

'Take care,' Kirill whispered.

I had no other choice and stepped forward.

'Yes, comrade,' I said.

'Comrade! That's rich!' Genrikh retorted but he made nothing more of it. 'Put your head here,' he commanded me, pointing to the air a few centimetres from Styopa's face.

I did as I was bid. Genrikh jammed his index finger hard into Styopa's ribs. The pickpocket inhaled sharply then let his breath out as the pain subsided.

'So, English,' Genrikh demanded, 'what do you smell? The sea or the field?'

There was no alternative but to tell the truth. Had I lied, I would have been quickly accused of being an accessory: besides, Genrikh had made his mind up.

'The sea,' I admitted. 'I can smell fish.'

The words were hardly out of my mouth when Genrikh gave

the nod. Two of the *blatnye* seized Styopa by the shoulders, pinioning his arms and thrusting him face down on the table. Another grabbed his legs, swiftly binding them at the ankle with a belt. Unable to move, a fourth *blatnoi* tugged Styopa's right arm out from his side and held it there. In one fluid movement, Genrikh twirled round and brought a short-handled axe down on Styopa's wrist. It went clear through to jam in the table. The severed hand jumped away from the forearm, the fingers scrabbling as if it had suddenly received a life of its own and wanted to make its getaway. Styopa passed out.

Genrikh prized the axe out of the table and said, 'Stick it in the ashes.'

The *blatnye* manhandled Styopa to the stove. Dark, heavy drops of blood stained the boards of the floor. They opened the little door to the fire and thrust his arm into it. There was a hissing sound as the glowing embers cauterised the stump.

'Don't think about it, Shurik. You could do nothing,' Kirill quietly reassured me as we returned to our end of the hut. 'Consider it just another lesson in the long semester of our university education. Remember it well, my friend,' he added grimly. 'Not only the man who laughs survives.'

5

The building began life as the stables on a stud farm owned by a landowner who was killed by revolutionaries in the winter of 1917, a local detachment of them using it as a temporary billet for several weeks whilst they denounced, drove out, rounded up and eventually shot the local gentry. For a while it was abandoned then altered to be used as a fodder store for the village. With communisation, it was further adapted to become the local grain store.

It is a wooden building with a steeply sloping shingle roof, two small windows which are perpetually shuttered and a barn door set in one end. The only part of the structure made of brick and stone, for even the footings are constructed of seasoned oak as hard as iron, is the stove and chimney which are original: the stove is massive and once kept the stallions warm through the deepest of winter.

When the unimaginable happened and the universe moved on, the red flag lowered from the flagpoles of the entire nation, if not removed from the hearts of all the people, and the barn was no longer communally owned but put on the market, Trofim and Tolya bought it.

As young men, Trofim and Tolya were conscripts together in a tank regiment in the Soviet Army. Whilst serving their time in the far-flung corners of the kingdom of the red bear, they were trained as battlefield mechanics and engineers, learning every skill from stripping a gearbox to heavy duty welding. By the time they were released back into civilian life, there was little they did not know about the various incarnations of the internal combustion engine and the vehicles into which they were put.

Both returned to the village of Solntsevo, the other side of Zarechensk, whence they had come, and were employed as mechanics: Trofim was sent to work in the bus garage in the town, Tolya assigned to the agricultural vehicles depot just outside it. In the exogamous tradition of their village, they sought a bride from 'over the arches of the bridge', as the saying went, from the neighbourhood rather than from their own village, and ended up marrying girls from Myshkino.

For years, as they travelled into Zarechensk every day, as Tolya laboured in the dusty wheat fields of summer repairing a combine and Trofim stood in an inspection pit under a leaking sump, they jointly entertained a dream of which even their wives were ignorant. It was a fantasy without hope of fulfilment for there was no chance for it to ever realise itself in a world of collectivised farming and state control. As Tolya put it when he knew there was no one around to shop him, the Party not only ran the farmers and the farms, it also told the crickets when to chirp and the birds when to sing.

Yet their day came and their offer for the old barn was accepted by the state. Now they are the proud proprietors of a garage, repair shop and forge which they have grandiosely named Myshkino Motors. Not only that. The sign which hangs above the barn door is painted in both Cyrillic and English alphabets. It was Pavel, Tolya's brother, who persuaded them to have a bi-lingual sign in a part of Russia where the chances of there ever appearing a Westerner – apart from myself, who does not count – were about as slim as finding a toad on a mountain top. Pavel had emigrated to America at the first opportunity after the end of Communism and, returning with wild tales of life in Detroit where, having been a vehicle mechanic in the Soviet air force, he also worked in a garage, he filled their heads with capitalist plans of expansion and development. As Russia grew richer, Pavel insisted, it would become a vehicle owning meritocracy, which is how he described Detroit, and every town would need a dealership. It was his plan to set up a chain of such franchises across Russia, selling both Russian and foreign cars to the newly motorised driving classes. Those who got in early would make a killing. It was time to prepare, to be ready.

Trofim and Tolya had spent all their money on tooling up their former barn and had scant reserves to squander on a further fantasy, but they agreed to hang a sign out in readiness for Pavel's Vehicular Revolution.

At first, the villagers scoffed at the sign. It was a waste of paint. Over the months, however, the garage became known far and wide because of its idiosyncratic notice. Curious farmers brought their tractors in for servicing or their bent ploughs for straightening and welding. Car owners in Zarechensk drove over. When Father Kondrati commissioned a new wrought-iron cross for the arch over the graveyard gate, the word got out. Myshkino Motors was the place to go.

Within two years, Trofim and Tolya took on an apprentice to train up and help them with their increasing work load. They also employed a part-time smith who operated an old forge and even shoed the occasional farmer's nag, filling the barn with the stench of horse shit and scorched hoof. Pavel kept their hopes, and his own, alive by periodically sending them showroom brochures of the latest American cars from which they tore the pictures to pin on a notice board next to the tool racks. Where some garages have pin-ups of semi-naked girls, Myshkino Motors had Chryslers, Fords and Oldsmobiles hanging from the wall. The most recent they have received shows a highway patrolman standing by the side of a shining Buick saloon, his revolver slung low like a cowboy's, his eyes almost insectile behind close-fitting sunglasses.

As I approached the garage, I could hear the sounds of mechanical activity. Someone was using a grinding wheel, the whine rising and falling as he moved it to and fro across a metal surface. When the noise dropped, it was replaced by hammering and the shrill of music on a cheap radio with a tinny speaker.

The day being bright, the interior of the garage was cast in deep shadow and I could not make out what was going on inside until I was quite close. In the centre of the work area was a distinctly derelict, old-fashioned Russian limousine of dubious provenance. The bodywork was black, the doors wide enough to accommodate the fattest of Party secretaries, the back windows darkly tinted and still hung with threadbare curtains stretched from chromium-plated rails. Dents in the driver's door and front wing ringed with rust bubbles were evidence of an accident in the distant past. The windscreen was cracked right across and starred by stones. The vehicle was raised on axle stands, a pair of legs projecting out from under the engine over which the bonnet had been removed.

Perhaps, I considered as I stood for a minute at the side of the entrance to observe the occupants at work, the car was evidence of the veracity, extant after so many decades, of Dmitri's story of the onion seller at the railway crossing.

Nearest the entrance was the apprentice who, standing before a workbench, was hammering seized bolts out of a chassis member from, I presumed, the limousine. With every strike of the hammer, flakes of mud and rust dropped to the floor.

The apprentice's name is Romka and he was once a pupil of mine. A studious child of eleven when I retired from Myshkino school, he was always polite, quiet, unassuming and diligent but never all that bright except, that is, at music. Give him anything with strings on it and he would be able to bow or pluck a tune out of in it hours.

At another workbench at the rear of the garage, sparks shot out from the grinding wheel. The air smelled of hot metal, cold oil, gasoline and the sun-warmed timbers of the walls.

'Shurik!' a voice shouted out. 'Happy 80th.!'

The grinding wheel stopped screeching and hummed, the pitch dropping as the power was switched off and the motor slowed. The legs protruding from under the old heap started to scrabble and Trofim began to appear, wriggling out on his back. His face was besmirched with oil, his hands blackened. For a moment, I felt an unpleasant stab of nostalgia: he might have been a miner.

Tolya walked briskly past the car, avoiding the handlebars of a motorbike and tugging off a pair of metal-worker's safety goggles.

'Good morning, Tolya. How's business?' I enquired.

This is my customary greeting for Tolya, like any boss around the world, loves to have an interest expressed in his company.

He put his finger and thumb together and kissed the air a few centimetres from them. To put his fingers to his lips would have been to have had the taste of oil and metal filings lingering in his mouth for the rest of the day. In a vain attempt to clean his hands, he wiped them on a cloth hanging from a nail on the wall then inspected them. They were no cleaner.

'Well, you know I want to shake your hand, Shurik. But...,' He shrugged. 'How're you feeling today?' He made a fist and punched the air. 'Ready for battle?'

'As I feel every day,' I replied. 'A little older, a little wiser.'

'So what wisdom have you learnt today? Or has it yet to come?'

'I have had my lesson for today,' I told him. 'Just now, in Komarov's shed. I discovered that spiders do not tackle wasps but deliberately cut them free from their webs to avoid a confrontation with a more powerful enemy.'

'And these were *Russian* spiders?' Tolya asked with a feigned incredulity. 'From the country that took on the wily Afghans? And would have tangled with the Yanks if the chance had arisen?'

'Indeed, Russian spiders,' I confirmed.

'Ah, yes!' Tolya retorted, as if coming at last to his senses. 'Of course, they are Russian spiders. Not *Soviet* spiders.' He laughed aloud, throwing his head back. 'There you are, Trofim. Proof we do live in a new world. Even the spiders have wised up.'

Trofim balanced a monkey wrench on the radiator of the car and slid his hands up and down his sides.

'Happy birthday, Shurik,' he greeted me.

'What did they give you, Shurik?' Tolya wanted to know.

'They bought me a very old icon of St. Basil. How much it cost, I dare not think.'

'But do you like it?' Tolya demanded.

'It is exquisite,' I replied and smiled at Trofim, 'but you should not have spent so much.'

'What use are dollars?' he responded, 'if you don't spend them?' He picked up a ball of cotton waste and rubbed it between his palms. 'Have some tea with us. I'm losing my patience with this old bitch.' He slammed his hand against the side of the limousine so hard that the monkey wrench fell off the radiator to chime on the concrete floor.

Romka provided an old steel framed office stool for me to sit on and drew four mugs of tea from a samovar they keep on the go at the back of the garage. This, too, is an indication of Pavel's influence for he has told them that American garages always provide refreshment for customers waiting whilst their cars are attended to in the workshop. Tolya leaned on the end of the bench, Trofim cleared a space and hoisted himself onto the work surface. Romka sat on the motorbike.

'What is this car?' I asked, pointing at the dilapidated limousine with my cup.

'It was the official Party car in Zarechensk,' Trofim explained. 'When the Party office was shut, it was given to the town mayor who used it for a few months but he did not take to it.'

'For a start,' interrupted Tolya, 'he is a liberal reformer and the car had connotations with which he did not wish to be associated. It was unreliable and broke down frequently, embarrassing him in front of other mayors. When the back seat broke free from its mounting and he found a condom down the back of the upholstery – that was it! He sold it to a farmer who couldn't afford to run it. It does only five kilometres to the litre. With a tail wind.'

'The farmer kept it in his barn,' Trofim took up the narrative, 'where hens nested and his dog whelped in it. He sold it to us last week.'

'The condom, by the way, was as second-hand as the car,' Tolya cut in again. 'It seems the last Comrade Secretary had a busy extra-governmental life.'

'And a deaf, dumb and blind chauffeur,' Trofim suggested.

'But what are you going to do with it?' I asked. 'It's a wreck.'

'We are going to restore it,' Tolya declared with more than a hint of optimistic pride, 'and use it as a taxi. The Myshkino Cab Company. That's what we'll be. Romka here is going to be the driver, on commission.'

'Will you paint it yellow?' I wanted to know.

'We've not decided. Black is out and so is red, for obvious reasons. We were thinking silver...' Tolya stopped. He caught up with my thinking. 'You're a vicious, irritating old bastard!' he exclaimed.

I affected an air of hurt innocent and said, 'What do you mean?'

Trofim broke out into a peal of laughter. Romka cottoned on, too.

'This is Myshkino, not Manhattan!' Tolya retorted but with good humour.

We sipped our tea. A swift swooped into the garage, circled over our heads and swung out into the sunlight once more. From the samovar, a thin plume of steam rose up to the beams which, for a brief moment, looked less like the supports of a barn roof and more like transverse pit props. Tolya embarked upon a comparison of the new Ford Mustang, of which he has recently received the latest sales brochure, with a BMW convertible. He favoured the American car for style, ingenuity and what he termed the fun factor, which phrase he spoke first in English with an American, Pavelian accent before translating it into Russian: Trofim preferred the German for its superior engineering and build quality. I paid little heed to their esoteric conversation and it was not until Tolya addressed me that I was jolted back to the present.

'You'll like this story, Shurik,' he said. 'I heard it in

Leontiy's bar. You know it? The one by the market in Zarechensk. They serve good coffee there and Andryukha's little minion pushes his wares round the table. Andryukha's walnut cake...'

'Are you going to tell us it? At this rate, the preface will be longer than the novel,' Trofim remarked.

'Now that the Cold War is over,' Tolya began, 'there was held a joint military exercise between the Americans, the British and the Russians. On a survival course, there were an American CIA officer, a British MI5 spy and a KGB operative. The three are sitting down round a fire on the edge of the forest. CIA says, "I bet I could go into the forest, catch a rabbit, skin it and have it cooking in fifteen minutes." "That's a long time,' says MI5. "I could do it in ten." KGB looks at them and says, "five minutes for me." So the challenge is made. CIA goes off into the trees. Fourteen minutes later he returns, pulls the rabbit inside out, discards the pelt and sets it cooking on a stick. MI5 goes off. Nine minutes later, he's back and his rabbit's in the pot, boiling. KGB goes off. Twenty minutes later, he hasn't come back. CIA says to MI5, "So much for the Russian threat! These rabbits are nearly cooked. Let's eat them." They eat the rabbits and then, lying back, they have a little doze.'

Tolya took a swallow of his tea and I swear I heard Dmitri's voice. Looking out of the garage door and across the road towards the river, there were some men standing down by the bridge, where the bus to Zarechensk stops. They were in a knot, talking to each other, and I should not have been the least surprised had one of them waved to me.

'Two hours later,' Tolya continued, 'KGB still hasn't come back. MI5 says, "Maybe he's in trouble. Bears. Wolves. Vipers. I think we should go and look for him. After all, we're all friends now." So CIA and MI5 set off into the forest. They follow KGB's trail. Eventually, they come to a clearing. Across the far end, KGB is standing. He has caught a fox which he has tied by its hind legs from a branch. As they watch, he beats the fox with a stick and shouts, "Come on, you bastard! Talk! Where are the rabbits?"'

Both Trofim and Romka laughed aloud at this tale which, ten years ago, would have had them rubbing shoulders with a team of benighted *zeks* in a mole hole or breaking stones on the Trans-Siberian railway. I also chuckled but, as I did so, I wondered where Dmitri is now.

It is twenty years since we parted, shaking hands in the rain on the steps outside the barrack hut in which we ate and slept and snored and farted and argued and occasionally fought with men who had been caught with their hands in the till, or their fingers on the trigger, or simply fallen foul of a system they thought protected them from pain, injustice and the corruption of power.

'So, Shurik, your time's come,' Dmitri said.

'I'd rather stay a while,' I replied. 'Go in the winter.'

'Why?' he questioned. 'The snow's gone now.'

'It's the rain,' I said. 'I hate walking in the rain.'

'Stay then. The office is dry,' he argued, using that old euphemism of the bad, red years: wherever you worked was your office, be it a tractor factory or a collective farm. Or a mine.

'Maybe not. I have no secretary,' I countered. 'What can a man do without a secretary? I have had enough of typing my own letters. I am,' I straightened my shoulders with false pride, 'going up in the world.'

'How far?' Dmitri asked.

'About two and half kilometres,' I said.

'Find me a place in your new office.'

I looked into his eyes and saw, way back in his soul, a terrible sadness.

'You will always have a place in my office,' I replied. 'A desk in the corner by the window, overlooking the park with a black telephone at one elbow and an in-tray at the other.'

'Made of...?'

'Steel?' I offered.

'Wood. Mahogany, polished, tanned as the skin on the breasts of a Burmese princess!'

'Consider it done,' I promised.

'And a calendar?'

'What are the pictures of?'

He thought for a moment then decided, 'The natural wonders of the world. One picture for each month. January will be the Grand Canyon.'

He leaned forward, embracing me and kissing me on both cheeks and I kissed him in return: then he took my hand, removing his work glove so that our palms might touch.

'Go carefully in the world, Shurik,' he advised.

'Good-bye, Dmitri,' I replied. 'You have my love.'

We did not shake each other's hand. We just held it, like sweethearts reluctantly parting on a railway platform, the train getting up a head of steam and a porter walking down the line of carriages, slamming the open doors shut. I even thought I heard the ticket inspector calling *All aboard*! but it was a guard yelling at me to move my arse over to the administration building.

'Have a good life, Shurik,' Dmitri half-whispered, 'A good life for a good man.'

I could say nothing. I was no better, nor no worse than any of those men whose names the world had forgotten and who existed only in an official dossier locked away in a Moscow vault as dusty as Gallery K for Khruschev who would crucify Khazars.

The guard grabbed me by the arm and shouted, 'You want to go, *zek*, or do you want to be planted for another 25 years?'

From the steps of the administration building, I looked back. Through a thin mist of breath condensing on the pane, I could see Avel's face at the window by the door of our hut. Something white moved next to it. It was his hand, tentatively waving. On the steps, Dmitri was still standing, watching me as I disappeared.

I do not know, but I should like to think that he is living somewhere in a quiet corner of the new Russia, telling his jokes just as Tolya does and loved by the people with whom he is spending his last years, just as I am. Yet just as likely, he has been knifed on a train, or in a back street in an anonymous town, by an

Armenian without a sense of humour.

I drained my tea and rose to my feet.

'It is time I was on my way,' I declared. 'I'm not halfway round my daily constitutional and you've a tired old wreck to rebuild. And paint yellow.'

Tolya slapped me on the back.

'You'll be the first passenger to ride with the Myshkino Cab Company!'

'Where to?' I asked. 'My funeral? It looks like a hearse.'

Tolya nudged me.

'To the church. For your wedding to the Merry Widow.'

I grimaced and walked to the door, the sun bright in my eyes. I could do with sunglasses in my final years. Perhaps, I thought, Pavel could be put upon to bring me back a pair from Detroit so that I might look like an ancient version of the highway patrolman in the picture of the Buick.

'Let me walk you as far as the bridge,' Trofim offered. 'That black bitch can rust a little longer.'

We set off down the road, passing two houses and Andryukha's bakery which, it being late morning, was shut. Everyone purchases their bread early on, allowing the baker to make his pastries then take off for a day's fishing on a wide meander a few kilometres up the river: in the autumn, the perfume of his baking bread mingles with the pungent odour of smoked fish. Alongside the bakery was parked the baker's recently acquired red Volkswagen. Trofim jerked his thumb at it.

'It's a Passat,' he announced knowingly, 'a stolen car, of course.' He shrugged, his hands opening out in supplication to inevitability. 'The gangsters brought it in. I saw it just before Andryukha paid over his money. He asked me to check it – brakes, steering, clutch – wanted to be sure he wasn't buying a wreck.'

'And was he?'

'No!' His snapped his fingers to emphasise Andryukha's good fortune. 'It was as clean as a pin. Well serviced, well maintained, no rust, almost new exhaust pipe. In fact the owner's handbook was still in it. So were his registration documents. Herr Gratz of Innsbruck will be missing his motor.'

We walked on in silence, the sun warm across our shoulders and our shadows short before us.

'What were you thinking of?' Trofim asked after we had gone some metres, breaking our silence.

'When?'

'When Tolya was telling his story. You drifted off. I could see it in your eyes. You were a million kilometres away.'

'A million years,' I replied but I did not elaborate.

'Do you think of them often, Shurik?'

'Increasingly so,' I admitted. 'As I get older, I think back to the past more than you would. It is the fate of the elderly, who have a somewhat limited future, to dwell in the history of their lives. Your turn will come, Trofim. Believe me!'

Ahead of us, the bus to Zarechensk pulled up and the gathering of men boarded it. The engine revved, a noxious cloud of dense diesel fumes belching from the exhaust to drift away over the river.

'You have a future,' Trofim said as the bus slogged past us, gears churning, to turn right at the junction by Andryukha's place. 'A long future. So! You are 80 today. But you are healthy. Doctor Levina told Frosya she had never examined a healthier man. Your heart's as strong as an ox.'

'That's as may be,' I answered.

We reached the bridge. As I do every day, I leaned on the parapet and gazed at the water below. It was as clear as glass. Fish flicked over the tumble of stones and lumps of weed-infested concrete, the remnants of the old bridge which collapsed in a storm eighteen years ago. The silver scales flashed on and off as they wove through the choreography of their piscine manoeuvres.

'Have you made up your mind, Shurik?' he asked, leaning next to me.

'Not exactly,' I confessed, watching the shoal of fish swerve with the precision of a well-trained regiment.

'Is it so hard? If I were in your shoes, I should know what I should choose.'

He was thinking of advising me but that was something I could not allow him to do.

'Do not tell me what I must or must not do.' I sensed I was sounding curt when I did not want to be. 'Forgive me, Trofim,' I went on, moderating my tone, 'but this is something I must decide, without any persuasion or opinion from you or Frosya. And with respect, my dear friend, you are not in my shoes nor can you ever be, thank god – if you believe in such an entity – for the world has moved on and I trust men will no longer tread the paths I have walked upon.'

'I'm sorry...' he began.

'There are no apologies necessary. It's just that...'

I paused. A kingfisher darted beneath the bridge, a tiny arrow of azure and orange dipping to the surface, its beak trailing the water. The fish broke ranks in panic.

'In Sosnogorsklag 32,' I continued, 'Kirill and my other comrades, for that is what we were in those days - comrades in the true meaning of the word, not in the Party sense – were a team. A family, even...'

Trofim did not look at me but at the fishes below the bridge which were forming up again. A small fair weather cumulus moved swiftly across the sun, its shadow streaking over the meadows leading down to the river bank.

In my mind, I saw Ylli again, lying by the stove, feigning dead like a whipped dog. Avel was there carving his chessmen and Kirill was looking up at me as the last few sparks of life flickered in the furnace of his soul.

'When I left the gulag,' I said quietly, 'I abandoned my comrades.'

'You were getting your freedom!' Trofim exclaimed. 'They would get theirs, in time. When they saw you leaving, you were fulfilling their dreams, their hopes. If you could go so could they, one day. You were not just going for yourself, but for them.'

'Perhaps. Perhaps not. That was – is – not the point.' I turned and leaned against the bridge parapet, facing across the road and downstream. 'I had nowhere to go, no one to go to, yet I had to leave and the truth is that I did not want to. We had been together so long, had survived together. That was it. We had survived, not alone but with each other's love and support. Remember, I was in the gulag for longer than you and Frosya have been married.'

The cloud passed and the sun shone down brilliantly upon the river. Beneath us, the kingfisher returned for another attack, dived at the surface and flew off with a minnow twitching in its beak.

Trofim put his arm around my shoulder. He has started to do this of late and I like the closeness of his body, the smell of his sweat mingled with lubricating oil. It is, how can I put it, an honest smell.

'Tell me, Shurik, why did you never go to Moscow, to the British embassy?'

I thought for a moment before I answered. It has been so long since I last asked myself the same question and yet, down through the years, I have never forgotten how it was for me in those weeks between stepping out of the gulag and arriving on Frosya's porch.

Until I reached the village, I was terrified of that brave new world outside the gulag, where decisions crowded in like hoards of snatching beggars, where I had no friends and no one knew me.

'I had to come here, for Kirill,' I replied. 'To tell you...'

'But after that?' Trofim asked.

'After that,' I mused, 'it was different.'

Once in Myshkino, my life had changed and not merely because I found myself out of the gulag and amongst caring friends. Here, once I had divested myself of my responsibility to Kirill, I discovered an intense peace such as I had never known and to leave would have been to forfeit it.

For a while, I did toy with taking the train to Moscow, presenting myself at the embassy, a man walking in out of the deserts of history. Yet the more I mulled it over, the more foolhardy such a course of action seemed. For all intents and purposes, I was long dead: it was better for all concerned I stayed that way. I was, by then, more Russian than British and to be resurrected would only have caused trouble. The diplomats would have had to come to terms with my imprisonment whilst the Russians would have had to account for it. My parents, were they still alive, would have had to adjust to my reincarnation and I would have had to try and adapt to a country I no longer considered my own and a way of life which had become alien to me. Furthermore, I considered, I would have gained nothing I did not already have in abundance for, in Frosya and Trofim, I had my family and all I needed to have and to give was around me in Myshkino.

'I owed my gratitude to you and Frosya and my allegiance to my comrades,' I said at length, 'not to my country. Friends are more important than flags, Trofim.' I became momentarily pedantic. 'You must remember that. It is a lesson for the future. And now,' I went on, raising my arm and sweeping it across the fields and the forest beyond, the houses of the village, the river, the church and Myshkino Motors, 'this is my country.'

Trofim tightened his hug for a moment then relaxed it.

'I must get back to the black bitch,' he announced. 'We've got to get the engine out and rebuild the gearbox. I'll see you this afternoon.'

'Yes,' I agreed pensively, 'this afternoon...'

'Are you worried?'

'At my age?' I retorted, yet I was and Trofim knew it.

'Don't be,' he encouraged me. 'Whatever happens, whatever you decide, we shall be with you.'

At the edge of the bridge, he halted with his back towards me.

'Frosya and I have never regretted one hour of your being with us,' he said, not looking round. 'Not one, single hour.'

With that, he walked away up the hill towards the garage from which, distantly, I could hear the grinding wheel whining like a banshee once again.

6

It was about half-past four, with dawn still nearly five hours off. A gibbous moon, small and stark in the frigid air, hung just a few degrees above the invisible horizon.

The arc lights shone down upon the compound, casting almost perfect circles of brightness upon the frozen ground. Over the previous few days, an unseasonable wind from the south had partially melted some of the snow which was piled in rock-hard drifts where it had been shovelled or blown against the sides of the huts. In its place, the ground was covered in an uneven centimetres-thick sheet of rough ice upon which the overnight frost sparkled with a harsh, exquisite beauty. Close to the wire, delicate ice pencils about ten centimetres high, caused by the freezing air and wind eddying round the iron stanchions, stood erect like opaque perspex models of ornate gothic spires. The light, fractured by the ice, coruscated.

If it were not for the moon and the lamps on their iron gantries, the whole panoply of the heavens would have been visible.

'Five-thirty's one thing,' Ylli complained in a whisper. His breath misted before his face and froze, the little syllables of steam dropping within a second of leaving his mouth to coalesce on the front of his padded coat. 'Five-thirty I have grown used to. Five-thirty I accept. But four-thirty. Four-thirty's another matter.'

Dmitri rubbed his gloved hands together and shuffled his feet.

'What do you think it is, Shurik?' he asked.

I slipped my tongue out between my lips and tasted the air.

'Minus twelve. Maybe fifteen,' I replied.

'Spring's coming then,' Dmitri said in a tone of ironic anticipation. 'Another few months and we'll be lounging on warm rocks in the sun like lizards.'

He grinned and huddled his shoulders the better to close the gap between the collar of his padded *vatnik* and the bottom of the flaps of his *ushanka* where they were fastened under his chin by a leather thong tied in a double bow.

'Another six months if we're lucky,' Ylli said, ever the pessimist, 'and then there'll be precious little lounging.'

'You think there's been a cave in?' Avel mused apprehensively.

'We'd be so lucky!' Kostya exclaimed, smiling vaguely at the reminiscent of our brief, amorous liaisons in the Gallery R mole hole.

'If there has, it'll not be like the last,' Dmitri remarked soberly. 'That was small, nothing much more than a rock fall. One tunnel blocked. An inconvenience rather than a danger.'

'That's not how it was for the poor buggers who were trapped,' Titian said grimly. 'None of them got out. They just walled up the tunnel.'

'It didn't do more than slow production for the week by ten or fifteen per cent,' Dmitri went on, preferring to ignore the fact that neither work unit had been rescued: there was no reason, in his mind, to dwell upon the fate of 14 other *zeks* who were no longer in the gulag. They had, one way or the other, got out and that was the end of it. 'No, you mark my words, this is different.' He thrust his gloved hands into his pockets and shivered, partly at the thought of what might lay ahead of us and partly at the fingers of air trying to probe his clothing, to wheedle themselves in through the material. 'We wouldn't be called out in the dead hours of the night just to clear a slide of stone. The first team down would do it. If it is worse, we're not emergency crew trained. No,' he repeated, 'this is an altogether different business.'

I turned to see Kirill making his way across the ice from the administrative building. He was accompanied by three guards and the duty officer of the night. They walked slowly, clumsily, keeping their balance only with difficulty. The guards had their semi-automatic carbines slung over their shoulders, their warm knee-length *tulups* brushing against their shins. They, too, had pulled down the flaps on their hats.

It occurred to me how colourless the scene was. The ground was grey with ice, the snow off-white against the wooden huts which, in turn, were jet black in the shadows or graphite-black where the light touched them. It was as if the bleak winter had robbed the world of its colour, as if we were temporarily living in a black and white photograph. The only fragments of colour, the only objects in the entire scene to remind us this was reality, were the red flag with its yellow hammer and sickle hanging limply from its pole under a lamp beside the guard-house and the red stars on the guards' hats.

As the little party drew closer, the six of us formed a line but the duty officer waved at us and ordered, 'Gather round. Form a group.'

We exchanged suspicious glances. Such informality was rare in the extreme. Had this order been given during an exercise halt on a convoy across the taiga, in a clearing by the side of a road through the forest, we should have braced ourselves for the stutter of a Degtyaryov light machine-gun and a handshake with the ferry-man rowing us over the river into eternal oblivion.

Kirill nodded his assurance to us so we broke rank and encircled the duty officer, seven prisoners and three guards hunching together in the glacial, Arctic night.

'Work Unit 8,' the duty officer began rather pompously, 'you have been chosen for a task which will go down in Soviet history. What you are to assist in the execution of is an honour for which I wish I had, myself, been chosen.'

He paused to let the import of his words sink in. We merely wondered what the catch was. The word *execution* was enough to set our minds mulling over the possibilities.

'In ten minutes,' he continued, 'you will be collected by transport and taken far from here. You are, of course, not to know the actual location. For security reasons. This will become apparent to you when you see the task upon which you are to be engaged. For the glory of the Soviet peoples. I need not tell you that escape is impossible. You will be beyond roads. In the wild country.'

I cast a quick look at the wire behind Hut 14. Over the other side, across the ditch filled with snow camouflaging the tangled barbed wire and metal spikes, the world slid uninterrupted to the horizon. If this was not the wild country, where we were going would surely beggar the imagination.

'Your guards,' the duty officer went on, 'are coming with you merely to ensure security. To obey regulations. And, perhaps, for your own protection.'

Dmitri gave me a quick look. We had heard that one before. I could see in his eyes what he was thinking. The rules had changed. Our lucky stars were no longer lucky, our guardian angels had been dismissed and were lounging about in their mess. Someone, somewhere far away in an anonymous office, had opened our dossiers and made a decision. The red pencil had wavered, the rubber stamp had banged down. We were going to be driven out into the bleak Arctic wastes and shot in the head.

Having made his pronouncement, the duty officer left and the guards stepped back from us to hover together, murmuring.

'They're as much in the dark as we are and just as worried,' Titian observed. 'Shit scared.'

'Security reasons,' Ylli pondered with mock incredulity. 'What the hell does security matter? Out here in the bloody Arctic? Who the fuck are we likely to tell?'

'Ylli, shut up,' Kirill silenced him, 'and go get the rations. They're waiting for you in the supply hut. Kostya, give him a hand.'

Ylli and Kostya slid off across the ice. Kirill waited until the two of them were out of earshot then, grinning broadly, announced, 'We're going on a little holiday, comrades.'

The transport arrived. It was a large Zil-151 truck, the back covered by a low canvas roof. We all piled into it, Ylli and Kostya tossing up three sacks of provisions. The trio of guards elected to sit in the cab with the driver so we were left to our devices in the rear. The engine roared, belching out a cloud of black smoke which disseminated into the darkness. The gears ground together and we lurched forward. At the camp entrance, there was no head count. The sentries just opened the gates and we trundled through without slowing, turning left – north – at the road junction a kilometre from the camp. In five kilometres, we drove past the entrance to the mine, the moon just touching the horizon to the side of the pit head.

'Here we go!' Dmitri remarked as the driver changed down into second to negotiate the single track railway crossing. 'Into the Grey Beyond.'

'What's in the sacks?' someone asked.

Kostya unknotted the ties and rummaged inside: loaves of hard bread, ten kilos of potatoes well past their best, two dozen cabbages the outer leaves of which were just turning rotten, three kilos of dried fish, most of it disintegrated into crumbs and two kilos of bruised apples.

'The feeding of the five thousand,' Avel announced caustically, 'with dessert.'

Despite the fact that our rations were exactly what we would have received had we remained in the camp, our spirits were raised by the food. It was clear we were going to be gone a while and were not being driven to our deaths: at least, not at the hollow end of a semi-automatic rifle.

I took the outside seat in the transport, by the tail gate. It was the coldest spot on board, for the breeze of the vehicle's motion curled in round the canvas hood, carrying particles of dusty ice thrown up by the rear wheels, but I wanted it and, as the truck made steady progress across the rolling landscape, I watched the sky.

Once the moon was down, the stars became visible, as clearly as if they had been cut from polished diamonds and scattered upon a backdrop of black silk. It had been a long time since I had seen them. In the camp, there were always lights blotting out the heavens.

The lorry bucking and sliding on the icy road, I studied the sky, identifying Lyra down close to the western horizon, Cygnus the Swan to the north and Draco the Dragon at a slightly higher elevation to the south. Traversing the sky, I passed through Cassiopeia and Andromeda to arrive at the Ram, identifying Botein at one end and Mesarthim at the other, finding the remaining stars – Sharatan, Hamal and the two whose names I did not know, even if they had them – faint but clear in the sharp cold air.

Gazing up, the opening lines of Chaucer's *The Canterbury Tales* came unbidden to my mind, dredged up from some long-forgotten classroom in a world I no longer remembered and to which I certainly no longer belonged.

> *'When that Aprille with his shoures sote*
> *The droghte of Marche hath perced to the rote,*
> *And bathed every veyne in swich licour,*
> *Of which vertu engendred is the flour;*
> *Whan Zephirus eek with his swete breeth*
> *Inspired hath in every holt and heeth*
> *The tendre croppes, and the yonge sonne*
> *Hath in the Ram his halfe cours yronne....'*

'What're you prattling on about?' Titian asked.

'Nothing,' I said, not realising I was speaking aloud. 'I was reciting a poem.'

'In English?' He did not wait for my answer. 'What was it about?'

'The month of April, when the spring comes.'

'It may be spring in April in England, but up here?' he replied trenchantly then, looking up, went on, 'You think they have the gulag up there on Mars?'

'What do you think?' I retorted.

He pondered the question for a moment then said, 'Not yet. But when men get there, they will.'

The dawn broke, a gradual process like the healing of a

wound. At first, it was indefinable but then one grew suddenly aware that it had happened, like the granting of a wish. A thin wash of light to the east spread gradually upwards and the day, such as it was, established itself.

Half an hour later, we halted in a gully at the bottom of which was a derelict bridge. Beyond it, the road petered out.

'How far have we gone?' Dmitri wanted to know.

'Five hours at not much above twenty-five kays an hour,' Ylli reckoned, 'makes it one hundred and ten, maybe twenty kilometres.'

'All down,' one of the guards called, coming to the rear of the truck and unlatching the tail-board. 'Take a leak but don't leave your peckers out too long.'

For a few minutes, we stamped about trying to get our circulation going, whilst Kirill set about persuading the guards to permit us to light a small solid fuel stove he had unearthed from a tool box in the back of the transport. They agreed and, using a bucket, we melted some snow to pass a mug of hot water round between us. Less than half an hour later, we heard a grumbling sound and a half-track appeared over the brow of the gully, slewing to a halt by the truck. We transferred our rations sacks across to it and, within minutes, were on our way in the second vehicle.

At three that afternoon, our backs aching, our arses numb and our ears ringing from the incessant cacophony of the half-track's unmuffled engines, we reached our destination.

✳

The tent in which we were billeted was pegged out at the end of a row of six on what, in the brief summer, would have been a muddy strand on the curve of a river about twenty metres wide. The sides had been piled up with turves to give added protection against the winter blast. Now, the mud was as hard as concrete and the river might have been made of marble.

We tumbled in through the flap of the door, all of us in high spirits. We had not been exterminated out on the tundra and our quarters were almost palatial. Politically zealous youths on a Socialist Youth camp weekend outing could not have been more boisterous.

Around the sides of the interior were ten bunks upon which lay straw-filled palliasses and piles of three blankets per bunk. In the centre was a stove, the chimney of which went straight up to a hole in the roof surrounded by a protective sheet of aluminium to stop the canvas scorching. Next to the stove were five oil lanterns, a pile of kindling and a box of anthracite kernels. On shaking them, it was found the lantern reservoirs were full of paraffin. A sturdy pine table had half a dozen chairs placed on it, seat downwards as in a restaurant at closing time and, to our astonishment, there were three deck chairs of the sort one might have found by the beach at a resort on the Black Sea, folded up and stored at the rear. Next to them was a barrel of fresh water, a ladle resting on a thin film of ice on the surface. A shelf bore an assortment of pots, pans, a kettle, aluminium plates and a mess tin full of cutlery.

Within ten minutes, we had stowed our provisions, staked our claims on the bunks, lit the lanterns, got the stove going and were boiling the kettle.

'Queer place!' Titian commented as we lay back in the lap of our lean but comfortable luxury. 'It's got all the facilities but it seems deserted.' He ran his finger along the frame of his bunk, collecting dust. 'The maid's not been in for a while.'

'No room service,' remarked Avel.

'I don't like it,' Ylli grumbled cautiously.

The air in the tent began to warm up and I started to feel drowsy. Kostya was already breathing deeply, on the verge of snoring.

'True story,' Dmitri began, leaning back on his bunk with his hands behind his head and his elbows stuck out. 'Peshkov published a novel called *Mother* in 1906. We all know it. Except

120

maybe you, Shurik. Seeing you're English...'

'I know Maxim Gorky,' I defended myself.

'The stereo-typical revolutionary novel,' Titian remarked.

'Which he wrote whilst living in the USA,' I chipped in, just to annoy Dmitri, allay my ignorance and prove my point.

Dmitri grimaced peevishly at me and went on, 'One day, Gorky met Stalin at a dinner in the Kremlin. Stalin says to him, "Alexei Maximovich, you once wrote a novel called *Mother*." "I did," agrees Gorky to the self-proclaimed Father of the Nation. "Well," says Stalin, "why didn't you write one called *Father*?" Gorky thinks about it for a second then answers, "It didn't occur to me. One has to have inspiration to write a novel."'

'Brave man!' remarked Avel, without much conviction.

'Bloody fool!' Ylli said, voicing Avel's true feeling on the matter.

Titian sucked his breath in and asked, 'Just how did Gorky die?'

There was a long silence. No one knew for sure.

'Not in the gulag,' Kirill announced at last. 'What happened to him at the dinner?'

'Stalin turns to Beria, standing next to him. Beria was head of the NKVD at the time. But he's still talking to Gorky. "I think, Alexei Maximovich," Stalin says, "you should give it a go. Have a try." His tone's encouraging, like a good father to a clever son. "After all, a try is not a trial." He breaks up the word *trial*. *Try-all.*'

'And did he try all?' Kostya asked, waking from his semi-doze but not opening his eyes.

The tent flaps parted and a man dressed like an intrepid Arctic explorer entered. His clothing was of the latest design. Not for him a padded groin-length *vatnik*, not even a calf-length *tulup*. His coat was thick and looked at if it was tailored from light blue parachute silk with bright yellow stitching at the seams. The cotton padding was deep and gave him the appearance of a colourful, muscular cartoon strip character. He pulled his *ushanka* off and stood with his arms akimbo.

'Welcome to – well, welcome to where you are, comrades.' He moved over to the stove. 'I see you've settled yourselves in. Do you have a team leader?'

Kirill got up from where he was sitting on his bunk and addressed the intrepid explorer.

'I am M938, team leader of Work Unit 8 at Sosnogorsklag 32 correctional camp.'

'Let's not you and me stand on ceremony. What's your name?'

We looked at each other, more puzzled now rather than suspicious.

'I am Kirill Karlovich,' Kirill said.

'Well, team leader Kirill Karlovich,' the man said and he sat down on the edge of the table, 'tell me, are you all...' He paused, as if deducing the word might insult us, but it was out of suspicion that he paused, not consideration. '...*ideinye.*'

'Yes, comrade,' Kirill confirmed. 'Ideological inmates.'

'No *blatnye?*'

'No, comrade.'

'Good!' He turned to Avel. 'What were you before you blotted your copybook?'

'Fighter pilot, comrade,' Avel said standing up, not quite to attention: it had been a long time since he had last addressed an officer and he assumed this must be one despite his multi-coloured garb.

'Saw action?'

'Yes, comrade. Korea, comrade.'

'And you?' he enquired, turning.

'Mathematician, comrade,' Titian said.

'In the military?'

'University teacher, comrade.'

'Which of you is the Englishman?' he asked. There was more than a touch of curiosity in his voice.

I rose to my feet.

'Number?'

'B916, comrade.'

'And what were you, Mr. B916 Englishman?'

'I was in the wrong place at the wrong time,' I replied.

I could sense my workmates tense up. There was a touch of the Gorky coming out in me. After a moment of silence, during which he astutely studied me, the man laughed quietly at my response, pulled a chair over and sat at the table, leaning forward on his elbows.

'I trust you are what I requested?'

'Comrade?' Kirill replied.

'I see. You've not been told anything. Am I in the company of experienced miners?'

'Yes, comrade,' Kirill confirmed.

'And am I to understand,' he went on, 'that you've brought your own rations?'

Dmitri pointed to the three sacks where they stood against the side of the table.

Leaning over and peering into one of them, he remarked, 'Staple stuff. Did they give you tea? Coffee?'

'No, comrade,' said Kostya.

'You'll need one or the other. You'll be working long hours. Some of it heavy work. A stimulant will be essential.'

No one replied to this: we were not about to apprise him of the fact that we usually worked longer hours than he could imagine with little more than a hunk of bread and a bucket of water to sustain us.

'You,' he pointed to Ylli, 'go to the fourth tent down, say Dr. Solovyov sent you and ask for half a kilo of coffee. Bring it back here.'

For a moment, Ylli stood quite still. We were all of us in a state of inanimation. Perhaps it was the thought of coffee which rooted us to the spot: perhaps it was the fact of one of our number being given the instruction to go and get something without so much as queue to join or a crowd to jostle.

'Well, what are you waiting for? Clearance from Moscow?

123

Get on with it,' Dr. Solovyov snapped, his impatience plainly evident.

Ylli darted out.

Kirill, not one to beat about the bush, asked, 'Why have we been brought here, comrade doctor?'

Ylli returned with a small tin. No sooner had he entered than we could smell the coffee. Feeling the glands at the back of my mouth tighten and begin to salivate, I tried to work out how long it had been since I had last tasted coffee, and failed.

The kettle was boiling by now. Titian, having discovered a battered and smoke-stained coffee pot, tipped a liberal amount of grounds into it, added water and stirred it vigorously with a bent aluminium spoon. Taking some dented mugs down from the shelf and blowing the dust off them, he filled them with piping hot coffee and handed them round.

With each of us grasping a tin mug of black coffee, Dr. Solovyov settled back in his chair.

'You are here,' he commenced, to a chorus of appreciative slurping, 'to partake in one of the most astounding scientific discoveries yet made in the whole of the Soviet Union, possibly in the world this century. Your part in this venture is to excavate, under my direction and that of Dr. Nedelko. You will be shown what to do in the morning.'

'How long shall we be here?' Kirill questioned.

'Meteorological reports suggest we have ten days at the most. It has been decided to make as much use as we can of this temporary and uncharacteristic break in the weather pattern. It won't be long before it's back to blizzards as usual. We have to work as quickly as we can, but that is not to say we sacrifice care. Everything we do – you do – must be conducted with scrupulous attention to detail and orders.'

'What are we to dig for, comrade?'

Dr. Solovyov drained his mug of coffee. He drank with the speedy ease of a man accustomed to such luxury. The rest of us had only been sipping at ours, savouring every drop.

'Follow me and I'll show you.'

We gulped down the rest of our coffee and hurried out of the tent. As we approached the guards' billet, they gathered up their rifles but Solovyov waved to them not to bother. They sat down again and watched us go by.

The sun, which had been up for less than six hours, never rising higher than twenty degrees from the horizon, had set by now. In the afterglow of evening, the first stars re-appearing, we trudged after him along the bank of the river. It was clear that it was not a permanent feature of the landscape. The banks were sheer and freshly cut. This was a watercourse which came and went every year. When the ice thawed and the summer rains came, this river would change course and the bed would become a dry gully like that in which we had stopped to rendezvous with the half-track.

'I might have guessed we'd be digging something. What do you reckon it'll be?' Kostya thought aloud as we walked along a mud bank.

'I think,' Ylli declared, 'we're going to dig out a satellite. I've heard they sometimes come down in the north. I think a satellite has crashed to earth and we are to be the poor sods sent to recover it.'

'Start praying you're wrong,' said Avel.

'Why?' Ylli responded. 'What can a defunct satellite do to you?'

'Kill you,' Avel replied. 'Slow and sure. Some of them have little nuclear reactors in them. If one of them's cracked open you'll have radioactive shit all over the place.'

'In that case,' I reasoned, 'the good doctor would be wearing protective clothing.'

'And he isn't!' exclaimed Ylli. 'You ever seen kit like his coat?'

'No,' Titian said. 'It's nothing like that. The camp's semi-permanent. That tent's not just gone up. It's been there a while. A year or two even.'

'How do you know?' Dmitri queried.

'For one,' Titian explained, 'the turves outside were cut last summer. The grass roots are virtually non-existent or brittle as glass which means they dried out before being frozen in the autumn. If they were recently cut, the roots would be alive. Second, I turned my palliasse over.'

It was a trick every prisoner learned. As soon as you were assigned a new bunk, you turned the mattress, poked about in the cracks of the frame. There was always the off-chance that the previous occupant had left behind a razor blade, a few grams of coarse Ukrainian tobacco or some other contraband neither the guards nor his fellow prisoners had come across.

'And what did you find?'

'Mosquitoes.'

'*Mosquitoes*!' Ylli exclaimed.

'Dead mosquitoes. A whole drift of the little buggers. Enough to fill a cook's ladle. That tent's been sprayed with insecticide. You don't get mosquitoes in the winter. So the tent's been there at least since last summer.'

Dr. Solovyov stopped at the edge of a sheet of ice jutting out from the muddy shore and pointed through the fading daylight to the far bank.

'What do you see, comrades?'

We looked at the earth bank, the evening sky above it. I could just make out Andromeda and the galaxy bearing its name.

The doctor switched on a torch, directing the beam at the earth bank about three metres from the rim. In the frozen soil was a dull white streak.

'What do you think that is, comrades? I shall tell you. It is the remnant of the largest mammal ever to roam the land. What you are looking at, comrades, is the last two metres of the right tusk of a female hairy mammoth.'

With that, he snapped the torch off with all the showmanship of a ringmaster in the Russian State Circus.

*

We were reluctant to retire to our beds that night. The freedom of being able to loll about the stove without being jostled by the *blatnye* and our fellow *zeks* was one to savour as long as possible. Somehow, even our rations tasted better.

For long periods, we did not speak. The oil lamps glimmered and, way out on the dark landscape, an Arctic fox barked intermittently, sounding like an old man with a rough cough.

'At least it's not a satellite with a strontium-90 payload,' Avel observed, putting down his latest chess piece, a bishop he had started shaping from a lump of anthracite he had carefully selected for its consistent density from the fuel box and polished with a square of discarded cloth he had discovered under his bunk.

'What're they after, though?' Ylli pondered, ever suspicious of the seemingly most innocuous motives of officialdom. 'I mean, what can you learn of use from a dead elephant?'

'This isn't just an exercise in scientific progress,' Kostya answered, 'not just a search for knowledge. It's for the glory of the USSR. It's a piece of jingoistic oneupmanship. The next time Solovyov goes to an international symposium, he'll stand up and declare, "We in the Soviet Union have dug up a mammoth." The Americans will get cross. They'll start searching Alaska like crazy. You know of the Space Race. What we are doing is contributing to the Mammoth Race.'

'That may be true. Probably is,' Titian concurred, 'but they'll find much of use. For example, what the animal ate.'

'Who cares what a dead elephant ate ten thousand years ago!' Dmitri retorted.

'From its diet,' Titian began to expound, the academic in him coming to the fore, 'we can tell what the environment was like, what plants grew here, what the climate was like...'

I let my mind wander for a moment, losing the thread of their conversation. It was several minutes before I was jolted back to the present by Kirill holding out the pot of coffee which had been simmering on the stove plate.

'What are you thinking, Shurik?' he asked as he refilled my mug.

'I was wondering,' I replied, 'if in ten thousand years, someone else will come along over the tundra and dig me up: and I was trying to guess what conclusions they might draw from their find.'

Kirill laughed quietly and ran his eye disapprovingly up and down me.

'Judging by you, Shurik, they'll have a pretty poor opinion of modern man. Dressed in grimy clothes, with lice in what little hair he has not shaved off, crabs on his bollocks, dirt under his fingernails with a mulch of cabbage and potato in his guts.'

'With coffee,' I added, raising my mug in thanks and sipping from it.

'That'll confuse them,' Avel said. 'A shitty diet with a luxury tropical plant added to it.'

'This all pre-supposes you'll be buried just under the surface,' Dmitri remarked. 'What if you buy it half a kilometre down on Gallery D.'

'D for Dzerzhinsky, first Chief of the Cheka,' Kirill butted in.

'Or they chuck you in a pit of quicklime?' Kostya added.

'In that case,' Dmitri said, ' the secret of your belly and your balls will be safe for eternity.'

Avel opened the door on the stove. The heat of the fire seared out. I could feel it burning my face. He tossed in some anthracite, first checking for any useful pieces he might carve, and slammed the door shut with his foot.

'They'll learn nothing of the truth,' Titian said after a few moments, holding his hands out to the stove which, now the anthracite was catching, was beginning to glow a dull orange around the firebox. 'Nothing of the real history of this place. Of us. All they will have to judge us by will be a few artefacts which they will interpret in the light of their own time. If they have no prison camps, how will they know of life here, now? They cannot.

History is a lie. It never happened. We only think it happened as we believe it did.'

'And what of books?' Ylli argued.

'Books rot,' I said.

'Or can be burned,' Avel added.

'What does it matter? History is written by winners, not losers,' Titian remarked. 'You don't read history books filled with defeats and failures. Only victories and successes.'

Dmitri leaned back, his chair creaking as he tipped it onto its rear legs.

'History. Death. Quicklime. Winners and losers. Who gives a shit!' he rebuked us. 'We're the losers. History's fucked us up good and proper. And who cares if we go into a pit of acid or the incinerator at the top of shaft K – for Khruschev, King of the KGB. Listen: three men are walking through the countryside. It's a sunny day. One's called Titian, one's called Ylli, one's called Shurik.'

He paused and scanned his assembled audience, grinned and winked. Kirill and I exchanged looks: Dmitri, ever indomitable, ever laughing when the odds were long or the dice loaded.

'They talk of this and that,' he started. 'Rounding a corner in the road, they come across a field of sheep. One of the sheep has seen sweet, new grass on the side of the road and stuck its head through the fence to eat it. But it's got its forequarters stuck between two posts. The three of them stop and gaze at the sheep. "I wish that was Tatania Alexandrovna, the farmer's wife," says the first one, wistfully. "No," exclaims the second with a dreamy look in his eyes, "I wish it was Ekaterina Vasilyevna, the nurse at the clinic." "I wish it was dark," says the third.'

To punctuate the punch line, he slapped his hands together. His palms cracked like a pistol shot.

'Who's who?' Ylli asked after our chuckling had subsided.

Dmitri grinned again and said urbanely, 'My friend, which one would you like to be?'

For a while longer, we sat about the stove, laughing and

talking and listening to Dmitri as the Arctic fox wandered off, its barking fading away. Ahead of the others, I lay on my bunk and tugged the blanket up to my chin, the last I heard being Avel's chuckle and Dmitri's voice before I drifted off into a sleep which, for the first night in more years than I could recall, was utterly without dreams.

*

The first day, we dug an oblong trench on the top of the bank, six metres by four and down almost as far as the carcass. The next day, excavation began in earnest.

Our spades and pick-axes put aside, we were handed triangular bricklayer's trowels with which we were instructed not to dig but to scrape the soil back, bit by bit. It was frozen solid but, as soon as it was opened to the air, it became friable and crumbled quite easily: it was like digging in compacted crushed ice. Dr. Solovyov and his colleague, Dr. Nedelko, stood over us every moment we were at our toil, guiding us, watching the ground as we edged, centimetre by centimetre, down to the mammoth. Even the guards and the two expedition staff – Spasskiy, the half-track driver and a cook-cum-jack-of-all-trades called Fedin – assembled at the edge of the trench to observe developments.

Halfway through the second day, the southerly wind picked up. Nedelko studied his thermometer.

'We need ice,' he ordered Fedin. 'Get to it.'

'Ice?' Ylli repeated incredulously from the bottom of the trench. 'The dirt down here's frozen solid.'

'But as you uncover it, comrade,' Solovyov explained, somewhat impatiently, 'it may thaw. That we cannot allow. The mammoth must stay well below zero at all times.'

In one of the supply tents there was an ice-making machine. Fedin started it up. A black puff of diesel scarred the sky before it reached the top of the river bank to be diffused by the wind. It seemed a gross and cynical violation of the ancient landscape to so pollute it and for the reason of making ice in one of the coldest places on the planet.

At around noon, I was first to expose the mammoth. The beast was lying horizontally on its side and I uncovered it at a point midway between its legs and about halfway down its body from the spine. Everyone crowded round at my discovery.

'Give me your trowel,' Solovyov ordered. I stood up and handed it to him whereupon he knelt where I had been and commenced carefully scraping away at the soil to ratify that what I had revealed was, in fact, mammoth and not something else.

'That's it,' he confirmed after a few minutes. 'You're all more or less down to it. Go very slowly from here on. A millimetre at a time. No clumsy digging, no hurrying.'

We continued scraping. Soon, every one of us had our own patch of rock hard carcass before us. The skin was leathery in appearance, rough and covered in a thick layer of bristly hairs. Over about an hour, I uncovered an area fifty centimetres square. At last, Solovyov called a halt and crouched beside us.

'So, comrades,' he said, 'what do you think of it?' He was unable to contain his ebullience, had to share it, even with prisoners.

'Remarkable,' I admitted. 'How old is it?'

'Around 22,000 years. Soil samples taken from the bank during the summer suggest that age when subject to carbon dating.'

'How did it die?' Kirill asked.

'That is what we want to know,' Nedelko replied. 'We have found other mammoths in the Soviet Union. In that respect, this one is not unique. Indeed, this is number 30 something. But the others have all died from obvious natural causes. The last I excavated in Poluostrov Taimyr had got stuck in a tar pit. The one before that, on Ostrov Komsomolets, was crushed by a fall of rocks from a cliff. But this one...'

'What's so special about this one, comrade doctor?' Dmitri asked.

'This one,' Solovyov answered, standing up and looking down at the areas of exposed skin, 'was not crushed by stone, or drowned in a pond, or sucked into a tar pit. It is, from its size, not a fully mature adult so we doubt it died of old age. It might be diseased, in which case we may learn why the species went extinct, or it might have died in a fight with other mammoths.'

'But that assumption,' Nedelko cut in, 'is not likely. We know from studies of modern elephants that whilst they do fight from time to time, they rarely fight to the death.'

'So?' Ylli said.

'So think,' prompted Solovyov curtly. He was clearly exasperated by our ignorance or lack of imagination. 'How do animals die – especially land animals – if they do not succumb to disease, die of senility or have an accident?'

We stood for a moment puzzling the scientists' quandary: then the possibility dawned on us.

'How will you tell, comrade doctor?' Kirill asked at length.

'Tell what?' Ylli said, who had not yet arrived at our deduction.

'Tell if it was hunted,' I told him.

'A bloody great mammoth like that!' Ylli retorted. 'By what? A sabre-toothed tiger would have a problem.'

'Perhaps there are spear wounds,' Solovyov said quietly, answering Kirill's initial question and ignoring Ylli's importunate outburst. 'Perhaps we shall find arrowheads. Axe marks. Who knows?'

Even Ylli was silent now as we all stared at the square of exposed prehistoric creature.

Avel's voice was not much above a whisper. 'So we're not the first poor sods to slave away up here,' he said.

'Internal exile goes back a long way,' mused Titian.

The sun went down and the air chilled. Fedin piled crushed ice over the carcass as a precaution and we retreated to our tent. We were, I remember, subdued that night. The wonder of uncovering the mammoth was somehow diminished by the thought that we were not just touching an extinct creature but that we were, through it, possibly in tactile communication with humanoids who had lived out their lives in these barren wastes long before we were sentenced to join them.

For three more days, we worked on the mammoth. As more and more of it was unearthed, the more astounding became our discovery. The creature was almost perfectly preserved. It might have been an unbutchered carcass hanging in a cold store. Although somewhat desiccated, the flesh was firm, the hairs of the shaggy coat pliable and the toe nails, when we reached the end of the first leg, were as polished as cow's horn. It might have been dead twenty-two months, not twenty-two millennia.

Despite being frozen, on the fifth day it started to give off an odour. It was not unpleasant, not the pungent perfume of putrefaction, but a delicate animal scent such as one might come across in a stable or byre, a mixture of bestial sweat, masticated vegetation and steaming dung.

By the end of day six, we had uncovered the entire right side of the mammoth, one of its tusks bending up into the air like an exposed root. The only part of its anatomy which seemed to be damaged beyond reconstitution was its eye which had collapsed. Now half exposed, the two scientists started their work of investigating the creature's demise. Using butchery saws and sharp knives, they began to open the carcass along a line of incision running from behind its ear to the inside of the rear leg.

At first, they slit through the skin which they folded back or sliced off. The subcutaneous layers of fat were yellow, the colour of tallow or bees'-wax. Beneath that, the muscle tissue was dark red, almost black, striated and shot through with streaks of light grey gristle. This was cut away in blocks and stored in insulated boxes of ice. When Nedelko finally made an incision into the body cavity, the smell we had experienced increased tenfold. As the two men tunnelled into the carcass, samples from internal organs were taken – the lungs like huge grey sacks of stiff india-rubber foam, the liver the colour of ebony, the heart a maroon black, the intestines a dull military olive, the stomach layered with veins. All the time they worked, crushed ice was piled onto the mammoth.

When it melted or was crushed under our boots, it became tinged with the delicate dark scarlet of the creature's blood.

All the while, the southerly wind kept air temperatures only a few degrees below zero. Every evening, Nedelko spent twenty minutes at the radio transmitter in the half-track, conversing with the meteorologists, confirming that the weather was not going to change. At night, we could hear the ice on the river shifting, expanding and contracting with eerie creaks and screams.

With the excavation finished, for it was decided not to attempt to dig out beneath the carcass, we were set to other tasks. Titian and I were put in charge of storing samples in bottles of formaldehyde or methyl alcohol, labelling them and putting them in compartmentalised boxes for the journey back to civilisation. Kirill and Avel were responsible for carrying the samples to us from the excavation and ensuring we knew what they were. Ylli was set the task of helping Fedin keep up the supply of crushed ice whilst Dmitri was instructed to remove the exposed tusk and saw off four of the teeth, leaving them in situ in the jaw bone. Kostya, meanwhile, assisted with the actual dissection, holding back sections of flesh, dumping the gurry in a pile a hundred metres off.

At last, in the middle of day nine, Nedelko received a radio message that the winter was on its way back with a vengeance, driving the high pressure back south. Solovyov declared the investigation was to draw to a close. They had cut right through to the left side, taken out most of the viscera in the front two-thirds of the carcass and were satisfied that they had sufficient samples to keep them busy for some months.

We stood around the edge of what we no longer saw as a palæontological trench but the grave of an awesome beast and gazed down upon the mutilated body. None of us spoke. It was a solemn moment. The low Arctic sun shone in our faces, the ground hard under our feet. The wind carried a vague hint of the threatening resumption of winter.

'What's going to happen to it now?' Kostya said, breaking our silence.

Solovyov replied, 'You're going to re-bury it in ice and soil. If our study of the samples turns up anything puzzling, we may need to return for more. As for the detritus we have dumped over there,' he pointed to the heap of intestines and organs, 'we shall incinerate it. Spasskiy,' he turned to the half-track driver, 'get a jerry can of gasoline.'

When the heap of orts was thoroughly soaked in petrol, Solovyov ran a trail back a safe distance and, striking a match, tossed it onto the ground. We watched as the flames raced towards the pile and exploded. A dense cloud of steam and oil billowed into the sky. The odour of burning flesh drifted over to us to taint our nostrils.

'We never found if it was hunted or not, comrade doctor,' Kirill remarked as Solovyov and his colleague returned to the excavation site.

'It would seem not,' Solovyov said. 'We found no indications and there were no internal injuries. Not that I expected any. You would be hard put to bring down such a beast with a Kalashnikov, never mind a bone club and a wooden spear. Of course, the left side might show injury.'

'To kill it outright would have been beyond primitive man's abilities,' Nedelko added. 'They couldn't bring such a creature down in one. They would have to wound it severely and follow it until it bled to death. That would probably mean hitting it from all sides. And the right was undamaged. Current thinking has it that when man hunted the mammoth, he killed it by driving it into a pit.'

Once more, we looked down on the carcass in the trench. Fedin was already starting to dump ice on the creature's forequarters.

'I want about twenty centimetres of ice over the whole thing,' Solovyov ordered, 'just in case. When you've done that, start shovelling the earth. But don't throw it down. You're not burying it but protecting it. Let the soil fall gently from your spades. We don't want it damaged.'

With that, he and Nedelko headed back towards the tents, deep in conversation. They were already planning their laboratory research programme.

'Well, you just going to stand there?' Fedin asked sarcastically. 'You heard him. Come on and fetch ice.'

Ylli and Dmitri slid down the bank and followed Fedin en route for the ice-maker.

'I wonder,' Kostya thought aloud when they were out of earshot, 'what mammoth must have tasted like. To the cavemen hunters.'

The five of us exchanged looks. We knew what Kostya was thinking. Kirill scratched his nose.

'Too risky,' Titian declared. 'What if it died of some disease transferable to humans?'

After a long silence, Kirill said softly, 'What does it matter? We're *zeks*. We're dead men anyway.'

The cut Kostya took came from what would have been, were the mammoth a beef steer, topside. It was a substantial piece of meat weighing about four kilos.

'How are we going to do it?' I asked as we tossed earth on the layer of ice.

'Make a stew?' Avel suggested. 'We've got cabbage and potatoes.'

'No,' Kirill decided, 'we roast it. That's what the cavemen would have done. They had no cooking utensils.'

That night, we erected a simple spit over a hearth of smooth river stones outside our tent, fuelling the fire with anthracite and timber obtained by chopping up a rations supply crate. Solovyov and Nedelko paid us no heed. They were in their tent and seemed not to have their suspicions aroused by our fire *al fresco*. The guards ignored us and, shortly after dark, went to Fedin's tent for a game of cards.

Dmitri, as chef d'éléphant, caked some potatoes in mud and placed them around the fire to bake. The meat took some hours to cook and it was late by the time it was ready for eating.

We sat in a circle round the flames, balanced on boxes and

barrels, except for Ylli who incongruously lolled back in one of the deck chairs. The flames danced upon our faces and hands, giving them a ruddy, primeval glow.

As Dmitri's knife pierced the meat, a delicious aroma wafted over us, stirring memories of our former lives which were, it seemed then, as far removed from the present and lost in time as those of the cavemen we imitated. The mammoth joint itself was hard on the outside and crusted with burnt tissue but within it was well cooked, rare only in the very centre. We held our plates out as Dmitri sliced off generous portions and served them.

I cut into my share. A pink, bloody gravy oozed from it as the knife severed the tissue which, to my surprise, flaked almost as if it was fish. I spiked a piece with the blade of my knife, hesitating as I carried it to my mouth: we were all vacillating for one reason or another. It was Kirill who, as usual, decided for us.

'What have we to lose, my friends?' he said. 'Tomorrow, we finish burying the past and return to the future.'

'Screw the future!' Ylli muttered.

'From the primeval to...' I began.

'To Sosnogorsklag 32,' said Kostya.

Together, we opened our mouths, like men taking part in some bizarre blood brothers' oath-taking ceremony, and ate.

The mammoth meat was gamey, rich, and mouth-watering. It was not at all tough, almost dissolving in the mouth. The juice which seeped out of it as we bit into it was slightly salty.

We chewed without speaking, lost in thought. It was not that we were overawed by the thought of what we were consuming but more that we did not have the vocabulary, the means of expression at our command, to speak. It was as if, by eating ancient meat, we had been temporarily transmogrified into primitive men with no language other than grunts and grimaces.

When we had consumed the joint, we ate the potatoes and sat back satiated, the heat of the fire playing on us.

'Only one thing needed now to complete the banquet,' Titian announced. He rose from his seat and walked to a snow drift behind the tent, returning with a bottle in the bottom of which were two of three centimetres of good quality vodka. 'Courtesy, albeit unwittingly, of Dr. Solovyov.'.

There was only sufficient for a thimbleful each. We held our mugs up in silent tribute to the mammoth and drank. The vodka was chilled and scoured my throat like carbolic.

Until after midnight, we all sat round the fire, drinking what was left of the coffee. Titian recounted bawdy tales of his student days at the University of Leningrad, Avel regaling us with stories of bravery in the skies above the 38th Parallel, of how he had engaged US Air Force F-86 Sabres and F9F Panthers over the Yalu River in his MiG-15, and Dmitri entertained us with a gamut of his jokes, filling our throats with laughter and our hearts with happiness. They seemed funnier than usual, I suspect because the vodka had gone to our heads, unaccustomed as we were to liquor, but I can remember not one of them now.

I kept my silence and thought how strange destiny was, that it should have brought me into the companionship of such a motley crew and given me such friendship in circumstances which were, I considered, as brutal as the world in which the mammoth had lived.

Glancing from one to the other of them brought to mind a definition of friendship although I could not place its author. A friend, it went, is one soul inhabiting two bodies. Yet here, in this bleak place of adversity and pain, we were not two but seven. And what we had between our disparate selves was something men who lived in comfortable amenity would treasure beyond health or wealth.

Later, as the fire died and the others took to their bunks, I sat a while longer outside the tent with the embers dying at my feet, the ice in the river crackling before me, the stars brilliant over my head and a taste of roast meat lingering in my mouth for the first time in years.

7

The unassuming church of Saint Lazarus stands on a grassy knoll across the river from the village with a fine, spreading walnut tree shading the main door. When I first came to Myshkino, it was in a state of semi-dereliction. One of the side chapels remained in use by a few old crones who hobbled up there once a week, or on feast days, to light a candle stub and chant a while, but the bulk of the interior was used in good years to store excess grain from Myshkino Motors' barn and, for the rest of the time, winter fodder, firewood, communal agricultural tools and spare parts for the village tractor which were locked in the seventeenth century vestment chest. In there, they were secure from thieves and moisture for the lid was a tight fit and the chest weighed at least five hundred kilos when it was empty, the hasp fashioned from iron a centimetre thick.

There was no village priest. The post had been vacant almost since the Bolshevik uprising. In 1919 the incumbent, a young man not long ordained called Father Mikhail, prophesied the future course of Russia. He was, in retrospect, exceedingly accurate in his vision but he kept it to himself. One spring day, he conducted the service, led the prayers, sang sturdily and gave the blessing: the next day, he was gone. His small tied cottage behind the church was empty, the fires in the stoves out and his wardrobe bare. For weeks, the villagers prayed for his safe return, scoured the countryside for his body and put out tentative feelers as far away as Voronezh. Six months later, they learnt from a deserter fleeing south that he had renounced his faith and joined the White Guard. He was never heard of again.

No other priest arrived as a replacement. The villagers kept the church going as long as they could but, in the face of the ravages of the weather, time and socialist dogma, it fell into decay and underwent its secular utilitarian transformation.

As the world changed, however, and the rolling clouds of Communism started to thin, the villagers gradually turned back to the church. There was no outward manifestation of this: it happened in their hearts and minds, far away from the tentacles of the Party and the KGB. Eventually, there arose a determination to restore it. At first, the excuse was that the building had a cultural connotation which should not be ignored. Religion, it was argued, was not the point. The church was a part of the village – and Russia's – heritage. After all, it was argued at a meeting with officials in Zarechensk, churches in Leningrad and Moscow had been preserved or restored to show to foreigners the history, the traditions, the grandeur of the Soviet past. The precedent had been set. That the chance of foreign tourists ever coming to Myshkino was about as great as a cake of cheese become a commissar was ignored.

I attended the meeting, with some reluctance. I wanted to keep my head well below the parapet. Certainly, the local officials had as little idea as to my own personal history as they had of the church itself but that was immaterial. In my mind, I saw them cast as overseers and, the night before the meeting, I suffered terrible nightmares in which I was dragged through a coal mine not unlike a darkened church, impaled upon an ornate altar and cut through with a compressed air-powered rock drill.

'Don't worry!' Victor Ivanovich, the village spokesman, assured me on the way to Zarechensk. 'You won't have to speak. You're just coming along to swell the ranks.'

'Like deer in the forest when the wolves are about,' his wife, Tamara, remarked. 'Safety in numbers.'

Her choice of metaphor did nothing to calm me and, as we climbed the steps into the local Party offices, my knees felt suddenly weak.

The meeting got under way with Victor Ivanovich stating the case. The local cadres, under the chairmanship of the local Party secretary, listened with the patience of officials who knew where their power lay. Tea was served. Cigarettes were handed round, the Ukrainian *makhorka* tobacco smoke dense and grey and, for me at least, unpleasantly familiar. Others joined in the parley. The current use of the church was discussed, alternative storage for the contents mulled over. Costs were bandied about. I sat in the back row, sipped my tea and kept my eyes down.

Suddenly, a voice from the front said, 'Comrade! You! At the back! Old man! What do you remember of those days?'

At first, I did not realise I was being addressed: then Trofim jabbed his finger into me.

'Shurik! The secretary's speaking to you,' he hissed.

A tsunami of terror washed over me. I looked up, slowly. If I had been closer to the front, to the table behind which the officials sat, he would have seen the abject horror in my eyes and suspected something. In a split second, I lived again the handcuffs, the KGB interrogators, the circus dwarf in Gallery B. B for Bulganin who had buggered us all.

'What do you remember of the old days, when the church was a church?'

Trofim, understanding my fear, nodded encouragement to me. I rose unsteadily to my feet, holding on to the back of the chair in front to keep my balance.

'Very little, comrade,' I replied, trying to contain the waver in my voice and control my knees which were quaking unrestrainably. Even addressing him as *comrade* was a crime: as a former *zek*, I should have called him *grazhdanin* for, being a miscreant, I could never be his comrade, only his fellow citizen. 'I was,' I did a quick calculation, knowing that the nearest I kept to the truth the less likely I was to snag myself up with lies, 'only three or four when the priest left.'

'But you remember afterwards? The villagers kept it going for a while, we understand.'

'My parents were not very devout,' I answered, wondering whether or not to add that they were, by their impiety, good Communists, but I decided against it. 'I only went to the church with my grandmother and then not very often.'

'Do you remember what the interior was like?' the secretary quizzed me.

I was, slowly but surely, being snared. Yet I had to answer.

'Not very well, comrade secretary,' I admitted. 'I remember it was always dark. There were candles lit – not very many – and a small red lamp hung from the roof. There were some icons and the wall behind the altar was painted with pictures.'

At one end of the table, a young woman clerk frantically scribbled in shorthand as I spoke. The very movement of her pen across the paper of her pad sent a shock of fear through me. She might have been recording my confession to crimes the conduct of which I was not even able to imagine.

'Anything else?'

'I remember the smell,' I lied. 'Always very musty.'

I made to sit down, thinking my interrogation was over.

'Comrade,' the secretary asked, 'what is your name?'

The clerk looked up. Her pen was poised. This was for the official record. This was going into the Myshkino dossier.

The blood must have drained from my face. My head swum and I fought to keep myself in check.

'Alexander...' I began.

'He is my uncle,' Trofim called out. 'He is one of the schoolmasters in our village.'

'Ah!' The secretary brightened up. 'Tell me, comrade teacher, what is your opinion as to what should be done with the church?'

I looked down at my knuckles. They were white as they gripped the metal stay of the chair.

'Just tell him!' Trofim muttered. 'Don't be afraid.'

'Safety in numbers,' whispered Tamara, sitting in front of me, not helping the situation much.

It was plain I had to say something. Silence would have roused suspicion and might have undermined the villagers' case, bringing them untold trouble in the form of petty bureaucratic hassling for months to come.

'I think,' I commenced, gathering my thoughts, 'the

142

restoration of the church would be beneficial to the community. It will bring a sense of awareness of the past in our young people. Is it not the case that, when the Revolution overthrew the old order, the palaces of the Tsar and his nobles were not destroyed, nor their treasures looted and dispersed, but retained in their grandeur for they belonged to the Soviet people. To the proletariat.' I began to warm to my speech, despite myself. 'So it is to this day that we, the Soviet people, may visit such places as the Winter Palace in Leningrad or the Terem Palace in the Kremlin to see and understand our cultural heritage. The preservation of our past is important to us, it gives us identity.'

I paused. All the officials were looking at me with an intensity that unnerved me and yet, at the same time, it bolstered my spirit.

'When the French overthrew their monarchy,' I continued, 'they destroyed everything. Palaces were looted, libraries destroyed, paintings burned. That was because they are a barbarian race. But we, the Soviet people, did not do this. We are civilised and realised the cultural importance of our past. Certainly, we removed the monarchy but we did not destroy that which made us.'

'And how do you regard the restoration of the church in Myshkino?' the secretary asked.

'I consider it the restoration of a facet of the past which will give continuity to the future. A man lives by his history and what he was is what shapes what he shall become.'

There was a long silence. The officials looked at me and I looked at the floor as I slowly lowered myself onto my chair. I felt drained, afraid and alone. Trofim took hold of my hand and pressed it between both of his: his skin was warm against mine which was chilled for want of blood.

For some minutes, there was a muted discussion amongst the officials. The villagers remained apprehensively silent. Every so often, one of the officials glanced up at me, tickling the hairs on the nape of my neck.

143

At last, the secretary declared that he and his colleagues would retire to consider their decision. More tea was served. I spilled half mine on the floor for I could not prevent my hands from shaking. The others gathered round me, murmuring their congratulations on my speech. Victor Ivanovich told me he could never have put the case so succinctly, so sententiously. After half an hour, the officials returned, the secretary coming across the room to me.

'Comrade,' he said, 'you are a most eloquent orator. I am sure you are just as effective a teacher. You are a credit to your village and to the Soviet people.'

I smiled politely and mumbled some suitably humble reply but, all the while, a rip tide of triumph was surging through me. The music of revenge, the exquisite rhapsody of retribution was playing in my soul. A thousand trumpets blared the fanfare of ironic victory. I had beaten the entire system, the order which had thrust me into a quarter of a century of oblivion, which had tried to destroy my spirit, to eradicate my humanity, to demolish my love of my fellow men, to quench all hope and which had caused the death of Kirill.

'Comrades,' the secretary addressed us from in front of the table, 'we have reached our decision. The church of Saint Lazarus in the village of Myshkino may be restored.' He drew himself up: he was about to prove to us what a generous man he was, worthy of his exalted position and his right to drive and fornicate in an official car. 'I have contacted the regional authorities responsible for such affairs and they have agreed a grant of four thousand roubles to assist with the restoration programme.'

The villagers applauded, we left the meeting and returned home where I was feted as being the saviour of the church.

Now, the church stands upon its knoll looking as if seventy-five years of socialism were little more than a thunderstorm in the night. The wooden walls are painted white, the classic Russian onion-shaped dome on the single tower painted deep royal blue with gold stars spattered about it, all of them with six irregular

144

points. Boris, who was responsible for them, had little concept of geometrical perfection but he was the only one of us who had the courage – some said stupidity, others temerity – to balance on a plank suspended by two ropes from the base of the iron cross at the apex. The window frames are painted in the same deep blue.

Inside, the church is simple. Two of the wooden pillars holding up the dome are decorated with frescoes adequately copied from a guidebook to the Monastery of the Transfiguration of Our Saviour at Yaroslavl. Red, blue, gold and ochre predominate, the paintings looking like the two dimensional portraits of a particularly gifted but artistically ignorant child. There are five icons in the church. Two are modern copies but three are genuinely ancient. Where they came from, no one is prepared to say even today in the liberal world of dollars and gangsters, but the rumour is that they were stolen from another church over a hundred kilometres away by a secret posse of villagers who went off icon-hunting one weekend just as the restoration was nearing completion. A brass candelabra capable of holding thirty-six candles is suspended by a chain from a pulley system. That, too, was stolen but from a scrapyard, not another house of worship. Only the little oil lamp with its glass cowl the colour of freshly spilt blood and the silver censer are original to Saint Lazarus. They were kept secreted away over the years by one of the old women who continued to use the side chapel and were only discovered when her son, inheriting her house, had to climb into the loft to replace some rotten joists and found them wrapped in moth-chewed lengths of velvet stuffed into a wall cavity.

Beside the church is the village cemetery, a mixture of ancient graves protected by leaning iron crosses and more recent, stark headstones. Of Father Mikhail's house only a raised platform remains. The house was, in the harsh years of the 1930s, gradually dismantled, cannibalised to repair the other houses in the village or cut up for fuel. Its destruction also lent the villagers some credibility in the equivocal eyes of the GPU officers who visited from time to time, checking up on everyone's Stalinist zeal.

Three years ago, with the church reconsecrated, Father Kondrati was appointed to the living. He is not yet thirty-five but, with his rampant beard, his black robes and his tall priest's headgear, not to mention his small circular spectacles sardonically reminiscent of those Leon Trotsky wore, he looks much older and distinguishedly patriarchal.

It was late morning as I approached the church, making my way slowly up the knoll from the bridge over the river. He was in front of the main door, sweeping the area of baked earth with a peasant's twig broom like a witch's sky chariot. It was not until I was quite close that he caught sight of me, stopped his labours and settled himself on the bench under the walnut tree.

'Shurik, it's good to see you,' he greeted me as I moved under the shadow of the tree.

'You always say that,' I responded, 'as if it is a miracle I've survived to see another sunrise.'

He smiled. I knew this not from the curve of his mouth, hidden in his facial foliage, but the sparkle in his eyes.

'Every day is a miracle,' he replied in the firm voice of a man certain of his god and his facts, 'whether or not you or I are in it.' He gazed about himself in the patronal fashion of a man of the cloth. 'Is it not a fine day?'

'Yes, it is a fine day,' I agreed.

The meadow pasture on the church knoll has been mown and the hay collected in. Over by the tree line, where a track disappears into the forest, a horse was standing with its head down, grazing upon the sweet new growth that has pushed up since the mower did its work.

'And it is your 80th. birthday which makes it...' he paused to work out the sum. Like many men for whom eternity is a certainty and therefore not an object of fear, he is obsessed with the mathematics of time. 'Twenty-nine thousand, two hundred days!' he exclaimed.

'Give or take a few, Father,' I reminded him. 'You must account for leap years.'

146

He looked sheepish for, although he is well educated in the ways of the church and the wiles of the sinner, he is not in those of Pythagoras, Euclid and their brothers in numeracy.

'Add another twenty. Or so,' he said then, raising his hands as if he was about to bless me, added, 'Whatever! It is an extraordinary length of time. Our Lord in heaven obviously believes you have a purpose here on earth, to keep you with us for so long.'

I did not make a comment for I do not share his sentiments, do not believe in merciful gods of love and a panoply of omniscient charitable guardian angels for I have been in a place on their earth, in their creation, where they had no power: and this was no time for either argument or reasoned debate.

'What will you do with your day?' he went on.

'What I do with every day. Live through it, experience what it brings, suffer its pains, or those which twinge my joints when the weather's damp or cold, and rejoice at its little pleasures.'

He looked at me with a sadness I could almost touch.

'I know where you learned this,' he said, as if he was privileged with the information.

'It is not a lesson taught just in the gulag, Father,' I assured him. 'It is presented to every human at some stage in their existence. A few heed it. A minority skip it and play truant from life's little university. Most ignore it. In the gulag, however, one has no choice but to attend every class and pay attention for the teacher is a cruel master who will brook no slackers, no day-dreamers, no skivers.'

'You do not regret those...' he paused again, to search for an appropriate word which, he hoped, would not upset me: little does he know that nothing disturbs me now. What is past is past. As Frosya says, you cannot unwind the wool of destiny.

There was a squeaking overhead, shrill and almost metallic. The priest welcomed the distraction for he felt uneasy pursuing the direction in which he had steered out conversation.

We looked up. Two squirrels were contesting in the high branches, defending what they hoped would be their winter store.

'Indeed, the world is one of conflict, Shurik,' the priest observed with a sigh of resignation. 'We cannot escape it and must come to accept it. Men fight for nations and squirrels fight for nuts.'

'There is little difference between the two. It is only a matter of dimension. The size of a walnut against the size of the world. Ultimately, the prize is one of possession.'

'You should be a preacher,' Father Kondrati remarked. 'You have the gift of making complexities simplistic.'

'No,' I disagreed. 'I simply see plain truths and comment upon them. It requires no skill and only a limited vocabulary.'

One of the squirrels, as if to prove the crux of our conversation, gnawed an unripe walnut free of its stalk. Gripping the nut, which was almost as big as its head, the squirrel headed off along a branch. The current overlord of the tree was incensed at the usurper's gall and set up a piping chitter as it chased its enemy. The thief faced about but was now at a disadvantage. It had its booty in its jaws but it needed its teeth for defence.

'What are we to see?' Father Kondrati said. 'The battle of the titans of Myshkino.'

'We are about to see two of nature's prettiest idiots lose all,' I replied.

The owner of the tree attacked, running along the branch, its tail up and quivering with indignation. The would-be usurper dropped the walnut which fell, hit a bough, was deflected sideways, ricocheted off Father Kondrati's hat and bounced across the beaten earth forecourt to the church. Free of its burden, the squirrel squared for the attack. There was a rapid scrabble. The monarch of the tree was overpowered, lost its grip, dropped to the bough below, admitted defeat and, scampering along it, launched itself into the air to land on the shingles of the church roof. After a glance back at the victor, the vanquished creature ran to the dome, skirted it and disappeared.

'Everyone a loser,' Father Kondrati declared, reaching up to ensure his headgear was not dented. 'One squirrel loses its

148

proprietorial rights, the other loses its bounty and the tree loses a chance to spread its seed. The nut,' he added, in case I had not grasped the image, 'is unripe.'

Looking at the dome, I considered how many men I must have seen in the gulag years driven from their rightful places to die, in the name of politics and ideology, and then thought of how Dmitri had once told me of the thousands who had perished in the name of religion and theology, gilding the dome of St. Isaac's cathedral in St. Petersburg. Apart from the literally hundreds who fell to their deaths from the scaffolding, or slipped from the walls, there were many who were poisoned, who died a most terrible death, in the most appalling agony, for the gold leaf on the dome, one of the largest in all of Russia, was applied with liquid mercury which the labourers handled without gloves, wiping the sweat from their brows with fingers impregnated with mercury, breathing air in which mercury misted, drinking from tainted buckets through lips lightly silvered and as deadly as a cobra's kiss.

And I thought, why should I regret the gulag years when it was simply my bad luck to be caught up in them, just as it was the ill fortune of tens of thousands of peasants to be enrolled and miserably perish for the glory of God.

History is filled with men who were just unlucky: I was one of their number but now, I am not.

I have learnt the lesson. Not that of forgiveness. I forgive nothing. Nor that of stoical surrender: had I surrendered, I would be now a broken man, a ghost on legs with a cigarette in one hand and missal in the other. Nor was it the lesson of hate. One cannot hate one's destiny.

The lesson I have learnt is to accept, not with docility but with understanding. I have learnt, in short, to come to terms with the inevitable.

Father Kondrati stood up. He whistled to the horse which raised its head, stopped its grazing and started to walk towards the walnut tree.

'My friend,' he said, 'I must be off. I have a sick man to visit on the road to Zarechensk.' For a long moment, he watched the horse drawing nearer then, without my bidding, he put his right hand upon my head, his touch light. 'May Our Lord,' he prayed, 'bless you on this your birthday, may he keep you safe and guide you through the tribulations of life and may you rest in the everlasting grace of his love.'

I did not want to hurt his feelings so I thanked him. He went over to his horse and, hitching up his robes, swung himself into the saddle, straightening his hat which had slipped a degree or two askew.

'Good-bye, Shurik,' he called.

'God speed you,' I called back and waved.

When he was gone, the staccato tattoo of hooves on the roadway lost in the shift of the breeze in the branches of the walnut, I sat alone and pondered my predicament.

In a few hours, I was going to be visited by what I anticipated would be a spruce young man in a well-tailored pair of smart trousers, with the crease perfect down his shins, highly polished shoes, a white shirt so brilliant it might have been laundered in concentrated sunlight, a black blazer with gold buttons and a dark blue tie upon which, I imagined, would be embroidered the crest of the University of Oxford. Or Cambridge. One of the two. He was going to arrive before Frosya's house in a dark and official-looking vehicle the paintwork of which would be as polished as his shoes. Certainly, it would not be anything like Myshkino's future taxi. Accompanying him, there would be a man whom I envisaged would look perhaps not a little unlike myself.

And, when he arrived, I should meet both my past and my future simultaneously and have to cast my die.

∗

From the realm of St. Lazarus, whom Jesus returned from the dead, I headed further up the knoll towards the woodland domain where immortal Sylvanus, with his caprine horns and hoofed hind legs, eternally trills his syrinx.

Starting a hundred metres behind the church, a track enters the forest by a permanently half-open ramshackle iron gate. The hinges are long since seized and the brackets are rotted through. Any attempt to swing it wide or close it now would snap it off. In winter, the track is a bleak, monochromatic avenue stretching for a kilometre or so to its first corner, the snow a mass of signatures of bear, deer, and fox. Now, in high summer, it is a dark, leafy tunnel filled with the shy song of invisible birds and shadows forever on the move as evanescent breezes zigzag through the trees. The track itself is a tangle of undergrowth and rank grasses which has not been disturbed for over a decade.

The original track was centuries old, nothing more than a meandering pathway through the forest to the east, used by both hunter and hunted. Eventually, it reached Gorelovo although I have never met anyone who has done the entire journey. Then, thirty years ago, it was widened to take timber trucks to a two thousand hectare area of felling where a sawmill was established on the side of a valley overlooking a river of black water which flowed sluggishly through the forest. The enterprise lasted less than a decade, the sawmill was abandoned and the track left to grow over, bushes and small trees taking advantage of the sunlight. Where once the twenty-litre diesel engines of the logging trucks roared and spewed now only the thunder of summer storms and the whisper of birds' wings breaks the quiet symphonies of the trees.

Passing through the gate, I walked for about fifty metres then halted. The track went on ahead, the undergrowth becoming more dense but, to the right, a footpath veered off to circumambulate through the trees, keeping roughly parallel to the edge of the forest where it meets the fields of Myshkino.

Looking down the overgrown track, I considered how I could go that way. Take the long route to nowhere. Disappear. The ground was firm. I would leave no footsteps. By dusk, the grasses and bushes I would have had to push aside would have reasserted themselves and there would be no sign of my passage.

In this way, I could vanish into the forests like the Merry Widow's husband. I would, however, do a better job than he had. Once gone, I would stay gone. There would be no half-gnawn legs and arms to be carried back, no chewed finger stumps to be chanted over by Father Kondrati, or wept over by Frosya. As I arrived in Myshkino, unannounced and out of the blue yonder or, more accurately, out of the black night of the gulag, so should I leave. That way, my sojourn in the village would become nothing more than a ripple in the pool of time.

It would be selfish of me. They would miss me and mourn my disappearance, would want to have had a lavish funeral for me, my bier draped in black cloth and strewn with white flowers, pulled by two black horses with plumes on their foreheads: or I might be towed to eternity by the Myshkino Cab Company. I do not want them to fuss and go to any expense over me but, when the time comes, they will. Be sure of that. My wake will be remembered for generations.

Considering all they have done for me, they deserve far better than to have me walk out on them, a deserter from reality who can no longer face the barrage of life's artillery. They owe me nothing. I am the debtor here. For, in the final analysis, I am not one of them but just one of a million bums cast out of the gulag to be swept along by a tide he neither understood not swam with: yet they took me in and loved me, clothed me and housed me, gave me purpose and self-respect.

One tiny cameo has stuck with me through the years. On my second day in her home, I came upon Frosya in her little kitchen, cutting up some meat. I approached the room silently, for I had no footwear other than the boots I had brought with me from Sosnogorsklag 32 and they were nowhere to be found.

She sensed my arrival in the door and, not looking over her shoulder, said, 'Good morning. Did you sleep deeply?'

'In truth,' I replied, 'not so deeply. I am unused to soft beds and lying down without my clothes on.'

152

'That is how they try to break you,' she declared, turning from the table to sweep the diced meat into a pot on the stove. 'A man who can never undress has no sense of himself. He loses his identity if he cannot, just once in a while, survey his naked body and be familiar with it.'

I was quite taken aback by her perspicacity and would have carried on the conversation were my feet not growing cold.

'Do you have my boots?' I enquired.

'Trofim has taken them to be repaired,' she answered. 'They are falling to pieces.' She cleared a space at the end of the table. 'Sit here.'

I obeyed her and watched as she sliced some fresh bread and placed it before me on a plate.

'Did you bring all your possessions from the gulag?' she asked.

'Everything.'

'You lost nothing on the way? Or were forced to sell it?'

'Quite on the contrary,' I told her. 'I gained a few items, like the scissors.'

'I see,' she said thoughtfully. 'So everything you own is in your bedroom. All your clothes...'

'Except my boots,' I cut in, my feet getting colder still.

She poured me a glass of warm milk from a pan on the edge of the stove.

'You need this to build you up,' she instructed. 'We must gradually increase your strength. Now,' she opened a drawer, removing a knife, a fork and a spoon which she put on the table in front of me. 'These are yours,' she said, 'to have in your room. You do not need to use them. We have plenty. But you must keep them.'

'Why?' I asked.

'Because,' she retorted, 'a man who has no personal cutlery has no dignity.'

I have never forgotten that gesture, that first debt.

And yet, I suggest, a man's passing, his last cavort in the tango of life, before he switches partners for the waltz of death, should be of his own choosing.

The track was tempting. If I stepped that way, towards distant Gorelovo, all my troubles would be solved. I would be able to choose now. No need to put off the moment that was coming, later, as the sun starts to dip.

I felt in my pocket. The letter was there, crisp and neat as a warrant of execution.

Once, many years ago, when I was no longer regarded as a newcomer to the village and still had sufficient strength in my legs, I did venture down the track but not alone.

That year was possessed of a balmy autumn. Spring had come early and the summer had lasted weeks longer than usual. When autumn finally came, the sun was still warm, the days cloudless and the nights not chilled until the early hours for the earth had stored up the heat of the long, dry months. The forests seemed to sigh with relief, grateful autumn was finally arrived and the effort of summer was done with. The leaves changed quickly but, because there was no frost to cut them free, they drifted down of their own accord, the trees remaining dressed for well over a fortnight in their glorious copper and fiery coats.

'We should not waste this magnificence,' Trofim declared one morning as we sat under the weeping silver birch, breaking our fast. 'A year such as this comes only once a century.' He produced a cracked leather-bound almanac he had recently picked up in the market at Zarechensk and thumbed his way back through it. For days, he had been absorbed in reading its contents. 'The last was in 1918.'

'In that case,' Frosya argued, 'you are wrong. This will be the second time in a century. So it must be only once in fifty years. On average.'

'You're a pedant,' Trofim chided her.

'And how do you intend not to waste it?' I enquired.

'I?' he replied. 'Not I. We. You and me, Shurik. We are going on an expedition.'

Frosya threw her hands in the air and said, 'I thought you were over expeditions.'

'Is a man ever tired of living?' Trofim rejoined forcefully. 'So long as true-blooded men have breath in their bodies and bounce in their balls, they never tire of expeditions.'

'So I'm to prepare for it?' Frosya asked. Trofim nodded eagerly and took hold of her hand. 'And how long for?'

'Three days?' he suggested, looking at me.

I shrugged, having not the least idea what he was talking about.

Throughout the remainder of that morning, Frosya busied herself preparing two Soviet army knapsacks, putting in them bread, cheese, a jar of pickled cabbage, some smoked fish and a dozen hard-boiled eggs. Trofim, in the meantime, went to our neighbour, Sergei Petrovich, and borrowed two ancient shotguns and a box of black powder cartridges which should have been in a museum. By midday, all was ready. Trofim instructed me what to wear and inspected me on the porch.

'Are the trousers thick material?' he asked, bending to test the cloth between his finger and thumb and nodding approvingly. 'Is your jacket warm? Lower extremities well catered for?' He gazed at my feet where I was wearing a pair of his own ex-Soviet army marching boots. Once through his inspection, he handed me one of the shotguns and a knapsack to the base of which was strapped a rolled blanket.

'We're staying out then?' I conjectured.

Trofim gave me a smirk befitting a mischievous ten-year-old who, fully aware of the concepts of right and wrong, had been caught red-handed with his fingers in the sugar jar. Frosya kissed first him, then me.

As she put her lips to my cheek, she whispered, 'Don't let him wear you out, Shurik. Be firm with him.'

'I'm not quite sure what we are doing,' I replied.

'Playing at boys,' she responded.

We walked down through the village, crossed the river, passed the church and headed off down the track. It was, as now, overgrown. Trofim led the way, pushing through the small, opportunist bushes which grew in the light but never reached above shoulder height because the forest deer were forever browsing on them. For at least fifteen minutes, Trofim did not speak. He walked staunchly ahead, forging a path I followed with the unquestioning obedience of a gun dog.

Finally, we arrived in a small clearing which had probably been a passing place for the timber lorries. Here, Trofim halted and stood quite still.

'What do you hear, Shurik?' he asked after a long silence.

I concentrated on listening to the forest.

'Birds and bees,' I replied. 'Maybe there is a hive around here.'

'What do you not hear?' It was a rhetorical question. He smiled at me, the smile of a man whose soul was at peace with itself and the world. 'Birds and bees,' he reiterated. 'No bombs, no bullets.'

'No Beria, no Bulganin,' I added.

As I spoke, I saw Kirill's face grinning from behind its mask of coal dust and I realised that, long before the gulag opened its maw and swallowed him whole, he must have walked down here on just such a day in just such an autumn, and thought just the same thoughts. A wave of love swept over me at this realisation. In every tree, in every drifting leaf, in every muted bird call, I sensed his presence and, for the first time since arriving in Myshkino, I came to understand why he had wanted me to come here.

It was not simply to tell Frosya of his love for her, his life and death. More, it was that, by being here, I was his ambassador, keeping his presence alive in a place he had never wanted to leave. So long as I was in Myshkino, so was he, by proxy.

For the duration of the afternoon, we followed the track. After some distance, it started to twist and turn, keeping to the contours of the land which became hilly, rising and falling in dales. At the bottom of each valley we encountered a boggy strip of marsh. Once or twice, we came upon the rusting girders of a bridge, the timbers long since rotted away and crossed on them, waving our arms out to maintain our balance. Most often we had to hop from sod to sod or run over the compact sponge of humus, our boots oozing the water out and releasing a scent of peat and fungi. At a trickling brook, Trofim filled a much-dented aluminium water bottle.

Just as the sun went down, we reached the area of timber extraction. The thick deciduous forest gave way suddenly to a vast expanse of young trees sprouting up above a dense jungle of briars, ferns and bushes. The track, coming out of the trees, ended in a wall of what appeared to be impenetrable vegetation.

'Where do we go now?' I asked, my voice quiet.

There was a certain solemn grandeur about the forest that seemed to dictate we did not speak loudly. It was as if we were in the cathedral of a host of wood sprites and nymphs.

'We leave the ways of men,' Trofim replied, just as softly, 'and follow the ways of beasts.'

Keeping to the edge of the forest, we had not gone one hundred metres when there appeared a narrow path vanishing into the vegetation. Trofim nodded at it and we set off to take its course. Just as the dusk started to deepen, we reached the remains of the sawmill.

'We stay the night here,' Trofim announced, pointing to a leaning shack.

*

'Is this where they found Vera Dorokhova's husband?' I enquired, leaning the shotgun against the wall by the door and lowering the knapsack from my back.

'No!' Trofim exclaimed dismissively. 'That drunken old sot never got this far. They found him less than an hour's walk in from the edge of the village fields. You know what they said?'

I shook my head and eased my shoulders. The knapsack was not heavy but it had restricted my muscles. My arms were tired from carrying the shotgun.

'They said he only got that far because his tank reached empty.' He mimicked holding a bottle to his mouth and made gulping noises. 'No vodka pumps in the forest...'

We prized open the door of the shack and entered. It was gloomy within, the roof leaning with a large hole in the centre. A pile of ammoniac black guano in one corner suggested the shack might be a winter roost for bats.

'This is our base camp,' Trofim announced grandly, unrolling his blanket and folding it on the bare earth floor. 'From here, we go out into the unknown.'

'I suspect,' I said, 'this is not exactly the unknown.'

'No,' he admitted, standing up and placing our guns against the wall. 'I have been here many times before. This shack is older than the saw-mill, older than anyone I know. Even you.' He winked and unbuckled the flap of his knapsack. 'They say the shack was built by my namesake.'

'Namesake?'

'Trofim the Bear-slayer,' he replied with a hint of pride. 'In the last century, about a hundred years ago, there lived in Myshkino a huge man. A giant. Legend has it he was two metres sixteen in his bare feet. Once, he was working in the fields around the village, in my field, as it happens, where the chicken run is now, when a bear which had been wounded by a careless hunter charged out of the trees and attacked him. They wrestled and fought like two men contesting the ownership of a horse. Or a woman. The villagers ran to his assistance, with guns and pitchforks – but what could they do? The two fighters were rolling about. At last, the fight subsided and Trofim stood erect. The bear lay dead. He had rammed his huge fist down its gullet and choked it to death.'

'And, presumably,' I suggested, 'Trofim was uninjured.'

'On the contrary! His forearm was badly mauled where the bear's teeth had bitten him and his belly was shredded to the muscle by the bear's hind claws. That's what bears do. They grip with their forelegs, bite with their jaws and rip your guts out with the back legs.'

'He died of his wounds?'

'Do heroes die?' Trofim responded with counterfeit incredulity. 'Of course not! He lived into this century. My grandfather met him. He still had the dents on his forearm from the bear's teeth and, when he took his shirt off to chop wood or mow hay, his stomach looked like a zebra's. All stripes.'

'How is it,' I asked, spreading out my own blanket, 'that the shack survived the timber felling operation?'

'The lumberjacks used it as a drinking club,' he answered. 'After all, it was Trofim the Great's lair so it seemed a suitable place for manly pastimes.'

'I thought he was called Trofim the Bear-slayer.'

'Whatever,' his namesake replied tersely.

Gathering a supply of fallen branches and twigs, we lit a fire on the bare earth in the centre of the shack. The smoke eddied about a bit then, as if finding its escape, drifted through the hole in the roof. Trofim produced a pan and we heated the water he had collected from the stream. It tasted faintly of earth but it warmed us.

For an hour or so, we lounged about our fire. Every now and then, far off, an owl hooted or a fox called. I was just beginning to get drowsy, the exertion of the afternoon catching up on me, when Trofim stood up, glanced at his watch by the light of the fire, scratched his hair and collected his gun.

'Time to go,' he announced quietly.

'Go!' I exclaimed. 'Go where?'

'To show you the wonders of the forest, Shurik. Leave your gun. One will be enough.' With that, he eased open the door and stepped out. 'Are you coming?'

I got to my feet, my muscles stiff. At the door, I stepped out to find Trofim outlined against a full moon rising over the horizon of the forest. It was huge, filled a third of the sky, and was dull orange as if the light playing upon it was not that of the hidden sun but the meagre flames of our little campfire. I could see every crater on its surface as easily as I could have seen the pits and lines of my own face in a mirror.

'It's like seeing a portrait of the history of time hung upon a black wall,' Trofim said.

For five minutes, we watched as the moon rose a degree or two higher, shrinking to a brilliant white orb. Trofim did not once take his eyes from it: he stood as if in silent worship.

'Just think,' he finally broke his silence, 'of all the other men who have looked upon that celestial face. Every human that has ever lived has gazed upon it and wondered. Not just Copernicus and Galileo, Tycho Brahe and Leonardo da Vinci. Ordinary people. Proletarians. Peasants and presidents.'

'Kings and kulaks,' I added.

Trofim turned his back on the moon. Risen higher now, it rode just over his shoulder.

'When she was a little girl,' he said, 'Frosya used to gaze at the moon and wonder if her father was on it, looking down at her. Her mother, you see, told her that Kirill was living on the moon.' He balanced the shotgun under his arm. 'What lies parents tell, eh, Shurik! Yet it was the truth, in a way. For all it was worth, he might just as well have been on the moon. And how could you tell a little girl about the gulag? When the Luna 2 moon probe landed up there, Frosya was ten. She asked her mother, when it returned, would it bring him back?'

A drift of smoke from the roof of the shack washed across the moon, momentarily blunting the edge of the craters. I cast my mind back to the gulag days and saw, as clearly as I did the moon over Trofim's shoulder, a colourless night upon which hung a red flag and through which Kirill walked in the company of three guards with their rifles slung over their shoulders, red stars emblazoned on their hats.

Trofim set off through the undergrowth. He moved with a certain stealth, holding branches for me to prevent them swishing noisily back and stepping cautiously when approaching an area of dry twigs. I did my best to imitate him yet still made a good deal more noise than he did but he made no comment.

After ten minutes, we reached all that remained of the

timber felling operations, a skeletal frame of rusty girders which had formed the basis for the saw-mill. Here and there, a few sheets of corrugated iron remained bolted to it. In the centre, partially covered in ground ivy, a circular saw bench stood slightly askew on a platform of rotting planks as thick as railway ties. Halfway up the frame was a platform, once the saw-mill director's inspection platform. Clearing creepers from the lower rungs of an iron ladder, Trofim began to ascend to the platform.

'We have the best seats in the house, Shurik,' he whispered as he beckoned me to follow him.

Once on the platform, we sat with our legs dangling into mid-air, our arms resting on one of the rails. All around us, bathed in brilliant moonlight, the new growth of trees prodded up from the undergrowth. A hundred metres to our left was a stack of felled trunks, abandoned by the loggers and now black and rotting, whilst in front of us glimmered a large pool.

'Just as on the moon,' Trofim murmured, 'we have a sea of tranquillity. There was always a clearing here because a spring rises out of the ground at this point. When the timber was being cut, they diverted the water away and the pool dried up. Now, there are no men, except you and me, and things are as they should be, as they always were.' He carefully laid the gun on the platform by his side, making sure the metal breach did not clang against the iron. 'Now, we don't talk. We don't move. We just watch.'

Within minutes of our falling silent, an owl landed on the girders above us, whoo-whooing strenuously. Its presence was our endorsement. Not a minute later, a deer materialised from the undergrowth and, with delicate steps, approached the pool. After raising its snout to test the air, twisting its ears to catch the slightest threat, it dipped its head and began to drink. The ripples fanned out across the still black surface, breaking into lines of coruscated moonlight. When it had drunk its fill, it stepped back. We could hear the suck of its hooves as it pulled its feet out of the marshy ground. Satisfied it was safe, it began to browse upon a bush until, quite suddenly, it was gone. No branches thrashed or twigs snapped. It simply dematerialised like a wraith.

The moon slid behind a cloud. Trofim touched my arm and nodded slowly over to his left. A dark shadow was moving towards the pool from the direction of the wood pile. The cloud moved on and there, in the full moonlight, stood a bear.

It was a young male, about three-quarters grown and yet already immensely powerful. Walking on all fours, its head was thrust forward in an almost belligerent fashion. The moonlight shimmered on its fur as if the creature were dusted with powdered diamonds. Its wet snout and eye glistened. Every movement it made was filled with the surety of its supremacy.

At the water's edge, it stopped yet, unlike the deer, it did not bother to glance around but immediately dipped its muzzle and started lapping noisily.

'This is how men were,' Trofim whispered under cover of the bear's drinking, 'before Adam sharpened a stone and cut himself upon it.'

When the bear had slaked its thirst, it sat back on its haunches on the soggy bank of the pool and proceeded to lick its front paws, running them over its snout as a cat might. Its toilet done, it swung round onto all fours and sauntered towards a bush into which it started to nuzzle, bending branches and grunting.

'Blackberries,' Trofim murmured.

For a while, the bear feasted on the bush, guzzling so noisily that, when I shifted my position to ease my legs which had begun to grow numb from the edge of the metal platform pressing on a nerve in my thigh, and a rusty bolt in the platform mounting squeaked, the creature paid not the slightest heed. At last, having gorged its fill, it returned to the pool, lowering its head to the surface once more.

Out of the corner of my eye, I saw Trofim's hand reach for the gun, feeling along the stock until his fingers touched the metal of the breech, cold in the moonlight. Very slowly, he lifted the weapon off the platform to bring it over the railing, the butt fitting into his shoulder.

'Watch!' he said quietly, and he aimed the shotgun at the bear. The bear stopped drinking. It raised its head, turning it from side to side. Moving quickly, with an agility belied by its ungainly shape, it set off for the cover of the bushes. I could hear its paws padding on the waterlogged soil. At the edge of the cover, it halted and turned, standing on its hind legs. It looked like a man in an overcoat several sizes too large.

'Don't shoot it,' I whispered, not raising my voice for fear that the bear, on hearing it, might decide to come for us.

The bushes parted and the bear disappeared. Trofim put the gun down.

'I would not shoot him,' Trofim said, no longer keeping his voice down. 'Russia has killed enough.'

He stood up and rubbed his legs: like mine, they must have grown stiff. We descended the ladder, Trofim going across to the pool to fill his water bottle. Taking no care to be silent now, we headed off back to the shack, put more wood on the fire and boiled the water, making tea which we drank in turns from a small mug Trofim produced from his pack. Warmed, we lay under our blankets on the earth as the smoke billowed up to the hole in the roof and the moon moved across the sky.

'Why did you raise the gun?' I asked.

'To tell him I was there,' Trofim replied.

'Why not just shout? Kick the platform? Clap your hands?'

'I did not want to disturb his peace,' Trofim said. 'I just wanted to let him know I was there, had the power but was not going to use it. And this he understood and left in his own time. If I had alarmed him, he would have run, terrified, and feared me forever more.'

A log on the fire shifted, sending a scatter of sparks upwards. Some made it through the hole in the roof, others fell to die on the earth floor.

'How much better,' he continued, 'to let your adversary know your strength rather than prove it for him. Animals appreciate such a demonstration. They are sophisticated, obey the laws of nature. Only men break nature's laws to supplant them with their own.'

I turned on my side to face him. He was leaning against his knapsack, staring at the fire. The flicker of the low flames danced upon his skin and shone in his eyes.

'Consider this, Shurik, how we insult the bear by associating ourselves with him. As strong as a bear, we say. Russia is the Bear, the Americans say. But have you seen a more noble animal?'

He punched the pack to make it a more comfortable shape and lay his head against it.

'And what do we do to this noble beast? We catch it, pull its claws out, file down its teeth and make it dance in Red Square to amuse the tourists.' He spat into the fire, his spittle hizzling on the embers. 'When I see a bear, Shurik, I am ashamed and put in my place.'

I dozed off and on that night. The ground was hard and my back, despite twenty-five years of exhausted sleep on a palliasse in the gulag, had grown accustomed to a bed. Yet it was not just the discomfort that kept me awake: as I lay there, I recalled that night I sat outside the tent, the stars above me, a taint of vodka on my breath. And mammoth. And, before me, just such a fire keeping the night and cold at bay.

Our expedition was taken a long time ago now. Trofim was younger then, employed by the state and unburdened by the proprietorial cares of Myshkino Motors: I was happy, free of the gulag, settled in my life with him and Frosya, no longer haunted by demons and unafraid of the uncertainties of the future.

8

During the day, whilst we were toiling underground in the mole hole, a blizzard rolled down from the north. By the time we surfaced into the night, a metre and a half of snow had fallen, inundating the surface crews. No sooner were we out of the cage and counted, work unit by work unit, than we were issued with snow shovels and told to report to the marshalling yards.

The wind which had heralded the blizzard had dropped by now but, in its vanguard, snow was still densely falling in heavy, lazy flakes which pirouetted to the ground. The locomotives in the yard had tried to make a getaway but could not and the snow plough, which usually cleared the branch line to the mine, was engaged in keeping the main line free until another could be sent up from the south.

'If hell were to freeze over,' Avel observed as we stood with our shovels waiting to be assigned a task, 'this is what it would be like.'

He was right. The lights around the pit head mustering ground and the sidings were only visible if you were close to them. The others were invisible in the falling snow, even as a distant glow. The sounds of the winding gear, the whining of the steel cables and the clatter of machinery and the cage doors were all muffled to nothing much more than an undercurrent of muted sound like the far off wailing of demented, disappointed souls. Even the loudspeaker system was useless for the sound of the overseer dropped within metres to the ground, as if frozen like the steam from our breath.

After ten minutes stamping our feet and huddling close together for mutual warmth, Kirill appeared from the gloom.

'Track six,' he said. 'Dig out the rear four trucks of the train and keep them clear.'

'Keep them clear!' Ylli explained. 'For how long?'

'Until the snow eases,' replied Kirill as if this was the most obvious fact in the world.

'It could snow like this for days,' Kostya said.

'Months,' Dmitri added.

'And what's the point?' Ylli went on. 'The locomotives can't get out until the snow plough gets here. And then what? It's not just snowing here. God's dumping the shit all over the land. The blizzard could be two hundred kilometres across and as many deep. We clear four trucks that can't go anywhere.'

Kirill's eyes were black in the shadow of the lowered peak of his *ushanka*.

'So you've a choice then, Ylli,' he remarked. 'You can dig the trucks out as the bastards want, or you can refuse and be shot – on the assumption that the guards in the firing squad can see you through the snow – or you can do a runner into the night, hitch a ride on the snow plough, commandeer it to Moscow and complain to the Politburo personally that this was a dumb-arsed order and they ought to get their thinking straight.'

We trudged across the mustering ground and over the tracks. Four trains of fully laden coal trucks stood idle, thatched with snow and looking like uniform rows of peasants' cottages with the windows shuttered and the fires gone out. Crawling under one of the trains we reached track six, turned left and made our way to the end of the row of trucks parked there. The last one had a dim red oil lantern burning in a bracket and casting a pink glimmer upon the snow piling up against the buffers.

'So where do we put it?' Titian mused aloud. 'We dig the snow off this truck and then what? If we put it by the track, it'll pile up and freeze into a rock-hard wall we'll have to chip out. If we put it too far over it'll block the next line.'

'Dump it on the far line,' Kirill decided. 'Let the surface crews shift it. It'll be their pigeon by then and we'll be down in the snug of the mole hole. No one's going to know who was responsible for what. They weren't taking notes of which work unit was assigned which task. The overseer was merely ticking off the tracks as he allocated the work.'

We set to on the last coal truck, working our way forward but, by the time the penultimate truck in the train was more or less dug out, the last was under another twenty centimetres of fresh snow. What was worse, every now and then a load avalanched off the top of the truck and either filled in our previous labours or fell upon us, freezing our faces and even bowling us over under the weight. After half an hour, Kirill disappeared into the blizzard for a while then, reappearing like a spectre, called us together.

'May I make a suggestion, comrades?' he began as we crowded together close to the side of the third truck. He spoke with the urbanity of the chairman of a Party meeting. 'This is frankly a bloody waste of our energy. Nothing can be done until the snow abates. I suggest we dig ourselves in and wait.'

'For what?' I ventured. 'If we are found slacking...'

'Don't worry, Shurik. We shan't be. The overseers are ensconced round the stove in the admin. office. The guards've hunkered down in the pit head building and the guard-house. Half the *zeks* have taken cover in the coal sheds and a number have even gone back down the shaft to Gallery B. Those left in the sidings are doing bugger all.'

'So we get cutting,' Kostya said and, raising his shovel, he trimmed out a block of snow the size of a small box.

Following his example, we cut loose blocks of snow and built a wall along the side of one of the trucks, Kostya filling in the gaps with compacted snow slammed in with the flat of his shovel. When one side was done, we did the other and both ends, leaving just a crawl-hole at one end. As we worked outside, Ylli worked within, flattening the snow that had drifted under the truck so that it made a smooth floor over the granite hard core of the track. In ten minutes, we had a truck-roofed igloo.

It was dark inside but both Avel and Titian had their lamp batteries charged so we switched one on. Within a surprisingly short space of time, the air heated up and we were able to remove our *ushankas*.

'Shame we've nothing to eat,' Dmitri remarked.

'And it looks like we'll not get any tonight, either,' Titian added. 'By the time the blizzard lifts and we've trudged back to camp...'

'Gygulevskoe,' said Kostya.

'What's gygulevskoe?' I asked.

'Russian beer,' Titian replied. 'The best.'

Ylli grinned and said wistfully, 'What I'd give for a beer.'

'Dream on!' exclaimed Dmitri. 'The only thing that looks like beer round here is your piss. And you can't drink that. It's flat.'

Kirill fumbled in his clothing and, pulling out three thin cardboard boxes rather like large pencil cases, declared, 'I think, when I get out of here, I'll become a *blatnoi*. As a law enforcer, I learnt a lot about the criminal mind but I was straight and made an honest crust. Next time around, I'll cross the road and earn a dishonest loaf.'

He handed the boxes round. I opened one. Inside, packed tightly together, were six dried herring.

'Where did these come from?' I enquired.

'Ask not and thou shalt be pleased,' Dmitri intoned.

'Two and a half each,' Kostya marvelled.

'But they're salty,' Avel commented.

Kirill nodded to me and indicated the door. I knew what he had in mind and slipped out of the igloo. The snow was still falling as heavily as before and there was no sound save the mutter of my companions and the minute reptilian hiss of flakes colliding.

Hanging from a bracket in the twilight under the next truck were five galvanised steel, ten-litre fire buckets. I checked one. There was no hole in the base and the handle was firm. Unhooking it, I set off along the train, moving from the dim areas of light into near darkness before arriving beneath the next lamp.

Suddenly, ahead of me in the gloom, I saw what I took to be a guard and was about to duck down when the figure saw me, stepping slowly back out of sight between two trucks on the adjacent track. For a moment, I pondered upon my situation but realised that if this had been a guard he would have challenged me, not slunk out of sight. I went on, not looking at the figure as I passed: it was probably another *zek* on the lam or a look-out for another work unit which had decided to skive.

At last, I came close to the locomotive. It was fired up, the cab glowing like the entrance to a furnace. Three or four men sat crouched about the open firebox like sentinels to the underworld. They were talking in low voices. Keeping my head down, I passed them by. Beneath the locomotive, the heat of the firebox and the shower of embers raked out each time a new load of coal was thrown in had thawed the snow. Water dripped all round from snow falling on the casing of the boiler.

I had thought to collect this melt-water but it did not reach the ground. The air was so cold, it froze in long icicles from the locomotive chassis. Cursing my luck and stupidity, I kept down considering my options. The best was to fill the bucket with snow and place it under the locomotive for the fire to melt it: but, I guessed, it would be frozen to an icy slush before I reached the igloo. I was about to despair when I saw a small brass tap connected to a copper pipe running the length of the locomotive, heading towards one of the huge pistons that powered the driving wheels. The tap itself was shut but the copper pipe was not covered in snow or icicles: it must, I therefore reasoned, be hot. I did not dare remove a glove to test it by touch. Instead, I dropped a pinch of snow upon it. It instantly liquefied.

Watching the cab, I placed the bucket under the tap and, very carefully, inched it open. There was a brief hiss of steam then a trickle of water which tumbled noisily into the bucket. I quickly turned the bucket on its side so the water did not rattle onto the base. In a few minutes, I had five litres of scalding water.

Setting off for the igloo, I reached the point where the figure had stood. This time, so as to be on the alert in case the man was a *zek* and readying to steal the bucket of water, I looked into the space between the trucks where he had stepped. He was still there. I briefly nodded a friendly greeting. He raised his hand and I plodded on. When I reached the igloo, the water was still hot. We ate the dried fish then drank our fill, the water tasting metallic.

Organising a look-out every quarter of an hour to see how the blizzard was progressing, we lay back in the comparative comfort of our igloo, occasionally talking or just resting with our own thoughts.

'Tell me, Shurik, have you ever been to Volgograd?' Kirill asked me, shifting himself over the snow floor and sitting by my side.

'Never,' I told him. 'The only parts of the Soviet Union I have seen are the inside of several detention centres, a few prison courtyards, bleak forests spied through the cracks in a box car door and the road between the camp and the mine.'

'When this is over,' he said, 'and a new moon shines in our sky, you must come with me. We shall sit by the river, drink vodka, eat caviar. The sturgeon in the Volga give the best caviar. Not black. Grey, like the eyes of an old cat past its mousing days.'

He leaned back against the snow wall, a little flaking onto his shoulder like dandruff, quick to vanish into the material of his coat. Titian poked his head out of the entrance and brought it back in, his hair speckled with huge flakes.

'Still coming down like the ash of a million freezing fires,' he said. I wondered if he was quoting from some unknown poem by Yi Yuk-sa.

'Downstream from the city,' Kirill continued, closing his eyes, 'the river turns south east, crosses desert and marshland to Astrahan and the Caspian Sea. Upstream, it runs beside hills, north of Kamysin. It's beautiful there. The forests come down to the river and you can walk in peace for kilometre after kilometre. Sometimes you see no one, just vessels passing. The crew wave to you. I know a place...'

His voice trailed off and I made no comment. When a man is

living inside himself, it is best to leave him be. One word at such a time can shatter a fragile world.

'We'll go there,' he declared after a long silence, opening his eyes and looking straight at me. 'You and me, Shurik, I'll show you. Then, after, we shall take the train to Zarechensk then the bus and go to Myshkino.'

It was the first time I heard of the village. Kirill uttered the name with such a sense of love and mystery, I found my mind beginning to try and draw in wayward strands of my imagination to shape it in my mind.

'Myshkino?'

'It is where my family comes from,' he said. 'Where I came from before the hand on the shoulder and the machine pistol barrel in the belly. My wife lives there now. At least, I suppose she does: she has no reason to leave for we have a small house there, once my father's. In Myshkino, she is amongst friends, can grow vegetables and keep hens. Maybe a goat. Survive. And she has my daughter...'

It was the first time Kirill had ever mentioned his family. I felt immensely privileged to be sharing this knowledge.

'I did not know...' I began.

'My wife is called Tatyana Antonovna. She is – or was – a school teacher. For young children. My daughter,' he closed his eyes to see her the better, 'is called Frosya. It is short for Efrosiniya.'

'How old is she?'

'When I was arrested, she was two. Now,' he thought for a moment, 'she is sixteen, seventeen perhaps.'

'Tell me about Myshkino,' I asked.

'Myshkino?' he answered thoughtfully. 'Myshkino is the real Russia. It is a village of maybe two hundred people. It has a church, a forge, a carpenter's shop, several farms – all you would expect of a small community in the middle of the world, far from machines and rancorous men who plot. A small river runs through the middle of the village and all around, beyond the fields, there is forest crawling with animals.'

'And what do the people do?'

'What do they do?' Kirill laughed. 'What can they do? In the summer they collect in their harvest and build their stacks of firewood, in the winter they toast their feet and talk of the summer. You would like it there, Shurik.'

He fell silent again. Titian checked the snow was still coming down. Dmitri, who had fallen asleep, started to snore. Kirill closed his eyes once more and I too dozed off to be woken a short time later by Kostya kicking the soles of my *valenki*.

The snow had thinned considerably. We could see ten trucks down the train. Kirill gave orders and we set to with our shovels. In twenty minutes, we had cleared our allocated trucks of snow and there was no remaining sign of the igloo.

'Typical!' Ylli exclaimed as we finished the job. 'We clear the last four trucks but no one was sent to do the rest.'

By now, it was not long to go to midnight. The sky was still clouded but there were breaks appearing in it.

'As soon as the clouds disperse,' Kostya observed, 'the temperature'll drop another ten degrees. If we're not back in the camp by then...'

We shouldered our snow shovels and set off in the direction of the locomotive, making heavy work of it through the snow which was now getting on for two and a half metres deep, nearly 40 centimetres deeper than when I had filched the boiling water. With every step, we sank in to our thighs.

Nearing the locomotive, I caught sight of something sticking up from the snow ahead of us. For a moment, it was hard to define its shape: then, just as I recognised it, Kirill gave a shout and started as best he could to stride out for it. I followed, the others in my trail.

Standing proud of the snow was the torso of a man. His head was shaven in the prison fashion and he was utterly naked, as chilled as a side of beef in a cold store.

'Allah have mercy!' Ylli murmured. Dmitri, never the

religious one amongst us, half-heartedly crossed himself in the close proximity of death.

We gathered in a circle around the corpse. The skin had gone waxen, even more so than the usual prison pallor, the ears almost translucent and the whole surface was covered in a fine dusting of exquisite crystals of ice. In the middle of the face, the glazed eyes stared sightlessly ahead above slightly-parted lips drawn into a thin, emotionless smirk.

'What the hell happened?' Kostya began. 'You think some of the *blatnye*...?'

'No,' Kirill pronounced, 'this was no killing. Revenge has not raised her bloody hand here.'

'What about theft?' Kostya conjectured.

'What can you steal from a naked man?' Titian mused quietly.

'Except life,' Avel said.

'They've taken his clothes,' Kostya suggested.

'No,' said Kirill. 'When they dig him out, they'll find his clothes in a pile round his feet.'

There was no need for further explanation. We just stood like mourners around a vertical grave, our heads bowed not so much in sympathy or respect, nor against the cold, but simply because it seemed vaguely appropriate.

'What do we do with him?' Dmitri asked.

'Nothing,' Kirill answered. 'What can we do? He's dead meat. Let's just move on. Say nothing. Pretend we never saw him. He won't care.'

As we filed off along the line of the trucks, one by one, I realised that the dead man must have been the lurker in the shadows.

'I saw him,' I confided in Kirill as we reached a gap in the trucks through which we turned towards the mustering area. 'When I went for the water. I thought he was a guard...'

'And now you regret not having stopped to talk to him,' Kirill said astutely.

'Yes,' I admitted, 'I could have offered him a mouthful of the water in my bucket. Maybe that is what he was looking for...'

'In nothing but his skin?'

'He had his clothes on,' I replied.

Kirill put his hand on my shoulder and said, 'Don't think about it. You could have done nothing. You were only an observer before the fact. He was already dead when you saw him.'

'He raised his hand to me.'

'Not his body, Shurik. His soul. He has been a dead man for weeks. It was only a matter of time. No one could have talked him out of it, reasoned him out of it.'

'I still feel responsible,' I said.

'You are not,' Kirill said, a little sharply. 'You are responsible for the living.'

We reached the mustering area where the other work units were massing, shuffling into lines under the arc lights. The guards started counting heads.

The body was discovered whilst the count was going on and was taken past us by two guards who carried it between them, stiff as a board: it looked like a lifeless shop store dummy waiting to be dressed in the latest fashions. There was no attempt made at decorum, to cover the corpse: in death, it had as little privacy as it had had in life.

'Do you know the poetry of Anna Akhmatova?' Kirill asked me as the body was tossed into the back of a parked truck, keeping his voice down so as not to be heard by the guards who were wandering about between the ranks.

'No,' I said.

'She wrote one line I saw inscribed on the wall of a cell I was held in,' he remembered, 'in Kiev. Such a line...'

'How did it go?'

'It was such a time when only the dead smiled,' he quoted, 'joyful in their peace.'

The count over, the guards ordered us forwards. We set off, heading toward the mine gates.

174

'Now is such a time, Shurik, my friend. Now is just such a time.'

Half an hour later, we were marching along the road to the camp, struggling through the deep snow, forgetting the man we had left behind, his dead eyes staring unseeing at the featureless iron flank of a truck full of coal.

*

'Two minutes,' a voice muttered in the darkness.

I turned over in my bunk, the topmost of the tier of four, taking care to hold the blanket fully to my chin. With our returning to the camp so late, the stove had not been lit and the air inside Hut 14 was well below freezing. Beneath me lay Avel, Titian and Ylli whilst across the narrow space between the rows lay Dmitri, on my level, with Kostya and Kirill beneath him. The bottom bunk was unoccupied: Korotchenko had been transferred a few months before and the accommodation supervisor seemed to have overlooked the fact.

A usually reticent and self-possessed White Russian from Irkutsk, we had pondered on his departure. He had informed us that he was being sent to a timber camp in the far north, towards the Finnish border, but we had our doubts. Only a fortnight before his transfer was announced, we had been sitting round the stove when he had suddenly started to talk. At first, no one listened. Everyone had a story to tell and most were basically the same, variations on a theme with minute twists of fate to differentiate them: life was normal, there was a knock on the door in the middle of the night, someone had a bright torch, a car was waiting, the interrogation was followed by a swift trial and a slow train journey and – here we were, miners all!

Yet as he got going, talking more to the stove than to those gathered around it, so we took to listening, the room gradually falling silent. I can remember quite clearly the point at which I joined his story. He was facing the stove, his cheeks flushed from the heat radiating off it. His eyes were narrowed to mere slits, as if he was leaning into a chill, brisk wind, and his hands were clasped before him with his elbows on his knees.

'...the cell,' he was saying as I joined the audience to his soliloquy, 'was in the police headquarters. About two metres square, it was. Three of the walls were stone but the fourth, facing the passageway, was a grill of iron bars about ten centimetres apart. The floor was smooth flags. No furniture, no bed or chair. Some straw in the corner, like an animal's cage. And mosquitoes. It was summer. They flew everywhere.'

Korotchenko fell silent.

'What's he talking about?' I asked quietly.

Avel, leaning against an upright supporting a tier of bunks, put his finger to his lips and said, 'You'll see...'

'If one stung you,' Korotchenko suddenly began again, 'the bite swelled up like a boil. They came at you all day long, not just in the early morning or evening. Even at noon, they would whine in through the bars of the windows. There was no glass. If you caught one...!' He smacked his hands together and stared at his palms. 'Look at that!' He pointed out his own hand to himself. 'Blood! The little bastard's already fed on someone and is heading now for you.'

'Where is he?' I whispered.

'Kirin, north China,' Avel replied. 'Shut up and listen.'

'I was shown in,' Korotchenko continued, 'by an officer. The cells were crowded. Chinese, mostly. Some Manchurians, Japanese stragglers. As I walked past, they watched me with sullen eyes and downcast faces. Finally, we reached the cell. She was in there, lying on the straw wearing a petticoat and a sort of loose-fitting blouse, both soiled with dirt and maybe blood. The mosquitoes bit her, too. They weren't choosy, not those mosquitoes. Mongolian mosquitoes from the desert rim. As soon as I came in sight, she was up on her feet, grabbing at the bars, grabbing at me. "*Har peen !*" she screamed at me. "*Har peen! Har peen!*" I asked the officer what this meant. He told me,

"Opium, comrade. She wants opium."'

'Who's he talking about?' I questioned Avel, somewhat annoyed at being left in ignorance. He had entered the audience before I had and knew what was going on.

'Shut up, Shurik!' he repeated.

'The other prisoners started shouting now,' Korotchenko went on. "Shoot her!" some shouted. Others, "Put her down!" as if she was a lame horse. The officer said to her, "No *har peen* for you, your majesty. No more good times for you, your highness."'

I dug my elbow in Avel's ribs and hissed, 'Who is it?'

'Radiant Countenance, Wan Jung, Elizabeth Pu Yi. The last empress of China.'

'At that,' Korotchenko reminisced out loud, 'she went berserk, banging her brow on the bars, screaming incoherently, scrabbling with her fingers to reach for us. I stepped back. A transformation came over her. "Bring me my brocade *cheong sam*," she ordered. In English. "Run my bath. Fetch me roast pork and glass noodles." "Watch now," said the officer. She turned and looked at the wall. "How beautiful the Forbidden City looks," she said. "I can hear the finches singing." Then, quick as that,' Korotchenko snapped his fingers, 'she was screaming for opium again.'

'Is this true?' I asked.

Avel nodded and said, 'Why not? It was rumoured she was taken by the Chinese Communists in 1946. No one knows for sure what happened to her. Except, of course, that she died.'

'How does he know all this?'

'Why shouldn't he? Korotchenko was sent as an adviser to the People's Liberation Army after the war in Europe ended.'

'I was on my way from Mukden to Vladivostok,' Korotchenko declared to the stove but answering my question, 'when I stopped off in Kirin. A week later, I went back. She was thin as a rake. Raving. Raving mad. Because she had no opium, she was hallucinating, going crazy, pulling her hair our, scratching her body like a flagellant. The cell was slippery with shit and vomit. They didn't go in. The guards refused. A Japanese woman with a small daughter was with her and begged to be allowed to wash her. The guards refused but they did hose her down from a fire hydrant. Her clothes clung to her. You could see her nipples like brown targets through the silk. Her petticoat was wrapped round her waist. You could see everything. The guards gave her no food. The next day, Kirin was bombed. I left. She was taken to Yenchi and I saw her there, a week later. She was babbling now. Totally out of her mind. Just before I travelled on to the border, she died.'

For a minute, Korotchenko was silent. We looked at each other. Even the *blatnye* were subdued, taking in the story.

'She wasn't the only one, you know,' he finished. 'We had others, too. Even Aisin Gioro Pu Yi, the emperor himself. And his brother Pu Chieh. I saw them in Chita.'

The lights dimmed, the signal that they would be switched off in ten minutes.

'Kings and cobblers,' Avel remarked soberly, pushing himself away from the bunks, 'paupers and presidents – no difference between them. They say in Hut 27, there's a general...'

The stove was stoked up and we all headed for our bunks except for Korotchenko who remained staring at the stove and mumbling to himself. In a fortnight he was gone. One of the *blatnye* stool-pigeons must have talked, Korotchenko was deemed to know too much and off he went, never to be seen nor heard of again.

'Two bloody blink-and-you-miss-them minutes,' the voice said again. It was, I now recognised, Dmitri speaking.

'What's two minutes?' I asked softly so as not to wake the others.

He replied, 'I reckon it took that poor bastard about two minutes from stripping off to ringing the doorbell to heaven. Not as quick as drowning but damn near so. And a lot less effort. No struggling against the natural desire to survive, to reach the surface. No waves to battle, no currents to defeat. No booming of water in the ears or the rush of the flood down your gullet. All he had to do was drop his pants and count to one hundred and twenty. What d'you think, Shurik?'

'I don't think,' I said. 'It was his affair, not mine. I've too much to think about to survive than to consider how to die.'

Dmitri chuckled, followed by a shuffling of blanket as he settled himself on his side, facing me.

'I wonder where he went as his blood froze,' Dmitri mused.

I knew what he meant. We all went somewhere when the going got rough, or the tedium started to tell, or the food was cold and late, or we were kept waiting at muster while the innumerate guards took another count.

'Where would you go?' I enquired.

'Me?' Dmitri responded. 'I would go... You know, Shurik, I have this dream – no, fantasy. I am not a *zek* nor a conscript. Nor am I a cook or a caretaker as I once was. No! I am the manager of an office. I sit behind a big desk with a telephone, a large blotter set in a frame of leather before me and a silver tray bearing my pens and pencils. Outside, in an anteroom, sits my secretary. She's twenty-two, got blond hair to her waist and her legs start in her armpits. Her tits are like two halves of an orange – firm, smooth and sweet to the tongue. I've tasted them. Believe me! And not in the stationery cupboard, either.'

'What does your office do?'

'It's...' he thought about it for a moment '...an Intourist office. I'm in charge of looking after important visitors to the Soviet Union. I fix up their hotel bookings, see they catch the right train, ascertain their car's on time, fix their tickets to the Bolshoi, ensure they jump to the head of the queue to see Lenin, hold the flight if they're late getting to the airport and line up a tart if they want one or the KGB needs a favour.'

'And,' I asked, 'what sights do you show them?'

'My office is in Moscow so I take them to Red Square, show them St. Basil's Cathedral and the Novodevichy Convent, give them a tour of the Kremlin. If they are English – like you, Shurik – I would take them to the Angliiskoe Podvorye. You know it?'

179

'No,' I answered. 'My visit to Moscow did not include a tourist guide.'

'It is the English Inn,' Dmitri continued, 'a building given by Ivan the Terrible to English merchants four centuries ago. It was their hotel in Russia. Peter the Great used it as a mathematics school. Not many people know about it. It is in the bad part of town.'

'What if I was an American?'

'Take you to the State Armoury to see the Tsar's crown jewels. Americans like monarchs.'

'And if I was French?'

'I would get special permission and take you on a two day visit to Barysav to show you where Napoleon Bonaparte had the crap beaten out of him.'

He chuckled again and turned over. In a few minutes, he was wheezingly snoring with his head under his blanket.

I did not fall immediately to sleep as I did most nights. Perhaps my dozing in the igloo under the truck had dulled the edge off my desire to sleep. Instead, I lay with my eyes closed and my knees drawn up to my chest, listening to the breathing of my companions and wondering where they were now.

On the bunk below Avel would be strapped into the cockpit of his MiG-15, sitting on a parachute he would never need to open, gripping the control column with his right hand, his feet depressing the aileron pedals, swinging himself in easy loops through the clear skies of the Far East, bucking high altitude thermals and soaring through clouds that appeared as solid as drifts of compacted Arctic snow but were as insubstantial as a young girl's dream of handsome men. He would be on a sortie that never had to end: his aircraft would never run out of fuel and he would never need to sleep. Encased in his aluminium bird, he would dance in the sky forever, as free and easy as a migrating martin.

At a lower altitude, on the second bunk up, Titian would be standing at a blackboard, a stick of chalk in his hand and the flies on his trousers lightly talced where he had forgotten to wash his hands before relieving himself between classes. He was murmuring in his sleep but this, I knew, was neither the unconscious recitation of a Korean socialist's poem nor a lecture to his students, for the classroom was empty save for him. It was instead a complex mathematical theorem to which he applied himself when he needed distraction. I could imagine him, in his mind, studying the calculations in an exercise book and tried to see what it was he was seeking to evaluate. For a moment, I let myself enter his dream and ran my eye along the incomprehensible line $Ca > M/2 \; Yb2 = 4x/v + p4 > m$

It was nonsense to me, and probably to him, but it kept him sane. Titian would survive. Ten, fifteen, twenty-five years. No matter how long they kept him in the gulag, no matter how protracted his sentence or tedious his life were to become, he would pull through because he had set himself a task which required of him the most ordered, methodical thinking of which he was capable, a process as far removed from Hut 14 or a rest period down the mine as Moscow was from the Milky Way. And, like the predicament in which fate and the powers-that-were in the Politburo had put him, it could not be brought to a satisfactory conclusion. He would never reach an answer but would be eternally occupied searching for one.

Ylli, I conjectured, was probably back in Albania, looking through pine trees across a sandy beach at the tideless swell of the Mediterranean, a glass of clear *raki* by his side and a pretty girl on his knee. Beneath Dmitri, Kostya twitched in his sleep. He was always restless at night, his body moving to the imagined roll of a ship far out in the Atlantic. His mind was filled with the howl of a storm bearing the promise of ice on the rigging and deck rails, the dull chime of the ship's bell tolling the watches and the creak of the steel plates of the hull as the sea tested the rivets and tried the keel. And underneath him, Kirill was back in Myshkino with Tatyana Antonovna and his daughter who was always two years old, and he was still a young man unwounded by fate and the whim of distant leaders.

And what of me? Where did I go when Kostya was riding typhoons, Avel the skies and Dmitri his secretary?

I had a place to go of which none of the others had so much as an inkling. I kept it quite to myself, never spoke of it to them, never admitted its existence.

It was a garden.

Where it was, in which country of which continent, I neither knew nor cared. It contained rain forest ferns and stalwart oaks, cacti and roses, lilac wisteria and lianas as thick as your wrist. Verdant lawns ran between copses of ash and elm, acacia and baobab. Desert palms grew next to Rocky Mountain pines. The pathways, of which there were many, were gravelled with chips of grey granite, strewn with shingle pebbles mixed with sea-shells or paved with Carrera marble. Here and there, overlooking magnificent vistas, were erected small rustic shelters, miniature Greek temples and grottoes of rough-hewn stone. In a matter of metres, I could pass from the close, luxuriant foliage of the Amazon Basin into the leaf-strewn mellowness of a European beech wood.

At the centre of my secret property, the size of which I never ascertained, there was a substantial water garden covering an area of about two and a half hectares. The pool was shaped roughly like a dumb bell, the bar between the two weights, as it were, traversed by an ornamental bridge not placed centrally but three quarters of the way along towards the eastern end, laid down according to the rules of an ancient oriental geomancy of which I was ignorant. To continue the metaphor, the weights were not equal, one being twice the size of the other, with a circular island in the middle. The bridge, which was highly arched but not stepped, was constructed of pine planks, the rail posts elaborately carved with gryphons and dragons, mythical beasts from the Norse sagas above a trellis of chrysanthemum blossoms cut out by intricate fretwork. It was an ancient structure, the pine having mellowed to a caliginous imperial ochre. The copper nails holding the structure together were an iridescent green with verdigris.

At one end, where the path turned towards the bridge, a lantern hung from a pole. It was square with a frame fashioned of rosewood and, in place of glass, it had tissue-thin rice paper stretched between the sides, stiffened with dope and brushed with lacquer. When the candle within was lit, the paper glowed with an ethereal translucence. It reminded me of light shining through flayed skin.

All along the bank, wherever the lawns did not come down to end in a flagstoned edging, willows draped out to weep over the water in which a wide variety of lilies grew, their pads spreading across the surface. In places, they were so large and strong as to afford small birds a platform from which to dip their beaks when drinking. Emerald green frogs the size of field mice could often be spied squatting on them, their throats ballooning out as they bloarted for a mate in the dusk or declared ownership of their part of the pond. Overhead and even by moonlight, if the moon was already up as the sun went down, huge dragonflies darted or hovered, their thoraxes polished brown as mahogany, their long abdomens a deep vermilion with their grotesque compound eyes as pink as the flesh of an over-ripe grapefruit. As they turned, the orbs changed colour like a rainbow of oil on a puddle.

Close to the bank at the farthest end of the pool, where the water ran off over a stone sill into a narrow stream overhung by mosses and ferns, there was an area of rushes and sedges which trailed their black feathery roots into the depths. There koi carp, many of them weighing well over a kilo, drifted aimlessly by. One was as pure white as milk, its individual scales edged as if with amber, but most were off-white with scarlet, damask and pale yellow patches. Where the water was shallow, shoals of golden orfe scudded here and there, disturbing the crested newts which hung in the water as if dead then wriggled with alarm for the cover of the lily pads, twisting in their flight to show their tan bellies decorated with black spots.

Over the gulag years, I frequently visited this garden. Sometimes, I went there in the early morning when the dawn mist drifted over the surface like the breath of the spirits of my departed enemies. It was then, if I was lucky, I caught a glimpse of the cerulean kingfisher with amaranth wings mottled with jade. It patrolled the shallows, returning always to the same branch from which it surveyed the water. Later in the day, mandarin ducks paddled about the lilies or waddled along the banks, their heads nodding as sedately as a dowager's at agreeable prayer. From time to time, if I stood quite still, a grey heron glided in, its stilt legs lowering in the last few moments before it alighted on the bank to step gingerly into the water, like a man testing the temperature with his toes. It tended, I noticed, to prefer to feed on frogs to fish or newts.

All around, there were the sounds of a glorious orchestra of bird song. Often, I lingered on the bridge oblivious of the pool and its inhabitants, swept away by the grandiose symphony reverberating in the air. After a while, I started to differentiate between the birds just as one does the instruments at a concert. A warbler in the reeds played on its liquid flute whilst a robin, saucily balanced on the bridge rail not a metre from my hand, piped its penny whistle. Standing alert at the water's edge, a blackbird in its sombre priest's suit, with a beak like an orange flame from hell, trilled its piccolo to a bird which I never succeeded in identifying, hiding in one of the willows, blowing a mournful tune on a Japanese *shakahachi*. Far off, a woodpecker added percussion as it drilled into one of the elms in a distant copse.

At night, the pond took on a different character. It was dark, almost foreboding and vaguely threatening, yet in a familiar way. The water, which in daylight reflected the sun and the clouds, and my own face should I lean over the rail of the bridge to stare downwards at myself, became as black and still as primeval sin. In the day, the surface was rippled by fry, tadpoles, diving beetles, water boatmen, aquatic spiders or mayfly hatching off the surface: at night, nothing moved it except the down-draft of a bat's wing as it flittered across the lilies, picking off midges on the wing. The fish seemed to hide, the dragonfly squadron disappeared to disguise itself amongst the stalks of the reeds.

When I came to the pond at night, I never disturbed its nocturnal peace with a torch. Only the moon, or the stars, or the lantern by the bridge illuminated my way.

Who lit the lantern was a mystery but not one that concerned me. It was sufficient that it was always lit should I arrive as twilight fell or in the middle of the night. There was never anyone else present. No groundsmen mowed the lawns, killed the moss encroaching upon it from the pond or tugged dandelions from its carpet. There were no bailiffs to patrol the pond or scoop autumn leaves from the surface, no gardeners to prune the bushes or tie back the ramblers. Over the many visits I made to the garden, I did not once encounter a single human being. Only animals, from every nook and cranny of the tree of creation, inhabited the place: and, no matter whether I came upon an hamadryad or a hungry lion, a tarantula or a Tasmanian Devil, I was never harmed. The cobra never struck, the lion never charged.

Such safety in my solitude never surprised me for this was my garden, exclusive to my use. There was no gateway in the long, high wall which encompassed it, no way in nor any way out. Not once did I ever invite a guest there. Not even Kirill. It did not matter. He never knew of my exclusion and, besides, there was no entrance he might come in by save a tiny door hidden in the far, dark caverns of my mind well beyond his or anybody else's reach.

9

Some way along the footpath, there is a fallen tree, brought down in a blizzard eleven years ago. The villagers have long since sawn off the trunk and branches for fuel or planks but they have left the tangled wizard's hands of the exposed roots. Over the years, these have been washed free of soil, the finer ends nibbled at by deer or robbed by birds hunting for twigs. The result is a sort of basket of gnarled roots which I have, with the aid of a sharp knife, trimmed and pruned into a passable resting place on my walks.

On reaching it in the early afternoon, I settled myself into my rustic seat which faces into the forest and away from the village. Beneath the trees, there is comparatively little undergrowth and I could see for several hundred metres. The ground was strewn with last year's dead leaves and, with the summer well into its last quarter, fungi were beginning to appear. When there was no breeze, the air was laden with their scent, the delicate aroma of decay. Every so often, a bird briefly dropped from the forest canopy to kick the leaves about, pecking at grubs or ants: jays hopped and squirrels skirred here and there, burying nuts for the winter.

Whenever I rest here on my constitutional, I have the vague yet distinct feeling that I am not alone. Seldom do I ever see anyone here: perhaps once or twice a year, someone passes by on the path and nods a greeting to me. They may stop and briefly pass the time of day, temporarily disencumbering themselves of a load of firewood, half a dozen birds or rabbits shot in the woods, leaning their axe or gun against the roots, but otherwise the woods are devoid of humanity. The path is a highway for deer, not men.

Were I to believe in ghosts, satyrs and the like, I could be convinced that the roots were one of their secret parliaments.

Maybe a hidden door exists at the base of the bole, a secret entrance to their underworld.

It is not a malign presence. I never feel I am threatened by it, that it wants to do me ill: it is more a matter that it is somehow in sympathy with me and would, if it could, befriend me, talk to me of my life and share my trials, tribulations and occasional nightmares.

I leaned back against the roots and closed my eyes for I had some serious thinking to do. The afternoon was progressing and it would not be long now before the dust in the lane would be disturbed by unfamiliar wheels and an unfamiliar knock sound on Frosya's door, chilling her heart and setting mine racing.

Since I slit open the envelope and read the letter, four lines of verse have drummed themselves through my consciousness. Try as I have to ignore them, they have refused to go away and have lingered like a hated tune. I could not place their origin and may have invented them, although I think not for I am not given to versifying: for all I know, I may have been misquoting them:

It matters not how strait the gate,
How charged with punishments the scroll,
I am the master of my fate:
I am the captain of my soul.

How they have taunted me with their blunt, cruel and ineluctable truth.

For so much of my life, decisions have been made for me.

In the gulag, we all knew where we stood. The lights went on: we left the camp: we marched to and descended the mine: we dug coal: we came up and returned to camp: we ate: we slept. No decisions were made with my involvement. We *zeks* lacked for none of the basic demands of a living organism, given the parameters of our situation, save our freedom. We were fed, after a fashion, clothed and sheltered. When we fell ill, we were provided with the most basic of medicinal care: if it failed well,

188

so what! Some other poor sod would be dragged off the street, or out of his bed, accused, tried and thrown into the system to make up the shortfall in manpower.

In short, we were treated in a manner no better and no worse than that with which a negligent farmer might regard his herd, or a lazy zoo keeper his cages of wild beasts.

It was all a part of the process of rehabilitation, of making us come to appreciate that Mother Communism, that buxom, grinning, snag-toothed wench dressed in a pair of dark blue overalls, with a scarf around her head and biceps like Popeye the Sailorman, would provide for us. She was our succour and our saviour as well as our slave-mistress and superintendent.

The whole idea was that, when we finally left the gulag, we would accept our lot, be grateful for the protecting arm of the Politburo, knuckle under to the socialist way and believe the improbable promises of the next five-year plan. We would work for the common good and receive our due share of the common profit. If there was one. And if we lived to see it.

Yet the gulag failed. We came out grateful enough for our freedom, but many of us had had our spirits as well as our health and strength dashed and, when we reached the village we had tried never to dream about, or the block of flaking concrete in the suburbs of an industrial town which we called home, and we found our parents dead, our wives old and sag-breasted or our sweethearts married off, we meekly acquiesced, asking no questions and making no waves.

No one was inclined to complain and not from fear of another stretch in a Siberian slammer. The decision had been made. Our fate was sealed without recourse or discussion and we accepted it for this was how we had been trained to see the world. As ants to the queen were we to the Kremlin.

So we went to the labour office and collected our allotted jobs in the grand scheme of things, travelled daily to the office or the factory, the railway marshalling yard or the power station and pretended to work whilst the Party pretended to pay us.

Thus it always was until politicians grew bored with playing their games and men grew tired of keeping the score.

There was, I knew, no avoiding the fact. As that damned poem stated repeatedly in the back of my mind, I was in command, the captain of my soul. Where I voyaged from that moment on was entirely up to me. My hand, and no one else's, was on the tiller. I had the maps and, although I may have been ignorant of where the reefs and shallows were, I had at least stars to steer by and a compass: and those stars were not Polaris and Cassiopeia, Alderamin and Capella in the constellation of Auriga but Frosya and Trofim turning through their orbits around Myshkino.

When I came out of my reverie, the sun was slanting at a greater angle through the trunks. I must have been there for over an hour, must have dozed off in my chair of roots. The jays were still at work hunting and gathering, but the other birds were nowhere to be seen. They would, I knew, be down by the river, slaking their thirst and taking their last drink before it was time to return to the trees to start staking out a claim to a perch for the night.

It was time to move on, time to come to a decision, time to set my course and hold my hand firm on the rudder, regardless of the tides and the currents of destiny. It was time to count as profit each day fortune allowed me.

For, after all, I was the master of my fate. It was a responsibility which came with liberty, and it scared me. It always has, deep down. Yet what is fate but nothing more than a melody of time, drawn from an instrument I can neither tune nor play, but only listen to from day to day.

✳

For a hundred metres or so, where the path starts to turn back towards the village, the forest is bordered by a wooden post and rail fence demarcating the end of the trees and the start of a wide meadow in which a large and ancient horse grazes all the day through. The animal is owned by Yuri, the schoolmaster under whom I taught in the last few years of my academic metamorphosis. In places, the fence has been recently repaired with sawn planks and nails but for some stretches the timbers, whole boughs merely trimmed of twigs, are ancient and attached to the posts with oak pegs. It is in one of these ancient lengths that the stile was constructed last year, by Yelyutin the carpenter, for my express convenience.

As I reached the style, and put my foot upon the step-board, the fence creaked. The horse heard the sound, raised its head from the short grass and pricked its ears. When I swung my leg over the stile the horse, going somewhat short-sighted in old age, caught a vague movement and, with the curiosity of the elderly, came shambling towards me.

'Good day, Bratan,' I greeted the animal. The name is colloquial and refers to a brother of whom one is fond. As throughout the world, everyone in Myshkino loves an old horse.

It recognised my voice and relaxed its ears. I was no longer an object of equine curiosity or a threat come out of the forest. Once it was by my side, it thrust its broad head out to be rubbed and I obliged the animal by running my hand down its long, bony nose.

'A fine day to be a horse,' I said, touching its shoulder which was hot from the sunlight. 'The air is warm, the sky is blue, the grass is sweet and mankind has turned to a new mule.'

The horse snuffled through its nostrils and I could smell the strong odour of grass sap on its breath.

'Ah! You don't know,' I went on. 'You've not heard! Well, Bratan, let me tell you. In Myshkino, the old forge at which, you were once shod, is now in a garage for the repair of self-propelled carts. Furthermore, it will soon provide vehicular travel for all the villagers, obviating the need for a saddle to be strapped to your old back and a steel bit to be shoved between your teeth.'

'However,' a voice replied, 'you do not need to be concerned for your hooves because they can still provide a shoeing service.'

I looked round the bulk of the horse to find Yuri walking towards it with a bundle of new-mown hay under his arm.

'Good afternoon, Yuri,' I said.

'Happy birthday, Shurik! You still talking to my ancient nag?'

'We old folk must stick together,' I justified myself. 'Besides, in real terms, he and I are the oldest inhabitants of the village. I have to find someone to talk to on my own level.'

Yuri threw the straw down, cutting the tarred twine binding it with a sickle-bladed, hooked hoof knife, rolling the cord up and pocketing it so that the horse did not ingest it.

'It's certainly true you won't get an ordered or intelligent conversation out of youngsters these days,' he said ruefully. 'The inhabitants of the classroom are not what they were in your day. And that day was not so long ago.'

Yuri touched the horse behind its left fetlock and it obediently lifted its leg so that he might inspect the hoof.

'Has he a problem?' I enquired.

'No, not really. He had a cut in his sole. He does it on purpose. To get sympathy.' Yuri looked up at the horse which had turned its head so that one eye surveyed its master. 'Don't you?' The horse tossed its head dismissively. 'Have you seen the stones in the river?' he went on, speaking to me again. 'Smooth as marbles. But he had to find the sharp one. However, I managed to purchase some veterinary mercurochrome in Zarechensk. Now that there are so few horses about, the medicines are cheap.' He studied the hoof and continued, addressing the horse more than me, 'You old folk are always getting minor ailments. We ought to have you...'

Yuri stopped himself but he knew the damage had been done. He is not a man who always thinks first before speaking. Like any teacher worth his salt, his brain has to be quick to counter the mercurial minds of his pupils but this can lead to a perceived social ineptitude and *faux pas* of the first order in adult company.

'Shot?' I suggested.

'I'm... I'm sorry, Shurik. That was stupid...'

'No, it was not,' I assured him. 'You cannot harm me with words, Yuri. Not careless ones, nor those spiked with malice. And yours are neither. You simply suffer from the mutable demands of your profession.'

'Profession!' he rejoined, lowering the horse's leg and moving round its head to check the next, glad to take the opportunity to turn the conversation. 'You have no idea, Shurik.' He instructed the horse to raise its leg. It slowly obeyed. 'In the old days, when I went to the village school and, later, when you taught in it, we studied. Some applied themselves hard, some not so. We did our sums, learnt our tables and theorems. πr^2. The square on the hypotenuse is equal to the sum of the squares on the other two sides. We chanted our spellings, recited patriotic verses, read our admittedly doctored history books and knew where to find Celjabinsk and Iskatelej on a map of the USSR even if we had not a clue what went on there. But now! The hypotenuse and the geography of Russia can go hang themselves. The little bastards don't know what the hell's going on in the Kremlin – and don't care! – but they can reel off the main cities of California and give you the name of Tom Cruise's cat.'

'Tom Cruise?' I questioned.

'A film star,' Yuri informed me. 'The boys worship him and the girls adore him. He is an action hero film star. Young, handsome...'

'And he is a cat lover?' I asked facetiously.

Yuri shrugged, turned his attention to the horse's hoof and found another stone embedded in the mud around the frog. Unfolding the hoof knife once more, he flicked it out and moved to the horse's hindquarters.

I looked down the meadow, across the river in which there is a line of stepping stones and up the other side to the village. The sun was beginning to lower now. The hour was drawing on.

The horse's hoof checked out, Yuri folded his knife up and

patted the horse on its flank. It whisked its long tail at him and took a few steps to the hay, arching its neck down to smack its lips at the fodder. Without speaking, we set off walking slowly down the field. We were halfway to the river before either of us spoke.

'Do you remember Lyuba?' Yuri asked.

I racked my brain for a minute. Over time, the memory of all my pupils has faded into a common blur except for Romka and he is only kept alive by my seeing him whenever I visit the garage.

'A small, diffident girl,' Yuri prompted me. 'Her mother had a withered arm. The child had no father.'

He spoke as if the lack of a parent was an accepted biological certainty, like the mother's deformity.

'Just vaguely. They lived in a small hut a little way down the Zarechensk road.'

'That's her. A quiet child, under size for her age, withdrawn into herself.'

'How old was she?'

'Nine or ten when you first saw her.'

'That must have been in '78. Did not the others call her Water Snail?'

'Because she always retreated into her shell,' Yuri explained. 'You know what became of her?'

'I have not the slightest notion,' I replied.

'She is now a librarian in the University of Minsk where she lives in a small apartment with her pet Samoyed. Twenty-eight years old, rather pretty but as yet unmarried. '

'The way you talk,' I responded, 'you might be lining her up for someone. Or fancying her for yourself. You would not be the first. That's the oldest pit a teacher in his middle years can tumble into.'

Yuri ignored my flippancy.

'Do you not want to know how I have discovered these facts?' he went on.

'I'm sure you're going to tell me.'

'They are printed on the back cover of her first book of

poetry. Good stuff it is, too. The critics love her. The book has a foreword by Yevtushenko. And do you remember Ivnev?'

'The name rings no bell for me.'

'His father was a labourer, worked on the railway. Track maintenance, fence painting. Nothing too taxing for the brain. You know what's become of him?'

'I assume,' I answered, ' he is still working on the railway.'

Yuri was slightly annoyed at my continual jibing and said, 'Not him! Not the father. The son. Ivnev is now a journalist in Moscow working for CNN, a world-wide American television company. I saw him the other night.'

'You saw him?' I responded, allowing a degree of scepticism to creep into the words. 'Where?'

'In Zarechensk,' he continued, picking up on my dubiety, 'and before you get clever with me, it wasn't in the bus station or a bar. I saw him at my sister's place. My brother-in-law's cousin lives in Germany and gave them a satellite television. He was on the American news, clear as the nose on your face. Along the bottom of the screen was his name.'

We reached the river bank and the stepping stones beside which were hoof-prints in the mud. Yuri squatted down to inspect them.

'Is this where the horse picks up stones?' I enquired.

'It could be,' Yuri responded. 'The children sometimes amuse themselves by throwing pebbles at the stepping stones. Some shatter into sharp splinters.'

All his talk of children had set my mind wandering.

'Do you know what happened to little Raisa?' I asked at length, as Yuri washed his hands in the river, scaring away a number of small fish which darted for the cover of the mid-stream weeds.

'Your favourite,' he replied, straightening up. 'A round, truly Russian face, always smiling.'

'And clever, quick on the uptake.'

'She went to study nursing in Kiev. Then she emigrated.

Now she works in a hospital in Canada, sends money back to her parents. Every month, sure as the moon rises, fifty dollars arrive. So,' he added, 'you do remember some of them.'

'Names are coming back to me,' I admitted, 'because you have oiled the cogs of memory.'

'Do you remember Davidov?'

'There were several.'

'Davidov, son of the panel beater in the Zarechensk bus garage. He is now an engineer in Germany, working for Mercedes Benz.'

'He was always crazy about cars,' I remarked.

'And Lado? Remember him? The boy who played with matches and burned Rysakov's hay rick to the ground. He's studying to be an architect in Moscow. And Ninochka, with her incredible blond hair, a mass of tight curls. You know, they used to say her family was descended from ancient Greeks who sailed up the Volga and got lost. Last month, she was appointed as a simultaneous translator to the Russian mission to the United Nations.'

Yuri put his foot on the first of the stepping stones. They are large, flat and firmly set on the river bed which, at this point, is shallow for once there was a ford here, before the bridge was built. I followed him and he paused three stones out, offering me his hand.

'I am not one of the children,' I reproved him. 'Old and doddery I may be but I'm not yet derelict.'

He smiled and carried on across the river. Some of the stones in the middle, where the current splashes over loose rocks just under the surface, were slick with water and I took, as I do every day now, great care not to slip.

'I trust the Styx will be as easy to cross when the time comes,' I commented as I reached the far bank, now accepting the offer of his hand to help me up the step from stone to shore. I have, of late, had to make a quick and undignified clamber to get ashore.

Side by side, we started off slowly up the slope towards the village, the houses above set against the sky. Ahead of us, close to the path, a billy-goat was tethered to a stake and chewing on a clump of weeds. To the right, I could see the Merry Widow's laundry hanging on a line, a drift of smoke lifting from a short chimney at the end of her house as she fired her baking oven. Farther down, in a corner of the field near to the river, someone had erected a large pile of wood for a bonfire.

'You are a devil of a man, Yuri,' I exclaimed. 'Your damned talk of Davidovs and Ivnevs has set my mind off.'

'Don't you want to remember those days? Were they that bad?'

'No,' I shook my head, 'of course not. They were good, golden times. Yet, recently, I have tried not to dwell in the past. A penchant for nostalgia is a sure sign that the Grim Reaper is running the whetstone over his scythe.'

'Do you know why those children have been so successful?' Yuri remarked.

'Because they are lucky,' I replied. 'Because the wheels of fortune have turned well for them.'

'That's not true,' Yuri responded. 'They have done well because you were their teacher.'

'I can hardly see how four years in the occasional company of an old *zek* can shape an entire life.'

'You didn't shape their lives, you opened them up. Before you came, their teachers were men and women of narrow vision who towed the Party line, preached the Party gospel and sang the Party hymns of praise. They were not small-minded because they were dolts but because that was the only way they could survive. Then you arrived and the world expanded.'

The goat stopped its munching and looked at us with shrewd hircine eyes brimful with mischievous evil. With like minds, we stepped off the path to detour the creature. Its curlicued horns invited injury.

'Few,' I quoted, 'have been taught to any purpose who have not been their own teachers. Those are the words of

Joshua Reynolds.'

'He was an artist, was he not?' Yuri rejoined. 'For painting that may be true but not for life. And if you are going to be sententious, Shurik, I can be too. A teacher affects eternity; he can never tell when his influence stops: the words of Henry Brooks Adams.'

'I taught English and a little elementary mathematics, the latter very badly.'

'And astronomy,' Yuri reminded me.

'I hardly taught that. It was merely an interest I had.'

At that moment, the goat decided to charge us, its head down and horns out. At the end of its tether, it was brought to an abrupt halt. Yuri laughed at the animal which backed off with a look of humiliation on its face.

'You broadened horizons, Shurik,' he continued. 'Before you stepped into the classroom, the sky was just a black space with lights and the world ended just beyond my horse. You gave them a new language, a whole new universe to explore.'

So as not to lose face, the goat had another but half-hearted lunge at us but we were now well out of its range and besides, it stopped itself before it reached the extent of the rope.

'What are you getting at, Yuri?' I wanted to know.

'Just that the people here admire you.'

'I know.'

'You have made a poet of a timid child and an architect of an infant arsonist. Two people survive into their old age because their daughter, whom you taught, supports them.'

'You will tell me next that Komarov's apples swell, Trofim's tomatoes ripen and Vera Dorokhova's bread rises because of my presence.'

'Don't be facetious, old man,' Yuri chastised me. 'You know exactly what I mean.' He paused and looked back across the river to where Bratan was still standing, head down to the hay. 'They are afraid, you know...'

He left the remainder of his sentence hanging in the air and we walked on up the hill to the road not far from Frosya's house.

Several of the Merry Widow's hens had flown from the coop by her woodpile and were scratching about in the dust, looking for seeds or grasshoppers.

'You taught the children English, yes,' he said at length. 'And maths and their way about the stars, yet you gave them so much more. What you brought to Myshkino was humanity. You may not realise it, even now, but you are to this day only the second person ever to return here from the gulag.'

'I did not return,' I reminded him.

'You know what I mean. Stop playing the pedagogue.'

'Who was the other?' I enquired. 'I don't recall a fellow *zek*.'

'He was before your time. Arrested in 1950, he was accused of anti-Soviet activities. Whatever the hell that meant! He can hardly have been an American spy or sabotaged the future of the USSR. He was a bus conductor. They sentenced him to thirteen years in the gulag and, during that time, he met a woman inside who was there for anti-social activities. She'd been a common whore in Moscow. They were both released round about the same time and wandered about before ending up in Myshkino. He built them a shanty on a scrap of rocky ground the commune had no interest in and earned a bit of money cutting timber in the forest. But he couldn't adjust, not even with his wife's love. And she did love him. Passionately, in her own way.'

'The gulag had conditioned him.'

Yuri nodded and continued, 'He hanged himself in the forest, just beyond the stile. It was my father who cut him down.'

A feeling of apprehension ran down my spine.

'Which tree?' I asked.

'It's not there now,' Yuri replied. 'It blew down in a blizzard, years ago. Only the roots remain. We chopped the rest of it up.'

'And the wife?'

'She was a mother by the time he killed himself, with a toddler. She stayed, grew a few vegetables, kept a nanny goat and some hens, like the rest of us. Her health was not good and she only worked spasmodically, cleaning offices in Zarechensk.'

'Still here?'

'No, she moved away in due course and died a year or two back.'

I tried to think who it could have been but arrived at no conclusion.

'Who was he?'

'He was Lubya's father.'

So now, after all this time, I knew why, when I sat in my forest throne and surveyed the leaves, I never felt alone.

'When you came,' Yuri went on, 'people thought it would only be a matter of time before they found you stretching your neck or blowing your head off with one of Sergei Petrovich's shotguns. Yet you were different. It was as if the gulag had somehow strengthened you. You had not become demoralised by it, broken by it.'

I smiled and thought of Work Unit 8, conjured up their faces in my mind, took a mental roll call, heard Dmitri's laugh and Kirill's soft, authoritative voice, saw again the snow flurries eddying round our legs.

'In you, Shurik, we saw that strength and were ourselves uplifted by it. We knew – at least, our imaginations told us – what you had been through, what things you had seen, things you had done. Where Milyukov was concerned – that was Lubya's father's name: the mother and child never used it after his suicide – we saw only despondency and surrender and it dragged us down. There, but for the grace of God and the KGB, went every one of us. Then you appeared that day, shambling along the road, and Myshkino changed.'

'You make me sound like some kind of Saviour of the Steppes.'

Yuri chuckled and retorted, 'Not quite so grand, old man. More a Harbinger of Hope.'

We arrived at the gate in front of Trofim and Frosya's house. The marigolds were wilting in the heat of the late afternoon but Frosya had just turned on the tap by the wall and the water was running down little trenches cut in the sun-baked soil. In a matter of minutes, the plants would receive their succour, the leaves would perk up and the flower heads would stand erect again.

'I shall see you later,' Yuri said, somewhat mysteriously: then he took my hand, not to shake it but to hold it in both his. 'Don't forget, Shurik. You mean something to us. To Myshkino.'

He relinquished my hand and set off down the lane. I watched him until he had passed Komarov's house at which point he turned up towards the school house. With him out of sight, I made my way up the path towards the house, my every step a conscious pace into the future.

10

Over about three months, we lengthened the mole hole by seventy-nine metres: then, in one day, we dug out over five metres. The coal seam we were following began to narrow and turn and, whilst the rock above remained firm, that beneath it became friable and richly fossiliferous. This made the coal easier to chip free from its surrounding matrix but it was still heavy going for the tunnel was less than one and a half metres high and three wide. Only one of us could work at the face at a time, back distorted and neck cricked, smashing the pickaxe sideways to lever the rock and coal loose.

We organised ourselves into a strict shift rota, based not upon time – for none of us possessed a watch – but upon effort. The worker at the coal face swung the pickaxe sixty times then surrendered the implement to the next man who started to labour at the rock as he moved to the sledge, waiting to tow it away. One person was usually absent with the second sledge, delivering the previous load to the central gallery and bringing back thirty centimetre square timber pit props when they were needed and fresh water, if he could find any. Usually, drinking water down the mine was stale and contaminated with dust. Two others loaded the sledge whilst the last two shovelled both coal and debris back from the face or shored up the roof. As soon as a complete cycle was achieved, we all downed tools for what we assumed to be fifteen minutes but which, subterranean time being beyond accurate computation, could have been anything up to twice that time. What usually set us to work again was a general consensus that our muscles were eased a bit.

In the rest periods, we lay about on sacks pilfered from the supply tunnel or sat with our backs to the wall, each sunk in his own private thoughts or making his own private escape.

I remember so very clearly, as if it happened only last week, the second rest break of that day towards the end of the third month in the mole hole. I had just finished my stint of chipping away at the under-belly of Mother Earth and was lying on my back on two sacks, my face staring at the roof of the tunnel. Set into the stone, as if engraved by someone working with a fine stonemason's engraving awl, was the perfect outline of a leaf. It resembled a frond of fern and was so flawless it might have been deliberately placed there by an ancient child goddess with a propensity for pressing flowers.

Ylli, edging past me, knocked the bare bulb hanging by its flex from the row of pit props. The light oscillated briefly. In the changing shadows, the fossilised leaf seemed to twitch as it must have done tens of millions of seasons ago in a Triassic breeze.

'Amazing, isn't it?' Titian remarked, following my eye. 'We're two kilometres down in the middle of a forest, looking at a leaf that once heard the roar of dinosaurs.'

'Reckon we might find one of those big motherfuckers of a lizard?' Kostya mused. 'Frozen in the coal like the mammoth was under the tundra.'

Titian embarked upon an explanation as to why that was unlikely but I paid him scant attention for the leaf above was sufficient for me. It was a ticket to leave the mine, leave the USSR, leave the pain and dust and smell of sweat for my garden. I turned on my side. Next to me, Avel had closed his eyes: from the look on his face, he was already shooting the clouds in his MiG-15.

In seconds, the others ceased to exist and I strolled along one of the gravel paths leading from the bridge over the pool to the temple to Athena on a grassy knoll.

From a distance, the temple looked to be a grand, imposing structure, circular with a surround of Corinthian pillars supporting the overhang of the domed roof at the top of which stood a statue of a Greek girl dressed in a flowing toga-like gown, one of her breasts bare. She was cut from marble, the white stone giving her firm skin a certain palpable translucency, the veins in the stone like the delicate blood vessels around her nipple.

My feet crunched crisply on the gravel which consisted not of sharp, grey granite chips but water-smoothed beach pebbles and tiny shells my every footstep ground to powder: and yet, whenever I next came that way, those shells I had crushed on my last walk had reconstituted themselves. Nothing was ever destroyed in my garden.

The temple, however, was not all it seemed to be for, as I approached it, it appeared to shrink in size until it was little bigger than a child's garden play-house. By stretching out my hand, I could touch the statue, feel the smooth curve of the breast which, despite its diminutive size, perfectly fitted the palm of my hand. It was always warm, as if the statue was in reality a young girl only just turned to stone by some wicked spell: that, of course, was unlikely for there was no evil in the garden, nothing so malign as to transform a living creature into inanimate marble.

On this visit, as I approached the temple, I heard a strange music coming from within. It was liquid, flowing as if performed on a flute or bass clarinet, the notes not distinct but merged into each other. If warm syrup could have been transfigured into music, I thought, it would have sounded like this.

Curious to trace the source of the music, I entered the building. How this was achieved I do not understand: the building did not grow in size nor did I, like Alice in Wonderland, consciously shrink. Be that as it may, my fingers gripped the polished bronze door handle, I turned it and entered. Immediately, to my intense disappointment, the music stopped.

Inside, the temple was devoid of all furniture save one chair. Positioned under the very centre of the dome, it was an ornate, throne-like seat of the Louis XIV period, opulently upholstered with silks and velvets of the richest, indescribable hues which were less like colours and more like tangible textures devised to caress and cosset both body and soul. Around the walls was a frieze painted in pastels but I was unable to make out exactly what it depicted: the interior of the temple was in semi-darkness except for a circle of soft light in the centre of which the chair had been placed. Possibly, the frieze consisted of classical rustic scenes of maids drawing water, cows wandering lush valleys in low sunlight, castles on precipitous cliffs, hovels tucked away beside rivers running through oak woods.

I required no invitation but went directly to the chair and sat in it. The door closed. It did not swing quickly shut as it might have done on a spring or hydraulic hinge but slowly as if secured by an invisible hand.

At first, all was silent. I sat quite still in the chair, filled with expectation. How long I remained immobile I cannot say. It might have been minutes, it may have been hours: and I cannot say when the music began again. It did not suddenly commence but grew gradatim, fragment by fragment upon the very air. As the temple might fill with water so did it with sound which contained no scales, no defined or recognisable notes, no tune. There was no structured score to be followed.

Closing my eyes, I leaned back in the chair which seemed to envelope me, fold itself around and cocoon me. The music rose and fell like waves upon a vast ethereal ocean until, hours later, the concert came to an end. As it had begun, so it finished, the melody gradually melting away like ice on a summer's day. I did not consciously hear it fade but came suddenly to the realisation that it was over.

Quitting the temple, and returning to my normal size as soon as I was out of the door, I found it was evening. The sun was setting over a copse of beech trees, the last rays golden through the shimmer of the branches. In the sky, a full moon was risen, casting a white gleam upon high, stratospheric clouds which, as I gazed up at them, darkened and became the fern leaf fossil over my head.

'What was yours called?'

I turned my head. Kostya was leaning against the wall of the mole hole beside me, chewing on a piece of bread.

'My what?' I asked.

'Your girl, Shurik! Your girl, the one you had. Jesus! Have

you had others we've not heard about!'

'My girl,' I replied, thinking hard. I was still partly in the garden where there were no girls, only statues.

'Yes! The little piece you shagged...'

'Valya,' I said.

'Mine was Lena.' He looked into the distance which was less that three metres away across the tunnel. 'Tight as a keyhole.'

'I'm amazed we managed it,' Titian cut in.

'Speak for yourself!' Kostya retorted. 'I was never lacking...'

'That's not what I meant,' Titian rejoined. 'I'm not doubting any of our manhoods. But the thing is, our diet is pretty turgid...'

'Shit, shit and more shit, some of it hot,' said Ylli.

'And mammoth,' Avel added.

We all laughed except for Titian who was determined to make his point.

'If your diet,' he went on, ignoring the interruptions, 'lacks vitamin E you can't get an erection.'

'A hard on,' Kostya said. 'We aren't in anatomy class.'

'In that case, we've all either lied like buggery to each other,' Ylli said, 'and not one of us has had his end away or, despite the crap food, we're still getting vitamin E.'

'Well, I'm getting vitamins a-plenty!' Kostya announced proudly.

'What about you?' Titian asked me.

'Truthfully, it would seem I'm getting my vitamin E,' I told him.

Kirill, who had been lazing against a pit prop, joined the conversation and said, 'You can be sure we're getting the very basic needs we require. They don't want to starve us. We might be *zeks* but we are also labour. We're not here because we sabotaged socialism, because we sold secrets to the British or helped someone jump a ship for Rio. We're here because the last Five-Year Plan, and the one before that, and the next one, needs so many tens of thousands of ants to see it through. We, comrades-in-coal, are nothing more than ants.'

'We live like ants,' Avel remarked. 'Under the ground most of the time and coming up only to forage about for food.'

'But with sufficient vitamins to fuck,' Kostya said, with finality.

Dmitri, who had been lying on a sack, sat up and said quietly, 'I hate all people, present company excepted. People can't be trusted. They'll rat on you, shit on you and do you in for a plate of porridge. They'll steal what they don't need and destroy what they do. People are the worst animals on earth.'

He spoke with such a conviction that it silenced us all for a moment: each of us, in his own way, looked for justification to this statement, and found it in his own experience.

'Heard about the Kuskova family?' Dmitri asked at length, breaking our thoughts.

He paused and looked from one to the other of us, ending on me. There was no humour in his eyes, no twinkling impishness.

'I'll tell you about them,' he continued, 'They lived in an apartment block in the city – Minsk, Moscow – I forget which. Doesn't matter. There was father, mother, *babushka*, two teenage sons and a daughter. Father's a clerk in some state office, mother's a nurse, *babushka's* old and toothless and the kids're at school or university. Late one night, they were all sitting round reading, playing cards – whatever. There's a heavy knock on the door. They go pale, look at each other. Visions of KGB uniforms and a man in a black leather coat. "Keep quiet!" father K whispers, "they'll think we're out." The knocking starts again, louder, more insistent. They all cower, pray no one's got a door ram. Again – knock! knock! Then they hear footsteps going away and their neighbours' door being rapped upon followed by urgent but incomprehensible voices. Then silence. They're scared witless but they want to know what's going on so they decide to send the daughter out to discover what's happening. She's a paid up, *bona fide* Party member, secretary of a youth organisation. Pretty, long legs, nice hair, firm tits. All the attributes to woo herself out of a pickle. She slips out of the apartment. Ten minutes go by then there's a heavy knocking on the door again. The family are silent. The knock is insistent again. Then they hear a muffled voice. "It's me! Alya!" The daughter! They open the door. "What's going on, Alya?" "It's all right!'" she says. "Nothing to worry about. It's only the building on fire."'

This time, our laughter was muted, wry.

'Time to cut coal,' Kirill announced.

We rose to our feet. It was my turn to take over the hauling of a sledge to the main gallery but Kostya had another idea.

'Shurik,' he asked, 'will you swap over?'

'Swap over?' I answered.

'Will you do my loading stint now and I do your pulling the sledge?'

I gave his request no second thought. My muscles were relaxed from my rest and my mind soothed by the music in the temple.

'Sure!' I agreed and I picked up one of the shovels.

At the time, I gave no thought as to why he suggested this, and why I accepted his offer. It was nothing more than a simple request from a friend although rarely did we exchange our rolcs: there was little to be gained by either of us from changing places.

Now, of course, I know it was scheming providence at work, tugging at my strings, re-setting the compass of my life. Had Kostya not made the suggestion, had I not accepted it, my life would never have taken the path that it has. Upon that one infinitesimal fraction of time hung everything.

We settled back into our routine. Ylli took his turn with the pick, Kostya and Titian pulled the sledges, Kirill and Avel shovelled back whilst Dmitri and I filled the sledges. Conserving our energies, none of us spoke. Conversation was usually reserved for rest periods. Nor did we slacken our rate of work. As a team, we worked well for we had come to understand the others' capabilities and had adjusted our pace to the lowest common denominator. In this way, no one was stretched, no one was criticised for holding the others up, no one was looked down upon.

In many ways, Work Unit 8 was the supreme irony. Two kilometres above us, Communism was failing in the bright light of day whilst we, state-confirmed dissident malcontents with KGB dossiers, guilty of something or nothing as the case may be, laboured in eternal darkness with dim bulbs in a structured, ordered team under one leader, everyone looking out for his fellow and doing his bit. If there was ever an example of socialism truly working it was the seven of us.

About halfway through Ylli's digging stint, he struck a particularly crumbling section of rock. The point of the pick went in to the shaft and, as he worked and levered it loose, fragments of coal and stone started to tumble down to his feet. By the time the pick was free, a hole had formed a good thirty centimetres deep and seventy in diameter.

Kirill called an immediate halt. Leaning forward, he sniffed at the hole like a bloodhound hot on the scent. Knowing what was in his mind, we stood motionless, making sure our metal tools touched nothing from which they might strike a spark.

'We're all right,' he announced at length. 'My lungs don't itch. No gas.' Stepping back, he surveyed the cavity and added, 'Better get this lot supported. Avel, go with Titian and get more props.'

Kostya being already absent with a sledge full of coal and debris, when Avel and Titian departed with the second sledge there were just the four of us left. Kirill issued fresh orders: we set about moving the loose rock Ylli had brought down, piling it up against the tunnel wall ten metres back, clearing the face area so the new pit props could be erected and bedded in. Kirill and Ylli moved the rubble back from the tight confines of the work-face, Dmitri and I taking it on down the mole hole. It was hard work. Without a sledge, we had to carry the débris on shovels, walking with our backs slightly bent.

Despite the slog of our labours, Dmitri's spirits were not dampened. It took a lot to get him down: he was, despite his fervent denigration of the entire human species, one of nature's optimists. As he crouched along, his shovel held out before him and his biceps tensed, his mind was working. When we had shifted about half the rubble, he stopped me by the spoil tip we were building.

'There's a pianist travelling by train across the Soviet Union,' he said, touching me on the arm in an almost conspiratorial manner. 'He's on his way to a concert, studying the score for his next performance. In the next seat, there's a KGB officer in plain clothes.'

'What score?' I interrupted. 'Tchaikovsky? Rachmaninov?' I suggested.

'How do I know, Shurik?' Dmitri replied. 'What does it matter? Stop being obtuse.'

'It's important,' I needled him. 'Details are important if you tell a story about the KGB. Details are everything to them. Rimsky-Korsakov?'

'You want to hear the story?'

'Not Borodin?'

I was not to know it but, as with Kostya's request to pull the sledge, my captious questioning was yet another intervention of fate's hand, slowing the wheel of fortune by a few crucial snippets of time.

'Right!' Dmitri said pointedly to silence me. 'Mendelssohn. Satisfied? Now can I go on?'

I nodded.

Dmitri gave me a sharp look for playing with him and continued, 'Being KGB, he didn't know the first thing about music and thought the sheet of notation was a code and the pianist an enemy of the state. "What is this, comrade?' he asked the pianist. 'Just one of the works of Mendelssohn,' the pianist replied. At the next station, he was dragged off the train and thrown in a cell. Six days went by before they lugged him into an interrogation cell. 'Right!" said the KGB officer. "You'd better tell us all you know. Mendelssohn's already confessed."'

I chuckled and said, 'Probably true. But why Mendelssohn? He was a German. Surely a Russian pianist would play a Russian composer.'

'He was Russian?' Dmitri retorted sharply. ' I said he was Russian...?'

Something touched me softly, almost inconsequentially on the shoulder, drawing my attention as a friend might coming up behind me in the street. It could have been an angel's wing. Instinctively, I turned.

By the glimmer of the last of our pilfered light bulbs, down towards the end of the mole hole, I could see Kirill. He was half bent with his shovel in his hand and looking at me. Beyond him, Ylli had his back turned. Something in me wanted to call out yet I held my silence.

A thunderclap struck me as physically as a fist, the sound ramming itself through my body like a charge of heavy electricity. It was as I imagined it must be in the very nucleus of a storm cloud, rising and billowing over sun-baked plains. My ears rang, my pulse raced, my eyes screwed themselves shut. My soul withdrew into the core of my body and crouched there, trembling. I was thrust to my knees by a force I could neither resist nor understand and a strange wind blew over me which smelled of rotting flesh and dead stone. A blast of tiny shrapnel spattered against me, stinging my ear lobes.

All was then black and silent save for a tribal drum beating close to my head in the jungle of the impenetrable night. I raised my hand to my face. My left cheek was damp and sticky.

Slowly, I gathered my wits. The tattoo on the tribal drum subsided and my ears began to pick up individual sounds again. At first, I heard my own breath coming in short gulps, then my heart racing followed by a noise like small waves breaking on a shingle beach: finally, I heard someone else breathing and a voice.

'Shurik!' The voice was low, cautious. 'Shurik!'

'Yes,' I replied, my own voice loud inside my head.

'My battery's fucked.'

It was Dmitri.

'You all right?' I asked.

There was a pause for a moment, as if he was checking

himself, before he answered, 'Fine. Is your lamp working?'

I felt along my belt to where the lamp, which Kirill had filched for me on my first day at Sosnogorsklag 32, was clipped. Tugging it free, I pressed the switch with my thumb. The battery was not fully charged, the beam consequently dim but sufficient to show me Dmitri's drawn face, his eyes staring through a mist of fine dust hanging in the air.

'Blessed Isaac!' he half-whispered: it was more a prayer than an expletive.

It was then I turned, swinging the feeble beam of the lamp. The roof supports were buckled and splintered: the roof over our heads had retained its integrity but it was lower by at least ten centimetres. Through the dust, where Kirill and Ylli had been, there was a sloping wall of rock and rubble.

I did not bother to try to stand. I scrabbled forwards on my hands and knees, jammed the lamp behind a prop that had eased itself away from the wall and began to tear at the rubble, throwing the rocks back behind me. Blood from a gash just beneath my left eye dripped onto my chest, fingers and the stones I was man-handling.

My mind was empty of all cogent thought. I did not bother to reason if what I was doing was either logical or sensible. Something instinctively told me to dig, regardless of the consequences. After some minutes of frantic scratching, I glanced over my shoulder. Dmitri was just visible as a vague figure on the periphery of the lamplight.

'Don't just stand there!' I bellowed, my voice flat in the confined space. 'Get fucking backup!'

Dmitri disappeared and I returned to my task.

As I laboured, I swore in the most foul-mouthed fashion, cursing my luck, the cave in, the overseers and the Politburo and the Supreme Soviet, the callous gods that had stuck me in the mole hole and buried Kirill.

In retrospect, I gave little or no thought for Ylli. Something told me, his having been behind Kirill, that he was passed rescuing. He was, I considered, already gone, his spirit heading for purgatory by way of a Mediterranean beach lined with pine trees wafting in a warm, onshore breeze, pretty girls with long legs swimming in the sea and waving to him.

A rock the size of a football came free. Too heavy to lift, I rolled it clear, thrusting it impatiently out of the way with my foot. A slide of gravel slid over where it had been.

'Fuck you!' I addressed the gravel, digging my fingers into it, paddling to either side like a dog digging for rabbits. 'Get the fucking, shitting fuck out of it!'

I reached another stone, tore at it with my fingers to get a grasp on its surface, tugged at it, rocked it back and forth and got it free. As it slid to the floor, I saw an opening. Thrusting myself forward, I lay with my chest against the rock fall and pressed my face to the hole. A warmth came out from it and I could hear a gentle hissing, like a punctured tyre slowly going down.

Grabbing the lamp, I held it next to my face and shone it into the hole. Not twenty centimetres in, I saw the top of Kirill's head.

The hissing stopped, started again.

With a renewed frenzy, I set to work on the rock fall, oblivious to the consequences of another possible cave in. In less than a minute, I had the fallen rock cleared from around Kirill's head, exposing him down to the shoulders. He was lying face upwards, his eyes shut and a pit prop across the chest. The rest of his body was buried.

Stepping back into the gloom, I ranged about for the water pail. Although some débris had fallen into it, there remained a few litres of water. I dragged the bucket forward and, cupping my hands, splashed water in Kirill's face, dripping it onto his closed eyes which I wiped free of dirt with my fingers. His breathing hissed again.

'Kirill,' I said, close to his ear. 'Kirill, it's Shurik.'

Collecting more water, I trickled it onto his lips, where it dribbled down the side of his mouth, soaking away in the loose stone. I tried again and his lips parted, his tongue flickering out to catch the liquid.

'It's Shurik,' I confirmed and gave him more water which he took in, gurgling as he swallowed.

His eyes blinked then opened.

'Shurik,' he murmured: it was half a question, half a rhetorical statement of wonderment.

'I've dug you out,' I told him.

'And what's the score?' he muttered.

'I'm here alone. Dmitri's gone for the rescue team.'

Suddenly, the light bulb flickered and came on. It was well below power but it provided more illumination that my puny lamp and gave me heart for it meant the mole hole had not collapsed between the coal face and the main gallery. The wire would almost certainly have split had there been another cave in.

'Have you got to Ylli?' Kirill asked. His voice was a little stronger now, as if the light had given him strength.

'He's too far in,' I said. 'You're pinned in by a support timber.'

'More than that, Shurik,' he replied. 'Much more than that.'

'Never mind about that. Just hold on. Dmitri'll be back soon. And the others.'

A faint smile played upon Kirill's lips.

'I can't feel anything, Shurik.'

Moving closer to him, I put my hand against his cheek as if he were a child in need of comforting, or a mistress who had placed her head in my lap. His stubble was rough and wet from the spilt water.

'You've cut yourself shaving, Shurik,' he said.

'Cut myself having a close shave,' I replied, touching my cheek. The blood was clotting now, tacky like half-dried glue.

It was then I realised how kismet had been manipulating me. Had I refused Kostya's request, I would now be hundreds of metres away in the main gallery: had I not questioned the nationality of Dmitri's KGB officer, I would like as not be dead.

'You go up the hill,' Kirill suddenly said, his voice a little louder, insistent. 'Go past the school on your right, and a house in

215

front of an orchard with a tumble-down shed next to it. At the top...'
He took a long hissing breath. 'You'll go, won't you, Shurik?'

'Go where?'

'Go to Myshkino.'

'Myshkino?' I had to think for a moment before I realised what he was talking about. 'Your village? You'll be going there yourself.'

'No,' he answered. 'Not me. You.'

'They'll dig you out,' I said and I realised I was stroking his face. It was like caressing fictile sandpaper.

'No,' he repeated. 'Not me. You.'

'Think of your wife,' I encouraged him. 'When this is all over...'

'Tanya Antonovna is dead.'

The light went out, plunging us in total darkness. It happened so quickly, I was startled. Then it flickered and came on again.

'When we were under the coal truck...' I began.

'I was lying, Shurik. To you and to myself. In the gulag, lies are often better than truths.'

'When did she die?' I said. 'And how could you know?'

'She has been dead two years. I was told.'

Assuming the camp officials had informed him of the fact, I said, 'Forget it! That's just a way they have of demoralising you.'

'They did not tell me,' Kirill muttered. 'I heard from a man from Zarechensk. It was influenza...'

'Then think of your daughter,' I almost pleaded.

'I think of her every day,' he murmured. 'Every day, Shurik.'

I gave him a drop more water. Bubbles formed at the side of his mouth, tinged with pink and I suppose I knew then he was dying but I could not accept it, would not allow him to surrender.

'You'll be out of here. Give them twenty minutes.' I said, almost frantically. 'Breathe slowly, evenly.'

I stroked some water over his brow.

'I'll go to my wife,' he murmured, 'but you, Shurik. You must go to Frosya.'

216

His throat rattled and he swallowed, his eyes screwing up with pain. When he opened them again, he stared at me.

'Can you hear them coming?' he asked.

I listened hard. No sound came to us down the mole hole and I shook my head. The light dimmed further then brightened once more.

'It's my turn to escape,' Kirill said. His voice was weak yet resolute, firm. 'Not for me a railway yard in a blizzard, eh, Shurik? They won't find me frozen solid, standing up like a stiff prick on its wedding night.'

He smiled again. A light shower of dust fell upon us from some movement in the roof. I splashed more water across his face and he blinked.

'You'll get out of here, Shurik. One day. But for me, I shall go the way of the mammoth hunters.'

'Don't talk. Conserve your energy,' I said.

Kirill closed his eyes and I thought he might be heeding my advice but, after a moment, he opened them and spoke again.

'Will you do something for me, Shurik?'

'Of course,' I replied.

My face was above his and I looked down into his eyes. They were as deep as wells in the dim light.

'Help me escape, Shurik. Put me out of my misery.'

'The rescue team'll...' I started.

'No,' Kirill said, his voice louder, insistent so as to silence my objection: then it subsided, the effort too great. 'I'll not make it to the surface. And if they do dig me out and get me to the sick bay, then what? My spine's severed. They'll shoot me like a dog run over in the street. This is the gulag, Shurik. This is the USSR.'

A spasm ran through him then which I could feel pass from his face into my fingers, touching the raw fibres of my nerves like a hot needle.

'You felt that, Shurik,' Kirill whispered then, after a pause, added, 'If you kill me, Shurik, I shall have won. The victory of self-determination. And the gulag will have lost.'

'How can I?' I pleaded with him.

'Because you love me, Shurik. Because, if you kill me, you shall share in my victory.'

I turned away from him. The dim interior of the mole hole grew misty through my tears, as if a molten dust was rising before me. From the distance, muted by the tunnel, came the sounds of men approaching. I could hear Dmitri's voice, urgent and coaxing.

'They're coming, Shurik!' Kirill said urgently. 'Be quick! Do it for love!'

'I can't.'

'Do it, Shurik. You must. Do it for love.'

For a moment, I looked at him. He was crying, tears slipping down the side of his head, coursing round his ear, making a channel of white skin in the clinging grey dust.

'For love, Shurik. For love.'

Bending, I kissed him on the side of his face. He tasted of coal dust and salt tears. The stubble of his unshaven beard was rough on my lips.

Glancing around, I saw one of the shovels lying half buried under the stones and gravel I had excavated. I picked it up, shaking it free of the rubble and weighing it in my hand as a man might test the balance of an axe before felling a tree.

'When you see Frosya, Shurik, tell her it was good.'

'Tell her what was good?' I asked.

'To die with a friend, Shurik,' Kirill said, his voice suddenly calm, resigned, almost seraphic. 'To die at the hand of a man you know.'

Averting my eyes, I turned round on my knees and, with all the power I could muster, swung the blade of the shovel at Kirill's head. It struck him firmly just behind the ear. The bone cracked loudly, like a small explosion, and an ooze of blood trickled out and down the stones. Kirill sighed, like a tired man easing himself into his favourite chair in front of the stove after a long day's grind.

11

She must have been looking out for me as I walked up the field with Yuri for, when I entered my room, I discovered that Frosya had laid out my clothes for me. On the bed, as neatly organised as if by the best trained of butlers, were lined up a white, freshly-ironed shirt, my best dark trousers and a smart jacket which had belonged to Trofim's father. My shoes, on the floor below the trousers, were as highly polished as a Cossack lancer's riding boots. On the table stood the chipped blue enamel basin filled with hot water, a thin skein of steam rising from it and catching the sunlight striking in the window. Beside it, she had arranged my razor, brush and block of shaving soap. A crisply laundered towel was draped over the back of the chair.

I took my time, shaving slowly and carefully, making certain I did not nick myself. Just as the skin on the back of my thighs is loose and gets trapped between the mattress and the edge of my bed, so do the lines of my face offer ample opportunity for daily, if involuntary, self-mutilation. And I wanted to look my best.

As I wiped my face clean with the towel, the material pleasantly scourging my skin, I happened to glance up at the framed monochrome photograph hanging above my books. It is faded at the edges, where the silver oxide has begun to deteriorate, but the central portion is still sharp and clear. It shows a young man in a trim uniform standing smartly erect beside the front mudguard of a truck. In the background appears what might be a barracks. He is smiling at the camera with an almost cheeky grin, his hands clasped before the buckle of his belt from which hangs, on his right side, a leather holster. The butt of his side arm is just visible. Everything about him speaks of pride and hope.

It is the photograph taken of Kirill on the day he passed out from the militia training academy.

Once a day, not necessarily in the morning when I rise, I

look at his picture and, divine supplication not being a part of my life, I think of him. There is no point in prayer, in asking some fictitious deity to protect him. He's long since been incinerated, or dumped in an unmarked pit of alkali somewhere near the Arctic Circle, and that's the end of it: Kirill will not be found, millennia hence, lying with the dinosaurs. And yet, by thinking of him, I keep him near me. The flesh dies as easily as a fallen petal rots, but love endures like stone.

Outside, I heard someone run up the path from the lane, their boots clattering on the porch. There was a brief muffled conversation followed by light and hurried footsteps approaching my room across the floorboards.

'All right, Frosya,' I pre-empted her. 'I'm nearly ready.'

'Romka's just been,' she said urgently. 'Trofim had a call from Zarechensk. They drove through there ten minutes ago.'

I opened the door. She took a pace or two back and ran her eye over me.

'Well?' I asked. 'Do I do you proud?'

'You look...' She came forward, put her hand on my arm and kissed me. 'Handsome,' she declared at last. 'Handsome and distinguished and... And dignified.'

'I have my knife and fork,' I remarked, smiling at her.

Frosya did not acknowledge my little irony but said solemnly, 'You have always done us proud, dear Shurik.'

Her fingers began to quiver, ever so slightly. I knew what was going through her mind. It had pestered her all day. Whilst I was out walking, she must have had a miserable time wondering.

'Don't be afraid, Frosya,' I calmed her, talking her hand. 'Be brave.'

She gazed momentarily into my face then averted her eyes as if she might find the truth there and discover it was not the truth she sought.

'Have you decided, Shurik?'

'Yes,' I admitted. 'I have more or less decided.'

'More or less?' she asked fearfully.

'More or less,' I confirmed. 'How can I be sure, a hundred percent certain? I am not a soothsayer.'

'But what if...?'

'Life is filled with what ifs,' I interrupted her. 'Neither you nor I can do a thing about them.' I placed my hand over hers to comfort her. 'Dear Frosya,' I said, 'allow me this much, that you trust me not to be, at least on this one occasion, the old dolt you know I am.'

She steeled herself. For a moment, her lips went into a narrow line as she told herself to be stalwart. Then, disengaging her hand from mine, she touched the lapel of my jacket and said, her voice not quite breaking, 'I'm a foolish woman.'

With that, she brushed past me into the room and, opening the bottom drawer of my chest, removed a thin, oblong cardboard box from it. I deliberately keep the box in there, with other objects I no longer need and a few garments now too big for my wasting frame, because I dislike it. It reminds me of the boxes Kirill produced beneath the coal wagon: ever since quitting the gulag, I have assiduously avoided the consumption of desiccated fish.

Tossing the box and lid onto my bed, Frosya turned towards me. From her fingers dangled a gold-coloured medal shaped like a star, in the centre of which was a hammer and sickle. The counterfeit gold has tarnished and, in one place, flaked off to reveal the base metal beneath.

'I nearly forgot your medal.' Very carefully, so as to ensure it was not on crookedly, she pinned it to my lapel, smoothing down the material and straightening my shirt collar. 'We were so thrilled the day you were awarded it. Do you recall that day?'

'Yes. The children in the school sang a song for me. A rather embarrassing song, if I'm not mistaken.'

'Embarrassing!' Frosya retorted. 'It was nothing of the sort.'

'It sang praises.'

'You deserved praises.'

'For what? For being a teacher?' I considered my words and

221

added, 'Perhaps, at times, the classroom was akin to a battlefield, but...'

'For surviving,' Frosya said. 'For being in Myshkino and surviving.'

In silence, she led me by the hand out to the umbrella of the silver birch. I walked slowly, perhaps more slowly than usual, for I felt suddenly tired.

The table was laid with her best crockery, two plates of *vatrushka* pastries and a bowl of Trofim's raspberries soaking in some kind of liqueur. On an upturned barrel, on loan from Komarov, stood an ancient, charcoal-fired samovar bubbling and hissing like a leaky steam train. Half a dozen chairs circled the table.

Trofim appeared, running up the garden, struggling out of his overalls as he went.

'They'll be here in twenty minutes!' he called out, stopping for a moment to hop about as he extracted his legs. 'Are you ready, Frosya?'

'Yes,' she replied, stressing the pronoun, 'we are ready.'

Once out of his overalls, Trofim came to the table and surveyed the spread.

'Everything set?' he enquired eagerly.

'Yes,' Frosya repeated, somewhat irascibly, 'everything is set. Except you.'

He made to pick up one of the pastries but Frosya pushed his hand away and briefly glowered at him.

'Get washed and changed,' she ordered. 'You look and smell like a mechanic.'

'I am a mechanic,' he retorted, 'and it's the smell of work.'

'Honest toil,' I butted in, taking his side to annoy Frosya.

'Honest, yes,' she conceded curtly, 'but filthy dirty.' She pointed at his hands. 'Look at your nails!' She scolded him as if he were a ten-year-old. 'Make sure to scrub them.'

Trofim briefly studied the clouds scudding over the village.

'And you, Shurik, are you ready?' he asked turning to me.

His excitement was abated now, replaced by concern. I

could feel a certain trepidation lingering behind his words.

'Yes,' I confirmed, 'I am ready.'

For a moment, Trofim studied my eyes, trying to put himself into my soul and learn my secret. I returned his gaze and let a hint of a smile out. He grinned and put his hand on my shoulder.

'You old fox!' he exclaimed then he ran towards the house.

'He hasn't called you that for a long time,' Frosya remarked. 'Do you remember?'

'Indeed, I do,' I answered.

Frosya followed her husband into the house and I turned my chair around so that, instead of facing the table, the lane and Myshkino beyond the garden, I looked up the slope towards the chicken run by the forest and recalled the time, years before, when Trofim caught a dog-fox.

It was a late August afternoon, not unlike today's. The leaves were just considering turning from the dark green of summer to the russets and browns of autumn. The chickens in the pen beyond the vegetable plot were beginning to return to their roosts in the ramshackle hen-house Kirill had made on his last leave before history in the form of a KGB squad caught up with him. Others were flapping in their ungainly fashion into the oak tree above the hen-house. Suddenly, they all started to kick up a boisterous palaver. Trofim arrived just in time to see a fox heading into the trees with a hen in its teeth. He ran after it, throwing a heavy stick at it, but the missile fell far short and the fox sprinted away in a blizzard of off-white feathers.

When he came back to the house, Trofim was furious and all for borrowing one of Sergei Petrovich's shotguns. He set off for our neighbour's house but discovered Sergei was absent on a hunting trip in the forest.

'Never mind,' Frosya stated stoically when he came back empty-handed. 'The fox should live and we have plenty of chickens. We can spare him one.'

His anger abating, Trofim begrudgingly agreed but, the next night, a cockerel went. He constructed a heavy wooden cage trap, baiting it with a live hen. Sure enough, the following morning, the door was down and a fox's snout was to be seen testing the air between the bars which he had already started to maul. Hoisting the cage onto his barrow, Trofim set off down the path with it heading for the gate. His intention was to throw the whole thing in the river and drown the occupant.

'So you have him,' Frosya remarked as he reached the porch where she and I were sitting peeling beetroots.

'The thief is in the dungeon,' Trofim replied triumphantly.

'And his punishment?' I asked.

'Ten years without the right of correspondence,' Trofim replied grimly.

I knew that euphemism: in the old days, when men were afraid to sneeze in case atishoo sounded like Stalin, it was the official court declaration of a sentence which inevitably led, within the hour, to a firing squad in the prison yard and a hastily excavated pit in the woods ten kilometres out of town.

Frosya put down her knife and went across to peer into the trap.

'He is so magnificent,' she said almost wistfully. 'Come, Shurik, look at him.'

I joined her and bent close to the bars. The fox was in its autumn colours, its coat a rich red-brown, its nose as black and shiny as an officer's polished leather pistol holster. The tip of its brush was dark and it had a white streak on its chest. As my face came into its view, it flattened its ears and snarled.

'Must you kill him?' Frosya asked, returning to her chore. 'Surely he will have learnt his lesson, being trapped. Now he will keep away from us.'

'And do what?' Trofim rejoined. 'Go after Arseny's chickens instead of ours? Or Roman's ducks? Besides, do criminals learn? What of the recidivist?'

Frosya shrugged. Both Trofim and I knew that shrug.

'Could you not take it far off into the forest and let it go?' I suggested.

'Then he would die,' Frosya said, 'more slowly than if you

threw him in the river. He would be out of his home range, competing with local foxes. They would chase him, attack him, wound him, tear his leg off.'

She dropped a peeled beetroot into a pail at her side and, for a fleeting second or two, I was back in Hut 14 and Genrikh was doing his stuff.

Trofim stood with his hands on the shafts of the barrow. He could sense the hidden admonishment in her words.

'If you want to drown him,' she continued after a pause, 'you can't do it in the trap. The trap will float. If you weight it, you'll not be able to lift it to drop it off the bank. Or over the parapet of the bridge. You'll need to take the fox out and put him in a sack.'

Trofim thought for a minute and lowered the barrow onto its legs.

'Very well, I shall keep the fox until Sergei returns. Then I shall borrow his gun.' He clapped his hands together. 'Bang! Finished. Quick, clean, no pain.'

'No correspondence,' I said.

Frosya started on another beetroot and observed, 'Sergei will be away three weeks. Masha told me. You can't keep the fox in the trap that long.'

At this, I could see Trofim was getting cross but he suppressed his anger.

'I'll sort something out,' he grunted and, turning the barrow round, stomped off along the path, going back the way he had come.

All afternoon, Trofim stayed away from the house. We saw him on occasion heading into the village but Frosya made no attempt to call to him. At dusk, he appeared on the porch with his arms akimbo.

'Right!' he said sharply. 'Come and see.'

We followed him to a patch of beaten earth in the middle of the vegetable garden, about halfway between the house and the chickens, where there stood a wire run about four metres long, two high and three wide with a wooden hutch at one end and a basin of water sunk in the ground at the other.

'Satisfied?' he growled.

Frosya smiled and put her hand on his arm.

'It's good,' she declared. 'It will do and, when the fox has gone, we can use it to raise chicks.'

'Won't he dig himself out?' I wondered aloud.

'There's five gauge mesh under the earth,' Trofim replied curtly. 'He's not going anywhere.'

Within a week, the presence of the fox was shown to have benefits. For the whole summer, the vegetable plot had been regularly visited by a number of the feral cats which lived around the village. Not only had they liberally used it as a feline latrine, spraying the cabbages and defecating on the radishes but they had fought with Murka, bloodily ripping her ear. Nothing Trofim could do dissuaded them from visiting: pepper had no effect and a salutary fistful of gravel only worked if you caught them in the act. However, the scent of the fox drove them away. What was more, the rats which habitually lived around the chickens also seemed to diminish in numbers and the rabbits which came in from the fields to denude the carrots disappeared completely.

Frosya stopped by the fox run regularly throughout the day. At first, the animal remained in the hutch during daylight but, growing used to her visits, it started to come out to laze in the sun. She gave it water, fed it scraps and, when one of Roman's ducks was hit by a passing lorry, she presented it with the mangled carcass. In a fortnight, she was able to briefly stroke it.

Her familiarity with the fox irked Trofim. He kept his annoyance under control until one evening when, on his way to lock the chickens up, he discovered Frosya sitting in the run with the fox lying at her side as she ran her fingers along its side.

'Bring it in the house, why don't you!' he exclaimed peevishly.

'He's not a pet,' Frosya answered calmly, 'he's a wild animal.'

Yet, when Sergei returned, Trofim did not approach him for the loan of his shotgun.

I visited the fox from time to time and it grew accustomed to my presence, too. Ever since the day it was released into its run, I felt a strange kinship with it. It was in prison, as assuredly as I had been and I was certain, in its own way, it felt as I had felt. Even dozing in the shade of the hutch, a luxury I had rarely been afforded in Sosnogorsklag 32, I could sense its heavy heart, its inner misery which did not show on the outside but which I knew dwelt far within the creature's soul. Perhaps, I wondered, it dwelt in its mind in a wondrous forest, lingering in dark corners of its canine subconscious just as the marvellous garden had done in my own.

'It is time,' Frosya declared one evening in late October, 'to let the fox go.'

'Let it go?' Trofim replied incredulously. 'You mean kill it? I could cure the pelt and we could sell it. Fox fur is fetching a good price in Zarechensk. Or you can have it,' he added with a certain sardonic touch to his voice. 'Your coat needs a new collar.'

Frosya ignored his remark and said, 'I mean let him go. Not kill him. He will do us no harm.'

Trofim snorted. 'No harm? The minute it's out of that run, it'll be through the hen house like a rabbit down a row of radishes.'

No sooner were the words out of his mouth than he realised what he had said, understood what Frosya's plan had been all along and grinned sheepishly.

'If I am wrong,' Frosya said, 'if the fox takes so much as a mouthful of feathers, you can fetch Sergei's gun and sell the pelt.'

The next day, the air chilly and the sunlight crisp, Frosya went to the run to bade the fox farewell. I followed her, entered the run for the first time and watched as the creature brushed against her legs, sniffing at the leather of her boots and raising its nose to catch her scent. She squatted down, the fox rubbing against her thigh and nuzzling her fingers for a titbit. She gave it an egg, warm from the nesting box. It took it delicately in its sharp teeth, not cracking the shell until it was a few paces off: then, holding the egg between its paws, it capped it at its pointed end with the expertise of a cook and lapped the contents.

'Do you think, Shurik, he is now – how shall we put it? Politically educated?'

I smiled and answered, 'Do you think I am?'

She laughed lightly and the fox, alerted by her laugh, stopped lapping and cast a quick, cautious glance at us.

'If he is not,' she reached out and stroked the animal's back to reassure it, her fingers drawing lines in the creature's fur which had thickened up for the coming winter, 'his coat will soon adorn someone else. In Moscow.'

The fox finished the egg, sat on its haunches and licked its muzzle. Frosya stepped back and we left the run, leaving the door open. At the edge of the vegetable plot, we halted and watched the fox.

For a minute or two, it remained where it was, its tongue wiping the last vestiges of yolk from its whiskers and licking traces of albumen off its front paws.

'Do you recall the day they left your cage door open?' Frosya asked quietly.

I made no reply, but I could remember it. Standing to attention in front of the commanding officer's desk, he handed me the release document.

'Prisoner B916,' he announced laconically. 'You are hereby released from your imprisonment. You have served your sentence. A travel warrant is arranged for you. You will be taken to the railway terminus at thirteen hundred hours. Collect your belongings from your hut, report to the quartermaster at eleven-thirty hours.'

He hammered several purple rubber stamps onto the document, initialled them and held it out to me. I took it in silence.

'Have you nothing to say?'

'Thank you, Grazhdanin Nachalnik,' I replied, nonplussed.

'Where do you intend to go?' he enquired.

I folded the document. My mind was quite blank. The inconceivable, the one thing none of us ever gave thought to except in the darkest of moments, for fear of creating a void of hope in our souls, had happened.

'Will you go home?' the *nachalnik* enquired.

I made no response. Home was not a concept with which I was familiar any longer. He grew angry.

'*Ubiraisya!*' he exclaimed impatiently. 'Go on! Bugger off!'

As I crossed the compound, my head was swirling with near panic: yet, underlying it, I felt a terrible sadness creeping over me like night moving inexorably across the tundra and, beneath that, I realised home, for me, was Hut 14. I could recall nowhere else. Memories of my early life a quarter of a century before had faded, like photos of the dead. A few names lingered but I could put no faces to them, no sound of a voice, not even a familiar location.

The only voice I heard clearly was Kirill's.

'Look!' Frosya said softly.

Quite suddenly, the fox had tensed. His ears were pricked and tuned to the main chance. His eye was bright.

'He has seen his future,' I whispered.

Frosya took my hand in hers, gripping it tightly. The fox looked at the open door, pressed his belly to the ground and started to slink slowly towards it. At the threshold, he halted and put just his nose over the wooden sill.

I had done much the same at the gate of Sosnogorsklag 32, had stopped at the white line over which no one could pass until counted off, waited a moment, tested the air as if I might smell the catch. Yet there was none. The guard by the door of the run-down prison bus shouted, 'You! Get a fucking move on!' And I remember, for a moment, I had not realised he was addressing me for it was the first time in 26 years that I had been addressed by a guard without his using my number.

The fox put one paw over the sill, tentatively, like a swimmer testing the temperature of the sea before stepping into the waves. I looked down. In my mind's eye, I could see my foot lift, go forward, cross the line.

'He's going,' Frosya murmured.

The fox, realising the coast was clear, moved warily out of its gaol and stood on the path, the sun glistening on its fur.

'Will he run for it?' Frosya pondered quietly.

'No,' I told her. 'He's no fool.'

Sure enough, the fox did not sprint for cover but made its way leisurely along the path towards the chickens. Its brush trailed behind it, swaying up and down to its step that had an almost jaunty pride about it which, in the same circumstance, my own had not for I was tired and afraid of what my future might hold whilst the fox was ready for whatever eventuality might arise. The hens, seeing it coming, took to the oak tree in a cacophony of annoyed clucking. The fox ignored them and kept going until it reached the edge of the forest. There, for a brief moment, it paused: and in my mind I, too, paused before putting my foot on the lower step of the prison transport.

'What is he thinking?' Frosya mused.

'He is savouring,' I said, 'the wonder of his liberty.'

Then he was no more, dissolved into the shadows of the trees as old as time.

'Are you sad he's gone?' I asked.

'No. I am happy. For him,' she half-whispered.

The door of the house opened and Frosya came out, walking swiftly over to check up on the samovar. Behind her, I could hear scrubbing as Trofim laboured to shift the grime of the garage from beneath his fingernails.

From the other end of the village, I heard a vehicle approaching. I could tell from the sound of the engine it was diesel powered. Yet this was no stuttering, smoke-belching Russian motor. This was a smooth-running, well-lubricated, expertly-maintained foreign machine. It was in a low gear and I could imagine the driver swinging the wheel from side to side to avoid the potholes and ridges in the lane.

Without hurrying – for who hurries at my age except towards the grave? – I turned my chair round and self-consciously straightened my jacket.

The hour had, at last, come.

*

The vehicle was large and dark green, an hybrid between an African game safari truck and a saloon, with wide diameter tyres on silvered wheels shaped like three pointed stars. The windows were tinted and, on the right hand corner of the bonnet, was a short, chromium-plated flagstaff with a tiny crown surmounting the top. Beneath it, a flag was furled in a white canvas sleeve.

It did not stop at the gate but passed slowly by, rocking gently over the ruts in the lane, the suspension smooth. I tried to make out the occupants but they were mere shadows through the tinting of the glass. A little way beyond the edge of Trofim's plot, it halted and turned round. On the rear door was mounted a spare wheel in a black cover upon which was the stylised drawing of a mountain peak, the word *Discovery* printed beneath it in script.

Back once more at the gate, it halted, facing down the lane towards the village. The engine fell silent. A man stepped down from the driver's door, opening the passenger door. At the same time, a tall young man in his thirties with a trim moustache and wavy hair, dressed smartly in immaculately laundered grey trousers and a dark blue blazer, came round the rear of the vehicle and stood deferentially to one side as a second passenger alighted. He was in his late middle age, balding and very slightly stooping. He wore a charcoal suit with a light pink cotton shirt, a maroon cravat knotted at his throat.

For a few moments, they stood by Trofim's gate whilst the driver removed a small attaché case from the front seat and handed it to the younger man. They exchanged glances then started forward, the driver swinging the gate open but not

231

following them as they made their way up the path.

Trofim met them in front of the house. There were brief introductions before they proceeded on round the corner of the house and across to the birch tree under the canopy of which I was seated at the table. The samovar domestically bubbled. A wasp, perhaps having abandoned Komarov's cider press, hovered over the pastries. Frosya, standing by my side, flicked it away then rested her hand on my shoulder, giving it a slight squeeze.

'We love you, Shurik,' she whispered. It might have been a plea.

The younger man with the attaché case came briskly up to the table, holding out his hand. I stood up, Frosya's hand slipping from my shoulder.

'Mr. Bayliss,' he greeted me in perfect Russian, 'how do you do? I'm Geoffrey Grigson, deputy head of mission at the Moscow embassy.'

'Mr. Grigson,' I replied, taking his hand. His fingers were firm, not too hard in their grip but resolute, confident. 'I'm well, thank you. Please,' I indicated the chair next to me, 'do sit down.'

He ignored my suggestion, placing his leather case on a different chair. There was a gold crown embossed just above the polished brass clasp.

'I am sure you realise who this is, from my letter,' Grigson said, urbanely. 'May I introduce Michael Tibble?'

The older man stepped forward. He was almost reticent, plainly ill at ease and unsure of himself. His face was grave, his eyes meeting mine then, for a moment, diffidently eluding them before returning to almost bore into me. Taking my hand, he held it rather than shook it.

'It is so very good to meet you at last,' he said in English. His voice was soft, kindly but in the detached way of a doctor at the bedside of a sickly child. 'I have thought long about this moment.'

'Welcome to Russia,' I replied, in English. 'And to the village of Myshkino. Do you speak Russian?'

'I'm afraid I do not,' he answered and I had the distinct feeling he was somehow afraid of me: certainly, he was in awe of me.

'Very well,' I declared. 'Whilst you and I speak, let us communicate in English but, if I talk to the others, it will be in Russian. I hope you will not mind. They may understand what we are saying but they are not sufficiently fluent in English to reply.'

He nodded and said, 'Of course, I quite understand. I am, I regret, a typical Englishman, reasonably articulate in my own language but ignorant of all others except a smattering of schoolboy French.'

I introduced Frosya first to Grigson then to Michael Tibble. Trofim guided everyone to seats, Tibble sitting opposite me across the table, Grigson at his side. Frosya fussed about at the samovar, serving tea and putting small plates before each of us.

'So,' I said at last, when the tea was poured and the cups steamed up into the shafts of late sunlight coming through the branches of the birch, 'you must now tell me. How are we...?'

'I am your aunt's son,' Tibble interrupted, eager to get the information out as if he was confessing to his interrogator. I had seen others behave just so before an overseer or a KGB inquisitor: speak fast, get it over with quickly. 'Your father, Alan, had a much younger sister called Marion who married Arthur Tibble, my father. He was a tailor, in Leicester. They had two children, myself and my younger brother, Stephen.'

'Then we are cousins,' I remarked, trying to recall him but with little success.

'Yes,' he said. There was a distinct sense of relief in his voice. His confession, as it were, was being believed.

'And now, if I may, let me ask you a few more questions,' I continued. 'My father, what became of him?'

Tibble looked afraid once more, embarrassed by the fact that he possessed the knowledge I was after.

'Your father,' he began, 'was my uncle. I knew him...'

'Mr. Tibble,' I cut in, 'do not be concerned for me. I am asking these questions out of curiosity. Nothing more. Your answers will not upset me, will not disturb me. I am – how shall we put it? – merely filling in a few potholes in the road of my life.

After an existence such as mine has been, there are probably as many as in the lane.' I smiled to put him at his ease: he half smiled back at me and picked up his tea cup. He needed desperately to do something with his hands. 'As you will by now know, having driven from Moscow, there are many potholes in Russian roads so it follows that there may be just as many in the roads of a man's life in Russia.'

'Your father died in 1968,' he said quietly. 'He had been ill for a short while, then pneumonia set in. He was in no pain...'

'And my mother?' I enquired.

'Aunt Bea...'

He paused and sipped his tea, putting the cup down on its tiny saucer. The china chimed for his hand was unsteady. This meeting was, I realised, and contrary to my expectations, far more of a tribulation for him than it was for me. I had expected to be the one who was afraid and yet now, faced with this man and the trim diplomat next to him across the table at which I have sat for years, I was quite composed, at ease with myself and the whole world. My heart was not beating more than marginally faster than usual. I felt calm and strangely serene.

'My mother's name was Beatrice,' I confirmed.

'Aunt Bea died in 1986. She was eighty-eight, living in a nursing home in the West Country.'

'Did you know her well?' I asked.

'Yes,' he said. 'I was her favourite, so to speak. After you went missing, she... She needed a son,' he added bleakly, almost guiltily.

'And was she ill also?'

'No, she passed away in her sleep after a tiring day trip to a matinée performance in the local theatre, with a dozen of her friends from the retirement home. Aunt Bea found a great delight in the theatre.'

Give all the detail you can, I thought. The more the merrier. Detail gives veracity.

'Thank you, Mr. Tibble,' I said. 'I am very grateful to you.'

A weight seemed to lift from him. He picked up his tea cup again but, this time, his hand was steadier. His confession had been heard and found credible.

At that point, I too sipped my tea but not because I had to find a diversion: it was simply that I was thirsty. Grigson snapped open the flap of his attaché case and handed me a manila envelope.

'The Foreign Office thought you might like these,' he said. 'They are copies of your parents' death certificates, your mother's final will and testament in addition to some of the correspondence which has accrued over the years.'

I accepted the envelope but did not open it.

'Aunt Bea's will,' Tibble volunteered, 'mentions you.'

At this juncture, he clearly expected me to remove the contents of the envelope, which was not sealed down: yet I did not for I had no desire to open such a Pandora's box of personal history. My history, I considered, looking around me at Trofim's vegetables, Frosya's flowers, the Merry Widow's house and, over to the side, the field with the belligerent goat tethered in it, was here, not in some faraway place represented by a few documents in an official envelope.

'I would rather not read these papers at present,' I said.

'Perhaps you should,' Tibble suggested tentatively. 'You see, Aunt Bea – your mother, that is – never really accepted that you were dead.'

'She believed,' Grigson interrupted, 'that you had been involved in a spying mission, had been caught and imprisoned. For years, she wrote letters to successive Foreign Secretaries every time there was a Cabinet reshuffle, to members of Parliament, to the Russian ambassador. She even wrote to Khruschev.'

'Did she receive an answer?' I enquired.

'Much to everyone's astonishment, she did. A personal one, at that,' Grigson declared.

'It's in the envelope,' Tibble said.

I handed the packet to Frosya and said, in Russian, 'This, dear Frosya, you must read. There is a letter in here from Khruschev. No doubt,' I added to Grigson, still speaking in Russian, 'it denies all knowledge of my existence? I was simply drowned after my car went into the Elbe.'

'Near Torgau,' Grigson responded, also in Russian. 'That was the official Moscow line. It was doubted, naturally and, to be truthful, the file was left open until the mid-Sixties. Reports from operatives and moles were received from time to time to the effect that you had at least not been drowned but, with an absence of concrete proof one way or the other, London finally concurred with the Russian statement and the dossier was no longer active. Moscow remained, of course, resolute. Your mother was, however, adamant that you had been working for MI5 and chased the matter for years. She wanted you exchanged for agents we had caught, demanded acknowledgement of your alleged espionage role and actually petitioned the Queen to have you awarded a medal. To be frank, your mother caused a bit of a ruckus and was regarded, according to inter-departmental correspondence, with no small degree of sceptical annoyance.' He hesitated for a moment then went on, 'I apologise now, on behalf of Her Majesty's government...'

I put my hand up and said, 'Mr. Grigson, there is no need for that and, as for a medal,' I added, touching my lapel, 'you can see I received one after all.'

Grigson smiled and replied, 'For meritorious service to the Soviet Union. Not exactly the medal your mother had in mind.'

Frosya held the letter out, a look of near wonderment on her face.

'It is from Khruschev!' she exclaimed.

'What does it say?' I asked.

'What do you expect?' Trofim replied sarcastically, reading it over her shoulder. 'A railway voucher to Sosnogorsklag?'

'It denies you ever existed,' Grigson stated, bringing our conversation back to English. 'The usual regrets but nothing more.'

'Yet now,' Tibble said, 'we know Aunt Bea was right all along.'

'I am curious to know how you discovered my whereabouts,' I said.

'Since the collapse of the USSR, KGB archives are now open to scrutiny,' Grigson explained. 'An historian going through the files stumbled upon yours a little over a year ago and contacted the embassy. They forwarded the report to London in the diplomatic bag and a senior secretary with a lot of years under his belt remembered the brouhaha your mother had kicked up. From there, it was just a matter of research, going through registration of births and deaths to trace relatives. Finding your cousin, we passed the information on to him.'

'When I received the information,' Tibble carried on, 'I contacted a society which looks into the matter of people who were lost in the gulag. They traced you. I then contacted the Foreign Office...'

'...and here we are!' Grigson explained.

Frosya returned Khruschev's letter to the envelope taking, I noticed, a peek inside as she did so: then she checked everyone's cup, refilling them and handing round her *vatrushki*. Tibble took one and placed it upon his plate but made no effort to eat it. I helped myself to two and set about consuming them. Frosya's pastries are the best in the village. Even Andryukha the baker has begrudgingly admitted as much.

'Tell me, Mr. Tibble, what is your job?' I asked.

'I am an accountant,' he answered, 'with my own practice. Tibble and Partners. I have two boys...' He reached into the interior pocket of his suit jacket and removed a brown leather wallet from which he extracted a colour photograph, handing it to me across the table. It showed two young men standing next to a woman wearing an ankle-length flower print dress.

'This is your family?' I surmised.

'My wife, Rosemary,' Tibble continued, 'and my sons. Simon is on the left. He is the younger and works with me in the firm. My older son has just graduated from university.'

'What did he study?' I enquired.

'Chemical engineering,' Tibble said.

I looked at the photograph once more but did not see this stranger's family: instead, I saw Frosya as a little girl beside her mother.

'What is your older son's name?' I asked.

Frosya put her hand on mine. She had understood the conversation and, with her intuition, saw where it was going. I gave her a quick glance, saw the fear in her eyes once more, and smiled to alleviate it.

'Alexander,' he replied quietly. 'Aunt Bea requested it. She did not want your name to die.' He picked his *vatrushka* up. It was no longer a pastry but a punctuation mark in the paragraph of his emotions. Yet he still did not put it to his lips. Instead, he returned it to his plate and continued, 'Simon is soon to be married and Alexander...' He gave Grigson a quick look as if he was about to enter upon an argument and wanted to be sure of his allies before he opened his mouth. 'My wife and I wondered if you would like... We would be honoured...'

I got up from my chair, my head brushing against the twigs of the silver birch, the leaves not much bigger than petals stroking my hair. Moving round the table, I stood by my cousin's chair. After a moment, he rose to his feet and faced me. Out of the corner of my eye, I could see Frosya watching me. I do not think I have ever seen her look so afraid, so terribly unhappy. Beyond her, Trofim was staring at his boots.

Opening my arms, I embraced my cousin, kissing him on both cheeks in the Russian fashion. He had not shaved since the morning and I felt the light scrape of his beard just as I had, all those years before, felt Kirill's unshaven chin scour my lips. He tasted salty, too: the tears were dribbling down his face.

'Cousin Michael,' I said, holding him at arm's length, 'I know your love for me is great and I, not you, am the honoured one. You named your first-born son after me. Had I died in the gulag, you would have kept me alive through him. And I know what you are offering me and I am truly grateful for it.'

I let go of him and took a pace backwards. The sun had shone on the wall of the house all afternoon, the warmth now radiating off it. He watched me for a moment then shifted his gaze to survey Trofim's ordered rows of beetroots and radishes, Frosya's tall dahlias nodding their heavy heads as if exhausted from the long summer.

'Have you lived here since your imprisonment in the... Since they released you?' he asked hesitantly.

Referring to the gulag seemed to embarrass him. Perhaps, I thought, the mere mention of the word prompted feelings of guilt and I thought how, throughout his life, he must have been pained whenever the word appeared before him, like Banquo's ghost at the feast of his everyday existence. And yet, what had he to be guilty about? Nothing. I was not his responsibility.

'When I was let out,' I told him, 'I came here to repay a debt to a close friend, a fellow *zek*.' I smiled. 'It's been a long time since I last used that word, an abbreviation of *zaklynchenny* which means prisoner in Russian. Frosya is his daughter. She and her husband took me in.'

He was confused, could not understand why I had not headed straight for Moscow, drummed my fists on the door of the British embassy, demanded succour and a passport, a plane ticket back to London and revenge.

'Have you repaid your debt now?' he ventured.

'No,' I said with a quiet assurance which I could see perplexed him, 'I have not. I shall never be able to settle that obligation.'

Frosya must have caught the drift of our conversation for she sucked her breath in and turned away, looking up the hill towards the chickens, into the sun. Her shadow was lengthening across the ground, almost touching my shoes. In the distance, one of the cockerels crowed. It was a cracked, imperfect *cock-adoodle-doo*, the *adoo* missing. It must be, I thought, one of the young birds yet to assert his presence amongst the hens.

'I know what you are offering me,' I continued, 'and I should like very much to meet your family, especially to meet the son who bears my name into the future, who will carry me with him long after I am nothing more than dust blowing across the steppe: but I cannot accept for I cannot leave here. This is my home.'

His face was a study in disappointment. He had, in his imagination, already taken me away to the genteel, damp, green shires of England. For a moment, I wondered if he was going to try and persuade me otherwise, yet he did not.

'Were I to come with you,' I added, 'I should be in an unfamiliar land, without friends. Here – well,' I remarked, smiling at him in the hope that this might help him to truly understand, 'I've grown used to the seasons. If I was to live away from Myshkino, my old bones would not know when to start twingeing at the onset of autumn.'

He returned my smile and replied, 'I understand.'

Yet I knew he did not – indeed, he could not – truly appreciate my feelings.

It was not just a reluctance to quit my friends: I was also afraid of leaving, afraid of what England might hold. I would be a stranger there, the thought of such alienation terrifying me. It was the same fear that had governed me upon my release from the gulag which had trained me to forget, never to think of what horrors the future might bestow. In the gulag, one lived only for the present: survival was not a matter of hanging on for years, but hours.

For just a moment, I felt an intense sadness that I had not at least sent a message to my mother, to let her know I was well, had made it through, had endured the nightmare. Yet it passed for I knew, had I done so, I would have been beholden to return to England, to face an unknown future for which I was unprepared. It is better she believed me alive rather than had confirmation of it for she was, after those gulag years, less than a vague memory to me and I had replaced her, over the long years, with Work Unit 8, then Frosya and Trofim and I should not have wished her to know I did not want to return.

Now, having trained myself to put aside the past like a unmemorable book, I cannot afford to indulge in such nostalgia. To go away now would be like fulfilling one of those forbidden dreams of how life was, as Valya put it, before the world ended. A trip down memory lane invariably leads to the embalmer's gaudy paint box and the undertaker's marble slab.

'But I had to come to you,' my cousin went on lamely.

'I know,' I replied, 'and I am grateful and very glad indeed you have made the journey. It has been good to meet. Perhaps, you will return to Myshkino? With your family?' I invited him. 'There is a house down the lane in which no one lives. It is the property of one Averky Ilich Izakov but he and his wife have emigrated and now it is empty. I'm sure we could ready it for you.'

He brightened at the prospect. His dream had been shattered but now it was reforming, like all dreams do, into a different, altogether more enticing entity.

'I should like that very much,' he said with a sincerity that touched me: then, realising that he was accepting an invitation he might not be able to fulfil, he cast a glance at Grigson who pre-empted his question.

'Quite easily,' the diplomat assured him. 'There should be no problem with visas but, if there should prove to be any glitch, we would be only too pleased to sort it out. I'm certain the Russian authorities would not put up barriers.'

Frosya turned to face me, her eyes rimmed with redness.

Going to her side, I kissed her on her cheek and said, in Russian, 'Frosya, Mr. Tibble and his family are going to visit us. Do you think the Izakovs' old ruin might be made temporarily habitable?'

She made no reply. She just looked at me and the tears welled up once more, running down her face unchecked. Trofim came over, put his arm around my shoulder. I felt his sudden strength, born of wielding hammers and twisting wrenches.

'So, Trofim,' I advised, 'you and Tolya had better get a

move on with that taxi of yours.'

For another hour, we sat under the tresses of the birch. The sun crept lower and the forest darkened into a black border between the warm earth and the cooling, fading sky. When we had eaten the liqueur raspberries, Trofim fetched a bottle of Komarov's distilled cider and we drank a toast or two. I talked of my life in Myshkino, answered my cousin's questions, told him of my days as a teacher, of the village, the villagers and their aspirations in the new Russia.

As the twilight began to deepen, Grigson announced that they had to leave and asked me to sign a few papers which he produced from his attaché case. Frosya fetched my pen from my room.

'These are preliminary formalities,' Grigson began to explain.

'I don't want to know,' I interrupted him. 'At my age, who cares? I don't need for anything.'

Without bothering to read them, I signed each page as required, but in Russian. It was then I realised I had not signed my name in English for over forty-five years.

'When would you like me to return?' my cousin asked as we shook hands by the vehicle. The driver, a Muscovite, had opened the doors, the scent of warm leather mingling with the perfume of Frosya's night stock, the plants opening their flowers, now the sun was down, in readiness for the evening's little moths which had spent their day in the goat's meadow.

'Don't leave it too long,' I answered. 'I'm an old man, I won't last forever. Come next month. In the autumn. The forests are exquisite as the leaves fall.'

'Very well,' he declared. 'Next month.'

As he climbed into the vehicle, Trofim suddenly spoke in English.

'Sir, Mikhail,' he addressed my cousin, 'what is this car?'

'A Land Rover,' my cousin replied.

'Lan'd Rover,' Trofim repeated. 'It's very good.'

The Muscovite leaned out of the driver's door and said in Russian, 'Forget it, friend. It costs more than your entire village.'

I unpinned the medal from my lapel and handed it to my cousin.

'Give this to your son. To Alexander.'

'What is it?' he wanted to know.

I was about to explain but Frosya, not to be outdone by Trofim's brief venture into English, said, 'It is the sign of a good man in Russia.'

12

The bonfire is dying down now, the ashes grey as newly spewed larva, the embers glowing like the heart of the world. The more substantial boughs flare every few minutes as a breeze fans them and, when one splits, it raises a display of sparks which rise into the sky and are lost amongst the stars. The thin smoke is delicately scented for some of the wood was donated by Komarov who has recently felled a diseased apple tree in his orchard, replacing it, as local custom demands, with a sapling initially watered with cider to – as Komarov puts it – give it legs.

All around the fire, people are sitting on chairs or benches which they carried into the field just after dark. Some talk, some laugh and joke, some stare at the fire, some at the sky, some at the black forest across the river where time is held captive. The children are here, too. The older ones tussle and chatter, the younger hold close to their parents because the night is dense outside the sphere of the firelight and they have been warned of the sprites which inhabit the shadows and snatch those that do not do as they're told. A few have fallen asleep in their mother's arms or curled up on the soft grass by her side, covered by a shawl.

I sit on my usual chair brought down for me from under the silver birch: it is the one to the shape of which I have grown accustomed over the years. I am wearing a thick woollen sweater which the Merry Widow has knitted for me as a birthday gift. Perhaps she is not so keen to bury me after all. At least, not in the ground. I suspect she would rather bury me in her somewhat capacious bosom or the folds of her bed. What does she see in me! I can hardly be a stud and she is still young enough – just – to want the occasional tupping.

My front is hot. The heat from the fire, even now that the flames have dropped and we have drawn our seats closer, is still intense, penetrating. If I were to sit a metre nearer, the wool on the sweater would scorch.

Frosya gets up and, with a long stick, rakes several potatoes out of the ashes, skewering them onto forks and handing them round. The skins are charred but the flesh inside will be soft, almost powdery and sweet. I recall another fire, under another sky long ago, and potatoes cooked in the ashes.

Trofim hands round bottles of Gigulovsky. He passes my chair, winks at me and hands me one.

Out of the darkness a voice says, 'What I'd give for a Russian beer...'

It is so loud, I almost turn round.

Perhaps, I consider, just as all my present friends sit here in the warm light of the fire with me so, in the chilly darkness, linger all my past comrades in adversity.

I glance up. A meteor sparks briefly across the sky. I do not consider it to be a fragment of a far-off place, to which I may or may not aspire when I shuffle off this one.

No. It is Avel in his MiG-15, chasing after eternity.

'So, Shurik,' someone calls from across the fire. 'It's your turn. Tell us a story.'

'I am no story-teller,' I call back.

'A man of your advanced years has a million stories,' Yuri says and, as he did this afternoon, immediately realises he's blundered again.

'Don't look now,' Komarov says, 'but your foot's in your mouth, teacher.'

'For a schoolmaster, you've a great taste in shoes,' Father Kondrati remarks dryly.

Everyone laughs but I am not that easily let off the hook.

'Come along, Shurik!' Tolya demands. 'Give us a tale.'

What shall I tell them? That I once ate a mammoth steak above the Arctic Circle? That I did not share my bucket of oily hot water with a man whose soul was frozen? Or shall I speak of Valya who, like me, right now, could smell burning apple wood?

There is another voice in the darkness. It is not as close as the other but comes from some way off, up by the tethered, belligerent goat.

'Come along, Shurik,' it chides me, 'tell them a good one.'

'Very well,' I concede, but not just to Tolya.

I take a swig of the beer to lubricate my throat and place the bottle on the ground by my chair.

'There was an Armenian,' I begin, 'who went on a tour of Belarus.'

In the darkness, there is laughter already. They know this one, my old comrades-in-chains.

'He was driving along one day when he saw a man selling something at the roadside. He stopped and got out. The man had a tray of small, round black balls. "What are these?" the Armenian asked. "They're learning pills," replied the Russian. "How much are they?" the Armenian enquired. "Ten dollars each. Hard currency."'

My! How they are laughing back there in the black corners of the night!

'The Armenian bought two and promptly ate them. "Blessed Jesus!" he exclaimed. "They taste like goat shit." "There you go," replied the Russian. "You're learning already."'

Tolya weeps with mirth. Komarov spills his beer. Trofim splutters: I have caught him in mid-swallow.

Up the hill, the truculent goat bleats once.

Someone has passed it by on their way into the future.

The laughter subsides.

'A good one!' Tolya congratulates me.

Across the fire from me, Romka is tuning his *balalaika*. Frosya and Katya, Komarov's wife, appear from the direction of a table set up by the river bank. They each carry a tray of glasses filled with *sukhoye*, a dry sparkling wine not unlike champagne. They hand them out to everyone, even the older children. I receive mine last. As soon as the trays are put away, Romka strums a few chords by way of a drum roll of sorts.

'Ladies and gentleman!' Trofim proclaims rather grandly.

'A long time ago, over twenty years, I came back from a hard day's slog at the office...'

'You never slogged hard at the office,' Tolya shouts. 'You could tell from the state of the buses.' He makes blurting noises with his lips, imitating a poorly maintained engine.

'A hard day's skive at the office,' Trofim concedes, 'to find a scarecrow on the porch. I thought Tolya had put it there. It was,' he takes his revenge for the interruption, 'dressed in his latest fashion.'

Laughter greets this turning of the tables. Tolya raises his glass in acknowledgement of this attack upon his sartorial tastes, but he does not drink from it.

'Coming up the path to my house,' Trofim goes on, 'you can all imagine my surprise when it moved.'

The fire gives his face a ruddy glow. The glass in my hand is cold and wet with condensation.

'I was all for putting it out in the vegetable plot,' he continues, 'let it earn its keep but – well, everybody, you know Frosya. A soft heart and a loving mind, except where I'm concerned. So, we made up a spare bed and the damn thing's lived with us ever since.'

There is a brief ripple of laughter around the fire. Frosya gives me a quick look, studies my glass to see it is charged. Trofim's tone changes, the jocular replaced by the sober.

'That day,' he says, 'Frosya and I simultaneously gained two things we lacked in our lives. We acquired in one stroke of the brush of heaven both a son and a father. From that moment on, our lives were enriched beyond our wildest dreams and, I hope you will all agree with me, our village became a different place. So, my friends...' He looks around and everyone stands. '...I ask you to drink to Alexander Alanovich Bayliss, the Englishman of Myshkino whom we all call Shurik.'

'Shurik!' they echo him, holding their glasses up, catching the light of the burning log in the centre of the fire which has suddenly flickered into life.

Nodding appreciatively, I accept the toast, raising my glass to them in mute gratitude for their friendship and then, at last, unable to resist it any longer, I turn.

I can see no one. Yet they are there, as sure as the fire is hot, the *sukhoye* is chilled and Frosya is loving.

And I raise my glass to them, to the past, to times you would think I should rather forget and yet which I cannot because I do not wish to. For, if I forget the past, I forget them – Work Unit 8 in Sosnogorsklag 32 – and that would not be right.

'What are you thinking?' Frosya asks.

'Do you really want to know?' I reply.

'I think I do already,' she answers, smiling at me with such love it takes my breath away.

The darkness is silent again. They have departed now, gone their ways into hushed oblivion whence I shall join them soon enough.

'I have spoken with Vera Dorokhova,' Frosya continues. 'Tomorrow, we shall start to tidy up the Izakov house. Now,' she picks up her stick, 'the next lot of potatoes should be done. Are you having one, Shurik?'

I decline and walk a little way from the fire towards the bank of the river. On the far side, Bratan stands watching the party. The moon is rising over the forest. It has not yet broken above the tree line but there is a pale glow where it will soon come into view.

Sipping my glass of wine, I think back over my day. In my imagination, I revisit my stroll around Myshkino, in much the same fashion as I used to stroll around my miraculous garden in the long gulag nights. One by one, I revisit Komarov's cider shed, the school, Myshkino Motors, the church, the forest and the house where, once more, I meet the cousin I did not, until Geoffrey Grigson's letter arrived, remember existed. I see him walk up the path, come towards me, unsure of himself. Finally, I see the envelope on the table.

After the embassy vehicle had driven down the lane and the dust had settled on Frosya's marigolds, I emptied the envelope onto the table. It contained, as Grigson had said it did, my parents' death certificates, the Khruschev letter, some correspondence to my mother on headed notepaper from several government ministries, a sympathetic letter from an under-secretary at Buckingham Palace expressing the Queen's regret, and my mother's will. I unfolded the document, typed on crisp legal stationery. One clause stood out from the rest, underlined in red crayon and initialed by both my mother and, I presume, her lawyer. It read, *In the event that my only child, Alexander David Bayliss, be not found alive on the centenary of my birth, then, at that time, the residue of my estates shall pass to Michael Ridley Tibble and his brother, Stephen Peter Tibble, or to their rightful heirs and descendants.* Attached to the last page of the will was a statement of account dated three months ago. My mother's estate, at that time, was valued at just over £412,000.

By hunting me down, my cousin has forfeited an inheritance of a considerable sum of money. That, I consider, is the sign of a true man.

The moon is just up. It is peering over the tops of the trees, the craters as clearly defined as the ruts in the lane.

Standing by the river, with Bratan snuffling in the new moonlight, I have made a decision. I shall write to my cousin and request that, from my inheritance, a sufficient sum of money be set aside to re-equip Myshkino school, with another sum to be placed in trust to provide two scholarships per annum for pupils to travel and see the world, that they, like me, can come to understand that there is evil and there is goodness, to learn the lesson that if you kill something of beauty, two uglinesses spring up in its place. The balance after these deductions shall be divided equally between my two cousins.

Or, not quite.

I shall also request that my cousin orders one of those Land Rover vehicles. It will be dark red, have a plush leather interior and air conditioning. Along the side, in both the English and Cyrillic alphabets, I shall have painted the words *Myshkino Taxis*.